Christmas Eve
COWBOY

Anthologies

SOME LIKE IT ROUGH

LORDS OF PASSION

HAPPY IS THE BRIDE

A SEASON TO CELEBRATE

MARRYING MY COWBOY

CHRISTMAS KISSES WITH MY COWBOY

LONE WOLF

Published by Kensington Publishing Corp.

Christmas Eve
COWBOY

DIANA PALMER

DELORES FOSSEN
KATE PEARCE

ZEBRA BOOKS
Kensington Publishing Corp.
www.kensingtonbooks.com

ZEBRA BOOKS are published by

Kensington Publishing Corp.
119 West 40th Street
New York, NY 10018

All Kensington titles, imprints, and distributed lines are available at special quantity discounts for bulk purchases for sales promotion, premiums, fund-raising, and educational or institutional use.

Special book excerpts or customized printings can also be created to fit specific needs. For details, write or phone the office of the Kensington Sales Manager: Kensington Publishing Corp., 119 West 40th Street, New York, NY 10018. Attn. Sales Department. Phone: 1-800-221-2647.

ZEBRA BOOKS and the Z logo Reg. U.S. Pat. & TM Off.

First Printing: October 2022
ISBN-13: 978-1-4201-5151-0
ISBN-13: 978-1-4201-5152-7 (eBook)

10 9 8 7 6 5 4 3 2 1

Printed in the United States of America

Contents

Once There Was a Lawman

DIANA PALMER

Chapter One

Thomas Kincaid Jones hated the little Colorado town of Raven Springs on sight. He was a city man, from Chicago. He liked the music of traffic, the horns, the eternal movement around him. Here, there was nothing to see, not much to do. Raven Springs, just a few miles out of Benton, Colorado, where he was temporarily assigned on a case, was the end of the world. It was a little town in northwestern Colorado, surrounded by majestic snow-covered mountains, with a small and tight-knit population that seemed to disdain any stranger. The holiday season had apparently been kicked off even before Thanksgiving, because the town was decked out in lights and Christmas decorations in the store windows. And Christmas was at least three weeks away.

He hated Christmas. It was a cold Christmas morning in Chicago when the woman he loved told him that she'd met somebody else and fallen in love, really in love, and that she was leaving him. He'd tried to talk her out of it. They'd been in an on-off relationship for months, and he'd been on the verge of proposing. He knew she dated other men, but he'd been fairly certain that there was no real competition. Well, not until that morning, when she'd hit him in the gut with her confession.

Maybe it hadn't been love as much as physical attraction

that held them together, but he'd felt lost when she left town. He'd decided then and there that he wouldn't ever let another woman get that close to him. Six years ago, that had happened. And while he'd had infrequent liaisons, he'd never loved any of them. If a woman could think of men as disposable, surely it was fair play for a man to consider them disposable. He was still bitter about Angie taking off with another man. Especially when he'd considered marriage for the first time in his life.

Just before she left, there had been one last, parting shot. She didn't really want to spend her life with a man in law enforcement who could be killed anytime he went out on a case. She hated guns. He'd thought she was just using that as an excuse. Probably she had. She'd never acted like she cared. He had a job, his service with the Chicago Police Department, and he'd been in Army Intelligence while he was in the service, in between law enforcement positions. Any man could be killed, by a car crash, a riot, a flaming meteor hitting the ground. Law enforcement had its risks, but so did life itself. He didn't dwell on that, anyway. He was a good shot and he had a solid background, starting at his service with the Chicago Police Department right out of school. He'd wanted something more adventurous, though, so even before Angie left him, he'd applied for a job with the Bureau. After months of checking and rechecking, they'd hired him. He'd had physical encounters with criminals, of course. One memorable one was right outside the local FBI office: two guys trying to kill each other over a girl. He'd stepped in, without thinking about it, and separated them. His reward had been a knife slashing into his chest. He'd subdued the suspect and called for backup, bleeding all the while. One of the local police officers, a man he knew, insisted that he go to the emergency room for treatment. He still had the scar.

It wasn't too noticeable, in the thick hair that covered the solid muscle of his chest. But it was long and deep.

He was a big guy, over six feet, not fat but husky and broad-shouldered, like a wrestler. He had thick black hair and large hands. His eyes were dark and piercing, and he almost never smiled. They'd called him Stone Face back in Chicago. Not in front of him, though. Not ever.

He was bored out of his mind. He was here on a case for the FBI. It was a federal crime, kidnapping, and he was partnering with local law enforcement to apprehend the perpetrator who'd left his heavily bound hostage—a young woman—to freeze to death in a lonely, unheated, mountain cabin.

Stuff of heroes, this assignment, he kept telling himself as he cleaned the .45 caliber automatic on a table in his motel room. Except he didn't feel like a hero. He missed the city. All you could hear in this place were barking dogs and even damned singing crickets! There was one in the room right now, driving him nuts. Why was it here in the first place, in the dead of winter? He'd tried to find it, finally realizing it was just outside the room, not in it. And he couldn't very well go to the room next to his, in the dark, trying to shoot a cricket. He imagined the occupant of the room would take offense if he asked to be let in on a search-and-destroy mission.

He knew his size could be intimidating. He'd played football in college, but he was a little past that now, at thirty-six. The job had become his life. He'd been with the Bureau going on six years now. He was comfortably settled, often applauded for his devotion to duty. Now, here he sat in this little dinky motel room in the back of beyond, listening to that damned cricket. It was absurd!

Before this came up in Raven Springs, Tom had been assigned another case in Denver. Since he was the closest agent to the small town, and the case he was on wasn't urgent, he'd been requested to help Jeff Ralston, the local sheriff, find the perpetrator who'd collected ransom for a dead hostage. The case had twists and turns like a snake, and it was especially sad at this time of year.

He was out of humor already, being reminded, every step he took, of Christmas. He wasn't looking forward to being stuck here for any lengthy period of time. Maybe the perp would feel guilty and present himself at the sheriff's office, hands outstretched for the handcuffs. He chuckled to himself. Sure. That was how it worked.

He'd just finished cleaning his .45 automatic and was putting away his cleaning tools when there was a knock at his motel room door. He holstered the automatic on his hip, and went to the door, one hand on the butt of the weapon. He was always cautious.

He opened the door a crack and was met by pale, icy-silver eyes in a pretty face, surrounded by long, blond, wavy hair that she was quickly plaiting.

"Yes?" he asked coldly.

"Do you drive a black Crown Victoria?" she asked politely.

"Yes."

"Did you park it in a driveway next to the motel?"

He blinked. "Yes."

"Well, would you mind moving it?" she asked curtly. "I'd like to get my car out of my driveway so that I can go to work!"

He held up his arm and looked at his watch. His thick dark brows arched. "It's almost eleven. What the hell kind of job do you have, pole dancing at a bar?"

Her eyes flashed pale lightning at him. "My job is none of your business. Will you please move your car?"

He shrugged. "If I must."

He followed her out the door. She wasn't tall. The top of her head came to his shoulder. She was slender and not bad looking at all. She had on a coat that had seen a lot of wear. There was a button missing on one sleeve. Her shoes were thick-soled and laced up. He wondered what sort of work she did. Maybe she cleaned offices. Didn't they do that at night?

He got into his car, started it, and backed down the driveway. He pulled in next to the curb and got out, locking it back up.

"Just for future reference," she said, "this is not part of the motel parking lot."

He pursed his lips and studied her. Indignant. Young. Very young. He glanced past her at a house that needed more repairs than he could take in all at once.

"I'll keep it in mind," he said.

For the first time, she noticed the pistol in its holster. "You're wearing a gun."

"Goes with the job."

"You're an assassin?" she asked with a snarky smile.

He glared at her. "FBI."

"Oh. The horrible kidnapping," she said. She nodded. "I knew her. Julie Crane. She was a sweet, kind person. She was standoffish if she didn't know you, but people understood why she was like she was. I can't imagine that anybody would hurt her. Of course, her stepfather has money, but they didn't get along. He was crazy in love with his wife. When she got lung cancer and went in for treatment, he went with her. He even hired a nurse to do private duty with her when she got really bad." She made a face. "Nobody liked the nurse. Julie certainly didn't—she said the nurse took credit for what Julie did when she cared for her mother. May

Strickland, that's the nurse, wouldn't even change the bed linen."

"Well, aren't you a buffet of news."

"You look like you'd need to eat a buffet twice a day," she returned, giving him a long look.

"I'm big-boned," he said resentfully.

"Salads are very good for you. So is yoghurt."

"I don't need health advice from kids, thanks."

She drew herself up to her full height. "I'm not a kid! I'm twenty-five."

"You're a kid. Drive carefully."

She made a face at him. "I always drive carefully."

He stood on the sidewalk and watched her back out. She went over the curb, almost hit his car, got into gear on the second try and putted down the street. The vehicle she was driving was pouring black smoke and it looked to be at least twenty years old. He shook his head. Talk about town characters, he told himself.

The next morning, he was sitting in Jeff Ralston's office, drinking coffee and going over witness statements.

"There was a kid last night who mentioned some things about the victim," he began.

"Who?"

"No idea. I was parked in her driveway next to the motel. Blonde, silver eyes, comes up to my shoulder. And twenty-five years old."

"Oh, yes. Annalisa Davis," Jeff replied with a warm smile. "She lost her dad last year." He didn't say how. That was Anna's business. "Her mother died a couple of years before that. She insisted on staying in the house, although it's falling apart around her ears. Proud as the devil. She won't let anybody help her."

Annalisa. It suited her somehow. "She's got a mouth on her," he remarked.

Jeff chuckled. "Just like her late mother. But she's a sucker for lost pets, small animals, and little children."

Something stirred deep inside him. He smothered it. The kid was years too young, and he didn't even know her. Best not to get involved.

"About the victim—" he began.

"Julie Crane," Jeff interrupted. "Her stepdad's filthy rich; he inherited all the money Julie's mother had, and it was a lot. He's kept the nurse who took care of his late wife. Her name is May Strickland. She and Julie didn't get along at all. I guess May wasn't mourning the loss. She acts like she owns the place, the maid, Alice, told my cousin at the grocery store. She convinced Granger Downing that he needed constant monitoring of his blood pressure."

Tom was taking notes on a phone app. "Did Julie get along with her stepfather?"

"Not really. She was autistic, but high-functioning. She could drive a car, cook, things like that, but she was hard to get along with if she didn't know you. Her mother loved her and took care of her. When she got sick, Julie took care of her. Her mother died of lung cancer, and Julie was left with her mother's husband and the nurse. She didn't like either one of them."

"Her stepfather, how did he feel about his stepdaughter?" he asked, looking up.

"He's an abrasive man when you first meet him, but he's got a soft heart. He liked Julie, but she made his life a misery," Jeff explained.

"Well, that dots a few I's," Tom mused. "I'll do a background check on him and the nurse."

"There's also a handyman, a friend of the nurse's, named

Billy Turner," Jeff said. "Two more unpleasant people you'll never meet."

"Doesn't bother me," Tom said imperturbably. "I'm used to unpleasant people."

Jeff just smiled.

His background check didn't turn up anything out of the ordinary. Granger Downing, Julie's stepfather, was a big noise among the country club set. He was loaded, although it seemed to be Julie's late mother who'd had all the money and he'd just inherited it.

He'd checked out the victim as well. Most people spoke kindly of her. She hadn't been a social person, but she had no real enemies that he could ascertain. *Follow the money* was a tenet that all law enforcement people tuned into. It was usually a good idea to do that. So Tom started checking into the victim's stepfather's bank account.

He was just coming back to the motel after a long and tiring morning when the smoke-pouring car-thing pulled into the driveway next to the motel. He got out of his vehicle and walked up to the young woman just getting out of hers.

"Rings and valves," he said.

She gave him a blank look.

"Rings and valves. Your car's pouring smoke."

She cocked her head and stared at him. She looked young and worn-out. "It thinks it's an old-time locomotive," she replied. "Don't pay attention to it, or you'll encourage it."

One eyebrow arched and his dark eyes twinkled.

"You're out early," she pointed out.

"So are you. Is pole dancing very lucrative?"

She glared at him. "I am not a pole dancer."

He smiled at her. "You're very young," he said quietly.

"Thanks, gramps," she tossed back.

He chuckled. She was a firecracker "What do you do, really?"

"I feed and water helpless things."

"That's a strange answer."

"It's the only kind you're getting, too," she said. "Why are you out so early?"

"Detecting."

"Oh, Julie Crane's murder," she said, and nodded.

"Yes. You knew her."

"She went to school with me."

"Care to enlarge on that a bit?"

"I would, but I'm asleep on my feet."

"How about coffee and breakfast?"

She hesitated.

"I have a testimonial from my district supervisor that I'm dependable and safe to be let loose around young women."

She laughed.

"Have you had breakfast?" he asked.

She shook her head. "We had a last-minute emergency, so I got off late. I'm starved."

"So am I. Who serves a good breakfast?"

"The new waffle place on the corner."

He led her to his car, pausing to put his computer and paperwork on the back seat.

"You're messy," she pointed out.

"I said you could have breakfast, not point out my bad habits."

"Sorry. I'll save it for after breakfast. And I buy my own, in case you need to know."

His eyebrows arched. "Why?"

"So I won't be accused of letting an FBI agent bribe me."

"I never bribe women with food," he said curtly.

"Oh, I see. You don't like women."

"Got it." He got in under the wheel and drove them to the fast food joint. They walked in together.

"Why don't you like women?" she asked.

"Because I used to be involved with one. She took off with another guy."

"Sorry."

He glanced at her. "You married?"

"Not on your life."

"Did you used to be involved with somebody too?" he asked.

She went quiet. "I want a waffle and bacon and black coffee, Sadie," she told the woman at the counter.

"I heard there was a flap on last night. You get it worked out?"

She smiled at the woman. "Just about."

"And what will you have, sir?" Sadie asked Tom.

"Same as her," he replied.

"How easy to please you both are," Sadie mused, used to people studying the menu for ten minutes only to decide they'd just have coffee.

"Only when it comes to food," Tom replied.

"I thought you were that sort of man," Annalisa mused.

"Oh, and separate checks, Sadie," Annalisa called back over her shoulder.

"Got it."

They found a booth at the back of the waffle house and sat down. She pushed back a wisp of blond hair that had escaped the braid she'd pinned around the top of her head.

"Don't you wear it down?" he asked, studying her.

"It gets in my way when I'm working," she said. She sighed, leaning forward with her chin in her propped-up hands. "I'm so tired."

She looked it. He wondered what sort of job she had. She was wearing a colorful shirt under her coat, with plain colored slacks. Must be a cleaning job, he told himself. She wasn't old enough to have a profession.

"Tell me all you know about Julie Crane."

"I covered most of it last night," she said. "She had some issues, but she was pretty good in school, especially with math. She was a whiz. She could do calculus and trig in the fourth grade. I couldn't even manage it in high school. She loved numbers."

"Did you know her well?"

"We were friends, sort of." She smiled sadly. "She gave me a necklace before she died. Real gold. I wear it on special occasions and think of her. I liked her a lot. I think she liked me, too. She certainly trusted me."

"Any evidence that the stepfather was doing things to her?"

"You mean . . . ? Oh, I see. No. He wasn't that sort. He tried to make friends with her, because he truly loved her mother, but she was jealous of him with her mother, and she wouldn't let him get to know her. Her mother was an invalid after the lung cancer started to work on her. She could barely get out of bed. Julie took good care of her, right up until the end; in spite of the so-called nurse who never did a thing she wasn't ordered to do! The cancer shouldn't have killed her that quickly, but I guess every case is different. I helped, until her mother's nurse thought I was trying to take over her job and complained to Mr. Downing. So I got handed my walking papers. That was sort of odd, you know, that the nurse objected to anybody helping her patient; as if she had something to hide."

"Julie sounds like a fine person."

"She really was, and what happened to her was so, so sad." He was taking notes. Any tidbit might be the key to unlock a case. He overlooked nothing. He said that to Annalisa, his dark eyes steady on her face.

"You never know when a tiny clue will blow open a case."

She nodded, and when he went back to making notes on his cell phone, she studied him. In his thirties, she surmised, probably on the wrong side of thirty-five. He was very good-looking. But she'd had her problems with men who thought the same thing about her. She'd been pursued by several, but she had no interest in them. She'd never felt anything at all with the boys she'd dated. She still felt very little. Men just didn't affect her.

Well, not until now. She studied that strong face with its chiseled mouth and high cheekbones and felt herself tingling all over. Odd reaction, especially to a man she didn't really know. He was everything she didn't like in a man. Big. Authoritative. Overbearing. He was also in law enforcement. That brought back really hard memories of her late father, who'd been all those things. Her father had dominated her completely, ordered her life, told her what to do, nitpicked everything. He'd run off any boys she might have become interested in. They couldn't get past him. He liked having Annalisa at home to do the housework and cook and take care of him. He wasn't losing that for some overheated boy who'd never stay with her anyway. He also wanted Annalisa to look after her mother and do all the housework when her mother's heart started to fail. Poor Julie had the same problems at her home, too. It was why Annalisa and Julie had been friends. Neither of them saw a way out that didn't involve tragedy. There had been no escape for Annalisa even after her mother died suddenly late one night of a major heart attack. Her father was too important in the community. He drank, a lot, but everybody protected him. Not that he was ever abusive to his daughter. He never lifted his hand to her. He was just overbearing and belligerent. And, at least, Annalisa was still alive. But poor Julie had died.

She threw off the memory. Everyone thought she missed

her dad. She didn't. She wasn't certain that she'd ever loved him. He'd been verbally, although never physically, abusive to her late mother. Despite the misery of her marriage, her mother was deeply in love with her father. She never stopped loving him, no matter what he said when he drank. She once told Annalisa that she didn't know why her father was the way he was, but that he'd been a good, kind man when she married him.

Annalisa's training had been a blessing. At least her father had agreed to that, and it was a good thing, because she had a job that she loved, that paid her expenses. Well, except for the house. It was falling apart over her head. She really didn't have the capital to fix anything. If it fell in one day, she'd have no place to live. She'd have to rent a room or something. Probably a good idea not to think too hard about that.

"Do you always brood over things?" her companion asked suddenly.

She looked up, startled. "How did you know?"

"Understanding body language is part of my job. I have all sorts of skills."

"I hope one of them isn't breaking and entering," she said calmly.

"I have not broken and entered anything," he huffed.

"Not ever?" she probed, eyes twinkling.

"I broke a door in once, where a woman was being assaulted."

"What about the man who assaulted her?"

"Oh, he ran into a wall and got a black eye. They suspected I'd done it to him, but the perp backed up my story very quickly." He smiled angelically.

"Good for you," she said curtly. "Men like that should be put in stocks in the middle of towns."

"There you go, getting medieval again."

"It wasn't me, it was you getting medieval," she shot back.

He grinned at her. His dark eyes twinkled. It impressed her. He seemed very different when he smiled. She smiled back involuntarily.

"Maybe we both should be living back in the dark ages," she suggested.

"Good luck finding a time machine, especially in my hotel. It has a cricket," he muttered. "A cricket! In the middle of winter, for God's sake!"

"The cricket is in a cricket box. The man staying in the motel takes it everywhere with him. It's a pet." She didn't tell him how she knew. The man was from out of town, but he was visiting a friend where she worked.

He gaped at her. "A cricket? He keeps a cricket for a pet? Why not a dog or a cat?"

"He said he had a dog. It tore up the floor in his kitchen, twice, and the cat he got to replace it ripped his furniture to shreds. He says a cricket can't do either of those things."

He just shook his head. "It takes all kinds, I guess. Maybe I can get used to it."

She smiled. "Earplugs," she suggested. "It's how I sleep late. My neighbor on the other side is in a band. He has drums. He practices early in the morning." She sighed. "It's a wonder that I'm not mentally disarranged."

"Except for wanting to put people in stocks."

"Even you must agree that some people would benefit from it," she pointed out.

He chuckled. "I guess so."

She finished her coffee, and stood up. "Thanks for the company," she said, and the tiredness showed on her pretty face now. "I'm going home to bed."

"Remember to put in the earplugs," he suggested. He got up too, and they both headed for the exit.

"I may need to double them." She laughed. "See you, Chicago," she added, giving him a nickname.

"See you, Raven girl."

"Actually, I feed ravens," she said, a little hesitantly. "They come every day to the back deck. My father hated them. He shot one. I buried it myself." She felt uneasy that she'd said what she did. "Forget I said that, please, people in town revered my father. They thought he was a great cop."

"Your dad was a cop?" he asked, surprised, as they reached his car and he opened the door for her.

She nodded. "He was chief of police here, in fact."

"How did he die?"

She bit her lip.

He moved a step closer. Just a step, but she tensed. "How?" he repeated softly.

"One of the local stores was robbed by an escaped fugitive. He ran and my father ran after him, into an alley. The perp spun around and put a bullet right through my father's head." She turned away. "It was a while ago."

"I'm so sorry," he said, and meant it.

She forced herself not to cry. It was a public place. She took a deep breath.

"Thanks for listening," she said after a minute. She turned and looked up at him with eyes that were still too bright. "He was a hero to the townspeople. But that was his public face. People are different behind closed doors."

"Some people," he agreed. "You never know until afterwards."

"You're not married."

"No. But I lived with a woman on and off for a few years. I bought a set of rings, the day before she told me she was leaving." His eyes were sad. "Sometimes you don't know people even when you live with them."

"I guess we're both clued in about that, wouldn't you say?" she asked.

"Do you want to get married?"

"No," she said at once. She drew in a long breath. "I just want to go to sleep. I'm worn out."

He nodded. His dark eyes twinkled. "Pole dancing can do that to you," he remarked facetiously. Whatever she worked at, she wasn't a pole dancer. But it was fun to tease her and watch her silver eyes flash at him. She had beautiful eyes.

She made a face. "You wish. Good night."

"It's morning."

She shrugged. "Whatever." Her eyes twinkled at him. "Different points of view."

"So they say." He smiled at her, and drove her home.

His smile made her heart flutter. She wondered about it all the way to her bedroom, but she was asleep before she puzzled it out.

Meanwhile, Tom was working a new angle on the kidnapping case. If the young woman was fine with people she knew, and the kidnapper had been a stranger, why hadn't she screamed for help? According to what he'd found out, there was a maid and a housekeeper who both lived in the home, and there was a security guard who was on duty outside after dark. He'd need to talk to all three of them.

He phoned the number at the Downing home and was told that Mr. Downing was too busy to come to the phone. This was after he heard Downing in the background saying hell would freeze over before he'd have anybody in law enforcement in his home, and the FBI agent could go to hell. Tom found that not only entertaining, but useful to know. As Mr. Downing would soon find out.

* * *

His first stop was Jeff Rawlings's office.

"You're out early." Jeff chuckled. "Want coffee?"

"I just had a cup, thanks. I need you to do something for me."

"Sure. What?"

"Pull Downing in for questioning in the death of his daughter."

Jeff made a terrible face. "If I do that, he'll sue me and the county and probably the governor. The man is nice, until something upsets him, but he has enough money and power to blow the pants off half the city council. He's dangerous."

"Is he, really?" Tom asked. He began to smile. "Okay, then. I'll do it my way."

Jeff was wary. "And what, exactly, is your way?" he asked worriedly.

Tom just smiled. It wasn't a pleasant smile at all.

Chapter Two

Several hours later, in the company of a fellow senior agent of the FBI from Denver, Doug Reynolds, both men got in the Crown Victoria and drove straight to the Downing residence. It was in a gated community, so they had to show ID. They flashed their badges at the guard, using their most intimidating expressions, and drove right up to the front door.

They knocked. The maid came, saw the two men, and froze.

"FBI," Tom said curtly, and showed his badge. His fellow agent did the same. They didn't smile.

"We need to see Mr. Downing at once," Tom added. He gave her the look again. It was intimidating.

"Come . . . come right this way. Mr. Downing and his, uh, May, his nurse are having dinner. They're in the big dining room . . ."

"How nice." Tom urged her ahead.

Downing was in his late forties, belligerent, without a hint of manners or courtesy. He yelled at the poor maid for interrupting his dinner and then glared at the newcomers while the older woman with him, May, went a pasty white.

Tom decided he had to have an interview with her—but alone.

"Get back to work, Alice, and next time you ask me before you let anybody in that door at night!"

The maid, young and scared, agreed, glanced with a rueful smile at Tom, and went back to her chores.

Well, what do you want?" Downing demanded. "You're interrupting my meal!"

"FBI," Tom said, producing the badge again. His colleague did the same.

"FBI?" His eyes grew big with surprise. "You can't just walk in here, without a warrant!"

"We're not searching the place, Mr. Downing. We're investigating your stepdaughter's kidnapping and murder, and if you have nothing to hide, you'll speak with us."

Downing was at a loss for words. He backtracked immediately when he realized why the men had come. "It was a tragic loss. My poor Julie. I was fond of her. She was like her late mother, gentle and kind, except for that unpredictable temper!" He shook his head. "I thought we had the ransom taken care of. Well, maybe I shouldn't have stopped by the country club after I delivered it," he added with a grimace. "I had some sizeable investments with a friend who was only going to be in town for a night. I was only there for ten minutes." He averted his eyes from the two agents' faces with a rough sigh. "Too late now to regret it. The kidnappers apparently just left her to die." His eyes met Tom's again "She was blue all over and cold as ice when I got to her," he added shortly. "Now I'm no medic, but I don't think that could happen in the few minutes between the phone call I got and the time I arrived at the destination to pay the money."

"Wait," Tom said. "You paid the money before you went to the country club?"

"Of course I did," the older man said belligerently. "I may be hard to get along with, but I'm not cruel. I wouldn't let so much as a stray dog die if I could save it with money!"

Tom was frowning and taking notes. "What time did you pay the ransom?"

"Let me see, it was seven o'clock that evening," he murmured, thinking back. After I left the money, I went to the country club and stayed for maybe ten minutes. Then, when I got the message where to find Julie, I went straight to the area the kidnappers said she was being held."

"You spoke with them?"

"Sort of," he said. "It was a robot voice, telling me where to take the money. When I got there, in an abandoned office, the door was unlocked, there was a note on the table that said to leave the money and get out and I'd get instructions."

"Did you?" Tom continued.

Downing nodded. "I got a text on my cell phone."

"May I see the message?"

Downing was reluctant and hesitated.

"I can get a warrant, if you need one," Tom said quietly.

Downing sighed. "No. I want to see the kidnappers caught." He pulled up the message and handed the phone to Tom.

Tom read the message. It was in stilted English and very brief. It gave a location and instructions, nothing more. Tom pulled up the number the call had come from, copied it, and handed the phone back. "Don't erase that," Tom told him. "If we catch the kidnappers, it will become evidence."

"All right."

Tom looked up the number and let out a muffled curse. "It's a fake number," he said curtly. "One used by scammers. There's a list of them online."

"I get those damned calls all the time," Downing said with some irritation. "The last one was from Russia!"

"I guess times are hard all over," Tom replied, "even there."

"What else do you need, Agent Jones?" Downing asked.

"Nothing more right now. There were no people at the place where you paid the ransom," he continued, "and you saw no vehicles nearby?"

"No to both questions. Julie's mother would be heartbroken if she was still alive. Julie had good days and bad, but she was kindness itself to her mother." Downing hesitated for a few seconds and averted his eyes. "If she died by the time I got to her, why was her body already cold and stiff?" he added after a minute. "Rigor doesn't set in that quickly, does it, even in cold weather?"

"I'll get back to you on that when we have the report from the crime lab," Tom replied. He glanced at May, next to Downing, who was fidgeting in her chair. The young maid, Alice, was hovering. She glanced at her boss and winced.

"I'll need to interview your household employees sometime in the next few days. I'll call first," Tom said, backing down a little from his initial confrontational stance now that Downing was cooperating. The man's new attitude had surprised him.

Downing just nodded. "That will be all right." He drew in a long breath. "We haven't even planned the funeral," he said after a minute. "No sense in that until we have her . . . her back," he said, refusing to say the word "body."

Tom noticed that. He got up, along with Doug. "Thank you for your time," he said formally.

"If you find out anything, will you let me know?" Downing asked. "I won't ask you to tell me any details that might hinder the case. I'd just like to know how it's going."

"I can do that," Tom assured him.

"Alice will see you out," Downing said, motioning to the

hovering woman. He reached for his coffee cup. "I don't understand why she was so cold . . ."

The two men walked behind the maid to the front door, out of earshot of Downing and his female companion, who'd looked very relieved when they got up to leave.

"He seems very mean," Alice said, her voice lowered. "But he's not really like that. I've been here for five years. He genuinely loved his wife. People say he just married her for her money, but they didn't see how things went around here every day. Julie had moods and she resented anyone coming between her and her mother, so she didn't like him very much."

Tom was taking mental notes. "No arguments over money?"

"Well, Mrs. Downing's nurse, May, has extravagant tastes. She moved right in, supposedly to take care of his wife when he advertised for someone to do private duty. She isn't the nurturing kind. I think Julie was resentful of that, too, because May was always hanging on her stepfather. Just not where his wife would notice. He was upset when the cancer was diagnosed and May had been a nurse in a nursing home at some point. She said she knew how to do daily care for an invalid." Alice made a face. "Poor Mrs. Downing was wet half the time and never had anything to drink or eat unless I took it to her. Well, except once, just before she died. May took her a cup of some tea that she said she wanted to try. That was the only kindly act I ever saw her do, too. I tried to tell Mr. Downing that Mrs. Downing wasn't really having anything done for her by anybody except Julie, but May could twist things to make him do what she liked, where his wife was concerned. She was always watching me . . . speak of the devil," she whispered without looking at the door.

"And that's how you get to Ray's barbeque," Alice said in

her normal speaking voice. "But don't turn off at the first red light, or you'll end up in Catelow . . . Do you need something, May?" she added, glancing at the hall doorway.

"What? Oh, no, no, he just wondered what was keeping you. He wants more coffee." May nodded at the men and went quickly back the way she'd come.

"See?" Alice asked.

Tom did. "Thanks," he said. "It's good to have some idea of the character of the people you deal with in cases like this."

"Mr. Downing's bark is worse than his bite, and Julie was an angel. May is out for everything she can get. She's supposedly monitoring Mr. Downing's blood pressure and looking after him while he mourns his wife. She convinced him that he needed that badly. Meanwhile her ex-boyfriend was hired to do odd jobs around here, but what he does mostly is watch May."

Tom pursed his lips. "You've been a lot of help. We'll be in touch."

Alice grinned. She ushered them to the front door. "Have a nice evening. Don't forget about the turnoff, now," she added to continue the fiction of giving directions, because she caught a glimpse of May hovering in the next room.

"No problem. We love barbeque. Thanks again."

"Well, wasn't that informative?" Doug asked.

"It's a dandy start, all right," Tom said, nodding. "I'm going to have a busy week." He glanced at the other man. "Thanks for coming down to assist. I thought I'd need a battering ram. Downing surprised me."

"You don't really know people when you have polite conversation with them. Anybody who works for them, on the other hand, is a great source of information."

"As we just found out. Well, let's get you to the airport."

They got into the car and pulled out into the road. "Downing's nurse at the table with him was almost dancing in her chair. Far too nervous to conceal a crime; it takes somebody with better nerves. A little sympathy and the threat of life in prison and she'll sing like a canary bird." Doug chuckled.

"I hear you." Tom turned the car toward the airport. "It was a horrible crime, badly thought out and poorly executed." He shook his head. "I won't mess up the case by speculating, but if you plan to kill somebody for money, you'd better have a plan that doesn't finger you before the body's cold."

"Amazing that they'd try it in a small town, as well, where people grew up together."

"Small towns." Tom made a face. "I'd go nuts it I had to stay here long. I miss Chicago."

"I like small towns," his companion said with a smile. "I married a girl from a little town south of Minneapolis. She couldn't stand life in the city, so I moved where she grew up. After a while, I not only got used to it, I actually like it there."

"I'd never get used to it," Tom said. "There's a guy in the room next to mine who's got a damned pet cricket. He takes it with him when he travels." He glanced at the other man. "First time I ever really thought seriously about homicide."

"Crickets are nice. You should stop gulping down your life and try living one day at a time," came the amused suggestion. "You'll be old before your time."

"I am old before my time," Tom replied. "Well, we're here," he said as he pulled into a parking space. They got out together and his companion picked up his bag.

"Thanks for the help," Tom said, shaking hands. "Have a safe trip home."

"No problem. I have to stop by the gift shop on the way

to my flight," he added with a chuckle. "My youngest boy's birthday is tomorrow. He'll be two years old." He sighed. "He wants a stuffed Pokémon. I had to write down the name so I wouldn't forget. There are dozens of those things!"

Tom grimaced. "You with kids," he said on a sigh. "I never thought about them. I move around too much."

"I move around, too. Kids are great. I can't imagine life without mine. All three of them," he added with a grin. "I hope you catch the killer," he added, somber. "Any human being who'd let a young woman freeze to death has no heart at all."

"Yeah," Tom agreed. "It's money," he added. "She was the only member of her family left, and her stepfather inherited. I'm not completely convinced that he didn't have some involvement, but he doesn't act as if he did. That woman, on the other hand . . ."

"Brutal, to let someone freeze to death on purpose," Doug said.

"And Downing was right on one score, rigor doesn't set in that fast. My best guess would be that the young woman was long dead by the time they got the ransom money. No witnesses."

"Exactly what I was thinking," Doug replied. "Better make sure the crime lab dots all the I's and crosses all the T's. This is going to be an evidence case."

"I'll make sure the evidence isn't tainted," Tom told him.

"I like being able to pay my bills and feed my family," the other man said. "But money is way down the list of things I'd harm somebody over. In fact, it's not even on the list."

"Same here. Greed." He shook his head. "It's landed plenty of people in federal prison. And if I can prove that anybody in Downing's household had anything to do with his stepdaughter's death, I'll help them right into an orange jumpsuit."

"I'll keep my fingers crossed for you."

* * *

Tom drove back to Raven Springs, dragged into his motel room and sat down. He was too tired to go out and get supper. He wasn't certain that he was even hungry. He'd spooked at least one potential witness. That woman sitting next to Granger Downing, May-something, she was high on his list. She knew something. He was going to find out what.

He pulled off his clothes and got into his black pajama bottoms. They were actually sweat pants, but he slept in them. He couldn't abide an undershirt in bed, so that went in with the laundry. He'd have to find a coin laundromat somewhere and get his clothes washed. It looked as though he was going to be here for a while. It was great to have Doug come out, Tom thought, nice of the man to come all that way. But it had produced results. Tom would sleep well, knowing they'd gotten somewhere.

He'd just climbed into bed and closed his eyes when he heard banging on his motel door. And he knew why. He groaned. There hadn't been a parking space in the motel's lot and he was so tired. He'd parked in the driveway again. Surely it wasn't going on eleven o'clock . . . ?

He looked at the clock. It was ten thirty.

He opened the door with a long sigh. "I'm sorry," he told the silver-eyed, furious woman in front of the door. "It was late and there wasn't a damned parking space and I was worn-out."

"I'm sorry, too, but I have to get to work." She was staring at him and became a little flushed with appreciation of that muscular physique, fascinating to her because she knew male bodies very well indeed. His was awesome. Almost perfect. She'd never seen a man so attractive in a pair of sweatpants.

"You could get a job pole dancing," she said with twinkling eyes.

He chuckled. "Stop ogling me. You're too young for me, kid. I'm older than dirt."

She looked up at him with a big smile. "Not hardly."

"Thirty-six," he said.

"Not bad, for your age," she said. "And I take back the bit about salads. There's not an ounce of fat on you."

"We're required to keep fit. So we can chase bad guys."

"I'll bet not many escape from you." She stared at him. "I'll stop ogling if you'll get your car keys and move your car." She hesitated. "There's a carport. It's made for two cars, but I only have one. You can park your car there, if you like."

"Well! That's a nice gesture. Why?"

"You're very good to look at. I haven't had a reason to ogle anybody since my favorite TV show went off the air."

"Which one?"

She cleared her throat.

"Well?" he prompted.

"*Game of Thrones.*"

"Wow."

She cocked her head again. "Wow?"

"You don't look the sort of person to like that show. There's all sorts of naughty bits in every episode," he added with a wicked smile.

"It was a great series."

"It was, until the last season. I didn't like the way it ended."

"Me neither. They're doing a prequel. I can't wait!"

He laughed. "I read about that. I'll be watching it, too."

She glanced at her phone and grimaced. "I'll be late to work."

"Can't have that." He went inside, slipped on his shoes, grabbed his keys, and went out the door.

"You're going to drive it looking like that?" she exclaimed.

He raised both eyebrows. She must mean the scar. He should have pulled on a shirt . . .

"You'll be mobbed by love-starved women!" she told him. "They'll all swoon!"

"The scar will put them off."

"What scar?" she asked.

He caught her arm and pulled her just a little closer. "This one." He took her hand and traced it.

She frowned as she felt it and pursed her lips, trying not to let him see that her pulse rate doubled and her breath suspended somewhere halfway to her mouth from the contact with that gorgeous male body. "That must have taken a lot of stitches."

"It did."

"And you think it would put a woman off?" she asked, wide-eyed.

"Wouldn't it?"

"It wouldn't put me off. If I was in the market for a man, that is. I'm not," she added quickly.

"That's nice to know. I don't have to worry about you jumping on me when I come to get my car in the morning."

She grinned at him. "You'll be perfectly safe." As she turned, she made a growling noise.

His chest swelled. He chuckled. "Stop that. I'm impervious."

She didn't say another word, but she couldn't stop smiling. And at least he hadn't noticed her reaction to him. She hoped.

He went to bed, still wondering what sort of work she did that late at night. She was intelligent. But she might have been forced by circumstances into a cleaning job. That was sad. It was admirable work, but she deserved better. He recalled her face when she'd touched his chest. It had been very expressive, like the sudden uptick in her heart rate and breathing, not signs an experienced law enforcement officer would fail to notice. Of course, he shouldn't have been noticing those things, either. She was far too young for him. Yet his own pulse had done some odd things when he felt her hand on his bare chest. He couldn't afford to get mixed up with a small-town girl who was too young for him. If only she wasn't so damned sexy! He fell asleep worrying it in his mind.

The next morning, he got up and showered and dressed. He really needed to find a laundromat. He had two suits and they were fine, but he had shirts and undershirts and underwear and socks that needed washing. He bundled it all into a zipper bag and started out the door and up the hill to his car.

She was just pulling into the driveway as he reached his vehicle.

"Going bowling?" she asked, noting the bag.

"Not hardly. To the laundromat, if you know where I can find one."

"Bring your stuff inside," she said. "I have some things to wash, too. We can put all of it in together."

"That's above and beyond," he pointed out.

She cocked her head and looked up at him. "I'm cultivating you," she explained. "That way if I ever get stalked by monsters, you'll come save me."

He chuckled. "I'd do that anyway."

"So, come on in."

She unlocked the door.

It was a small house, but neat as a pin, and she had some nice appliances.

"Have you had breakfast?" she called as she came back from the bedroom where she'd put her bag and kicked off her shoes. "I usually make something before I go to bed. There's no time to eat at work."

"I'd love breakfast. Can I help?"

"You can make the toast. I'll do the bacon and eggs."

He grinned. "Butter?"

"Real butter," she said, pulling it out of the fridge. "Fresh eggs from a lady down the road, and bacon from a man who makes his own and sells it to me."

"I've never seen fresh eggs. Only what comes from the corner grocery back home."

"In Chicago?" she asked as she pulled out a frying pan. "That's a very big city."

"Yeah, I guess it is."

"Were you born there?"

"No. I'm from Delaware, originally."

She broke eggs into a bowl. "Parents? Siblings?"

"Both my parents are dead. I had a sister, but she was in a bad wreck three years ago. They couldn't save her. They really tried," he added quietly.

"Most medical people do the best they can. But catastrophic injuries are almost impossible to heal."

"Her organs were . . . well, they were badly damaged," he said, choosing softer words.

"You won't shock me, by the way," she said, glancing at him. "I'm no stranger to injuries."

"Where do you work?"

"At the local hospital," she replied. "I'm a nurse."

"Damn."

She stopped as the burner heated, and looked at him. "What?"

"Damn! I thought you were a pole dancer." His dark eyes twinkled. "I was looking forward to seeing you on the job."

She chuckled. "That'll be the day. My grandfather was a Methodist minister. My grandmother had been a missionary. I lived with them from time to time. I have very old-fashioned ideas."

"No messing around, in other words," he teased.

"Exactly."

He glanced at her bare feet and laughed. "You don't like shoes, do you?"

"No. I'm on my feet all night. When I get home, all I want to do is relax."

"How long?"

"Have I been a nurse, you mean?" she asked. She frowned. "Let me see, I started training when I was in college, and then two years on the unit—five years, I guess."

"How old did you say you were?" he asked.

"Twenty-six. Today," she added, glancing at the calendar. She'd almost forgotten. She glanced at him, thinking he would have been a really nice birthday present. If she wasn't off men, and he was available. "And you're thirty-six."

"Not for long," he said on a sigh. "My birthday is next month. I'll be thirty-seven." He raised an eyebrow at the way she was looking at him. "Now, now, no ogling," he chided.

She stared at him with twinkling eyes. "Don't worry, you're way over-the-hill for a young thing like me . . ."

"Am I, now?" he interrupted. One big arm went out to whirl her to him as the other one caught her. She found herself held tightly against a suit that smelled of expensive cologne. Then a hard, faintly smiling mouth came down tenderly on hers and she stopped thinking altogether. He knew what he was doing, she thought dizzily, feeling her heartbeat race as that warm, possessive mouth became even more demanding, as if the touch of her had ignited him. It had ignited her, too. She stood on tiptoe, her arms going around his neck, as she coaxed him not to stop.

He lifted his head almost at once, watching her eyes open slowly, her face flushed with pleasure, her pretty mouth slightly swollen. "Now," he asked, faintly goaded, "still think I'm over-the-hill?"

She swallowed, hard, and moved back. "Not anymore," she murmured, her cheeks becoming pink.

He chuckled. "It's your own fault. You're very pretty," he added. "But I really am too old for you, kid. You don't even know how to kiss."

She glared at him. "They don't teach it in nursing school."

"No problem. I'm willing to do the honors, in between working this case."

She glared more. "I am not a project!"

His eyebrows went up over twinkling dark eyes. "Now when did I say I thought of you as a project? No, no. I think of you as an objective." His voice dropped, low, dark velvet. "Not a serious one, you understand. I don't want to get involved with you."

"Not that I want to get involved," she lied, "but is there a reason?"

"Yeah." He buttered the toast as it came out of the toaster. "I told you, remember? She fell in love with another guy and just left me."

"I'm sorry. But people don't really choose to fall in love, you know. It just happens."

"I thought she was in love with me." He went toward the door.

"You're leaving? But I'm cooking," she protested.

"I'm going to get my dirty laundry out of the car," he said.

"Don't get lost!" she called after him.

He threw up his hand and kept walking.

By the time he got back, she was finishing up the eggs and bacon and putting them on a platter. Her morning had gone from boring to exciting to disappointing all too quickly. She put the food on the table, followed by plates and utensils and a big pot of coffee, along with mugs to drink it from.

"I made coffee. It's pretty strong . . ." she began worriedly.

"If a spoon doesn't stand up in it, I don't drink it," he replied.

She laughed. "Okay, then."

She finished her eggs and glanced at him. He looked gorgeous in that dark suit with a burgundy tie and a spotless white shirt. She remembered the cologne he used when she'd been held against it earlier. He smelled nice. "You even look pretty good dressed," she teased.

He chuckled. "Give it up. I'm years too old to let you get under my skin."

"We can agree to disagree," she said pertly, and with a smile.

Breakfast was nice. They talked about commonplace things. Afterward, he insisted on helping with the dishes. She didn't have a dishwasher.

"There's only me here," she explained. "The washer and dryer, I really need. But I don't have that many dishes."

"Never thought of getting married?"

She shook her head. "I've been asked a time or two, but my parents' marriage was nothing to write home about. I think I'm better off on my own."

"That's what I thought until Angie came along and led me around by my libido."

She laughed. "What a way to put it."

"Nothing like the truth for getting through life."

"Well said."

"I can do the laundry."

"No," she said. "You're dressed to go out, so I expect you're investigating the kidnapping. All I have to do is put the clothes in and go to bed. By the time I wake up, they can go into the dryer."

"I appreciate that," he said. "I spend part of my life in laundromats and dry cleaners. And the repair lady."

"The repair lady?"

He opened his jacket to show the pistol on his belt. "Plays havoc with clothing, especially suit coats."

"Wow. I never thought of that," she said, eyeing the gun with no fear showing.

"Aren't you afraid of guns?" he asked.

"Heavens, no! Remember I told you my dad was a cop, but he was also a triple-A skeet shooter. I have a twenty-eight-gauge shotgun and I know how to use it."

He laughed. "I've very rarely seen a woman who'd pick up a shotgun, much less use it." He grimaced. "Angie hated weapons. I tried to explain to her that it went with the badge, but she never got used to it."

"Tools of the trade," she said simply.

He eyed her clothes. She was wearing a colorful paisley shirt with plain cotton trousers and a lanyard with a nurses' badge around her neck.

"Where's the white cap?" he asked.

"We haven't worn uniforms in years," she pointed out. "Scrubs are much more comfortable and easier to keep clean."

"I guess so." He studied her. "You look nice in that."

She flushed. "Thanks."

"Thanks for breakfast. And the laundry," he added.

"No problem at all. I'm Annalisa Davis, by the way," she said, extending a hand.

He took it in his big one. "I'm Tom. Tom Jones."

She looked at him, raised an eyebrow over twinkling silver eyes, and began to sing the Tom Jones song, 'What's New, Pussycat."

"I will tell everybody in town that you're a pole dancer," he cautioned.

She grinned and started to pull her hand away, but he kept it, smiling down at her. She made him feel warm inside, bubbly. He was a man who smiled very rarely. She was getting to him.

"Don't oversleep," he teased softly, and bent and brushed his mouth tenderly against hers. "And don't get attached to me," he added when he lifted his head. His expression was solemn. "I'm only a passing ship in the night. When I finish this case, I go home," he added.

"I know all that," she said. "I promise not to follow you, wailing all the while, on your way to Chicago."

He grinned. "Fair enough. Just so you know. I like you. But I'm not marriage material."

"Don't sweat it. Neither am I."

He let her hand go. "See you later."

"Don't speed, Chicago," she teased. "The cops here are on the ball."

"I did notice. And I never speed."

"Ha!"

She went toward the back of the house. "Lock the door when you leave, please."

"Will do."

He watched her every step of the way until she was out of sight before he let himself out, locking the door as he went.

There was a lot more investigation that he had to do before he could home in on a suspect, even though he was fairly certain where the trail was going to lead. First thing, he went back to see Jeff Ralston.

"Of all the people we might expect to get kidnapped, she was the very last one," Jeff told him. "Hell of a case. Very sad."

"I went to see Mr. Downing last night with another agent," Tom said.

"He's not quite what he seems," Jeff replied. "He took wonderful care of his late wife. He even tried to take care of Julie, despite her antagonism. His nurse May, however, would be number one on my list of suspects. Means, opportunity, and motive, all at once."

"Exactly." Tom sighed. "It's going to be a tricky case. We need hard evidence. Last night when we paid a call on Downing, the nurse was with him. Our being there didn't shake him, but the nurse looked as if she'd like to go out through a wall."

"May? No doubt," Jeff said. "She was supposedly working at a nursing home that nobody ever heard of. She stayed at the house while his wife was dying of lung cancer, playing up to him at every opportunity and mostly ignoring poor Mrs. Downing. Sweet woman," Jeff added sarcastically.

"Life pays us out in our own coin, you know," Tom replied. "What goes around, comes around."

"You can say that again," the sheriff agreed.

The news the next morning set a lot of people back on their heels. Granger Downing's friend, the nurse May Strickland, had put around some gossip that Downing was going to marry her.

Annalisa told Tom about it when he came to get his laundry late that afternoon.

"Hey, you didn't have to go to all this trouble," he said gently, smiling at the neat piles of clothing and his slacks and button-up shirts on hangers.

"It was no trouble at all," she replied with a smile.

"Do you know how long the Strickland woman's been associated with Downing?" he asked.

"Months," came the short reply. "She moved in when his wife was diagnosed with lung cancer, supposedly to nurse her. But Julie said all May did was try to seduce the boss. The nursing was done by Julie alone."

"What a lovely woman," he replied. "Does she by any chance keep poisonous spiders and vipers in her room?"

"No. Lucky them. If one ever bit her, it would die horribly."

He chuckled. He cocked his head, noting that her long blond hair came almost to her waist in back. Her silver eyes were unusually soft. She was wearing jeans and a pink tee shirt, and she looked good enough to eat.

"Stop that," she muttered. "You won't let me ogle you, so the reverse is also true."

"I'm not ogling," he said defensively. He smiled very slowly. "I'm trying to decide between the sofa or the big cushy easy chair in front of the fireplace."

She blinked and gave him a blank look. "You're after my furniture?"

"No, tidbit. I'm after you." He picked her up and carried her into the living room, where he dropped into the armchair.

"Why did you say it was a choice between my chair and my sofa?"

"The sofa is just a little more dangerous," he murmured as he stared into her eyes for so long that she felt hot all over.

"Dangerous . . . how?" she asked huskily because the feel of all that warm strength and the closeness of that wide, chiseled mouth to her own was giving her some problems.

"Well, honey, I can't very well lay you down in the chair, now can I?" he whispered against her mouth.

The endearment and the kiss melted her. She knew without asking that he rarely if ever used endearments, and she was grateful that he hadn't chosen the sofa, because she wasn't sure if she could survive the temptation he would present, stretched out on her couch.

"Deep thoughts?" he mused as his mouth teased her lips in the silence of the living room, unbroken except for the crackling sound that came from burning wood in the fireplace, and the hard, heavy beat of her own heart.

"I'm not . . . like this," she tried to get enough breath to explain.

He just smiled. "You don't encourage men to do what I'm doing," he translated.

"Well, yes," she replied huskily.

"It's okay. You're just overwhelmed by an unexpected attraction," he whispered.

She nodded. "Yes."

His teeth nipped her lower lip. His tongue slid sensuously under her top lip and his own lips caught it and caressed it slowly. "And now you aren't sure if you should stay here with me or lock yourself in the bedroom."

She laughed. "Yes."

His nose nuzzled hers. "You're only twenty-six," he whispered into her mouth. "I'll be thirty-seven soon. And this is just an interlude. I'm not a marrying man. But you're a marrying woman, and you're too honorable to cheat your husband by sleeping around."

Her breath caught. She drew back so that she could see his eyes. "How do you know that about me?"

He traced her mouth with a big finger. "Making quick assessments about people is part of my job," he said simply. "I've learned how to do it fairly well over the years." He studied her. "You'd race after somebody who dropped a dollar bill so that you could give it back," he said gently. "You'd stop and help an injured animal on the side of the road. You'd put yourself in danger to save someone you cared about." He smiled at her surprise. "I told you. I can read people."

She let out a breath. "Well, you've got me pegged pretty good."

He drew her close, so that her cheek was resting on his broad chest. Under her ear she could hear his heartbeat, hard and heavy.

"This is nice," she whispered, closing her eyes.

"It is nice," he replied, surprised. He laid his cheek on top of her blond hair. She smelled of roses.

"People don't hug anymore," she mused sleepily. "They even stay away from people they love and they'd rather text than talk."

"I text, but it goes with my job," he said.

"I sort of figured that. And this is Friday night, so the hospital is going to be full of people with injuries." She shook her head. "Snow is in the forecast, which guarantees that a handful of idiots will drive and run into other idiots, all of whom should have stayed home."

"I guess you stay busy."

"I'll bet you do, too."

"Pretty much. Crime is crime. We have shootings with injuries every weekend."

"But you stay and do the job," she remarked.

"Somebody has to," he said simply. "If we don't do our jobs, people die. It's a hell of a responsibility."

"One that I know something about," she said, and smiled. She yawned and curled her hands into the soft fabric of his shirt. "If I stay here much longer, I'll fall asleep."

He chuckled. "And if I stay here much longer, we'll be tastier gossip than the local news."

"Think so?" she teased.

"You'll see. But I really do have to go. I have a couple of

serious interviews to do at the Downing place tomorrow and I'll need to do some research first in our violent-crime database."

She lifted her head and stared up at him with soft silver eyes. "Don't get shot," she said.

He grinned. "I've only been shot twice, and that was overseas, before I went with the Bureau."

"Twice?!" she exclaimed.

He liked the concern in her voice, in her face. "Just in the shoulder and in a leg," he said. "Nothing serious."

She was lost for words. She grimaced. Her fingers went automatically to the deep scar across his chest. "You do dangerous work," she said softly.

He shrugged. "Any work is dangerous if you don't plan ahead," he said. "And since Angie walked out on me, I haven't minded the danger so much." His face was harder than stone as he spoke.

"Would she want you to take dangerous jobs if she knew?"

"It wouldn't matter to her," he said simply. "She never actually cared enough to worry about what I did, or if I was in danger."

She smoothed her fingers over his hard, beautiful mouth. "I'd care," she said, a little belligerently. "She couldn't have been much of a girlfriend."

His eyebrows went up. He didn't say a word, but his world turned upside down. He looked at her as if he'd never seen a woman before. His fingers went to her faintly flushed face and traced down her cheek to her mouth. "If you were involved with me, you'd care," he said abruptly.

"Yes." She cleared her throat. "But I'm not involved with you."

He smiled gently. "No, you're not. And you aren't going to be," he added softly. "I live in Chicago. I'd never adjust to life in the wilds of Colorado."

She sighed. "I guess not."

He bent and kissed her tenderly. "And on that note, I'd better go back to my motel."

"Not just yet," she whispered, her silver eyes searching his dark ones. "You could pretend you cared, just for a couple of minutes, couldn't you?"

One dark eyebrow went up. "Pretend?"

"I know, you hotshot FBI guys don't deal in fantasy," she said. "And I know you'll never want to settle down in Raven Springs, Colorado. But you could kiss me just once like you meant it, couldn't you?"

"Why?" he asked, his eyes piercing as they stared straight into hers.

She swallowed, hard. "Because I've never been kissed like that in my whole life, and I'm curious."

"You're a pretty girl," he said. "I can't believe that."

"I'm shy with most people," she confessed, studying his mouth. "I don't mix well. My father drove off any guys who weren't brave enough to deal with him, and nobody at work wants anything that isn't casual."

"Casual." He cocked his head. "You don't go in for one-night stands," he translated.

"Or any other kind," she agreed. Her eyes searched his. "But just one time, just to see what it would feel like. You know, if we were, well, involved."

His big thumb rubbed over her lower lip. He could feel her tremble. "You couldn't handle being involved with me, little violet under the stair," he scoffed tenderly.

"Are you sure?"

He nodded. "And I can prove it, too," he murmured as he bent his head and his warm, firm mouth came down on her lips . . .

Chapter Three

A few seconds after Tom curled her against his broad chest, she realized what he'd meant when he said she couldn't handle an interlude with him. All those years of practice that he'd had made her feel like a teen girl on her first real date. She had no idea that a kiss had so many emotions, or that it could make her want to do shocking things.

His big hand was just under her firm little breast, feeling the increasing acceleration of her heartbeat. He felt her fingers tangling in his thick hair. He'd never thought that his hair was sensitive to touch, but pleasure pulsed through him like a shot of rum when she did that. His breath caught and he lifted his head.

She looked into his dark, curious eyes, trying to make her mind work. "French fries," she murmured as her eyes lowered to his firm, chiseled mouth.

"French fries?"

She nodded. "You can't eat just one."

He chuckled softly. "When you get my age, you can," he teased.

She made a face. "Spoilsport."

He shifted her a little closer and bent to her mouth again. He loved the way she curled into him, the uninhibited way she responded to him. She wasn't coy or teasing. She loved what he was doing to her, and it showed.

"Sometimes honesty can cause problems," he murmured against her soft mouth.

"Excuse me?" she asked.

He studied her face. Flushed cheeks, swollen mouth, sleepy, hungry eyes. "Everything you feel is right there on your face, honey. You couldn't hide it if you tried."

She laughed softly and sighed. "Why bother?" she wanted to know. "You told me you had to study body language. Was it when you went through the Academy?"

"I studied a lot of things," he agreed. He smoothed back her disheveled blond hair. "But I learned body language doing interrogation."

"Can you really tell if somebody's thinking about committing a crime by the way they sit or stand?"

His dark eyes twinkled. "Depends."

"Depends on what?"

"If they're holding a gun at the time."

She laughed. Her eyes sparkled. "I like to watch TV shows about real police work."

He traced her straight little nose. "They can't show you most of real police work," he murmured. "It's not clean enough for family viewing."

"I worked in the emergency room for six months while I was training," she said. "It was pretty rough."

He nodded. "Pretty messy, too. I've been in firefights." He chuckled. "When I was a rookie cop, we had a call about a gang shooting. Two cars of us went screeching up to the scene of the crime. No people around anywhere, and one of the others heard a noise that he thought was an automatic being cocked. He started shooting."

"Was it a gun?"

"It was a washing machine switching cycles in a nearby

apartment with the window open," he continued. "He killed the car that belonged to the family with the washing machine."

"Ouch!" she said.

"The department had to buy the family a new car. And theirs was a really new car that the rookie killed. Expensively new."

"What did they do to the policeman?"

"He went back to his former profession."

"Which was . . . ?"

"Selling car insurance."

She almost doubled up laughing. "We get all kinds who think they're perfect for police work, but it takes a special mindset."

"And guts," she added quietly. She studied his face. There were lines there that a man of thirty-six shouldn't have. She drew her fingers down his hard cheek. "We had a policeman from Catelow shot late one afternoon. He stopped a speeding car, and it was driven by a man who was running from a murder charge. He shot the officer through the stomach." She curled closer to him and rested her cheek against his chest. "It took him several days to die. His wife said she'd lived with the fear of his being killed their whole married lives. She was in her sixties, and they'd been married for thirty-five years. He was about to retire, but he never made it." She drew in a long breath, inhaling a spicy, sexy cologne that clung to his warm skin. "She said a lot of women couldn't live with that day-to-day fear, which was why the divorce rate was so high in her husband's department. She was a sweet lady. I felt so sorry for her."

"The risk goes with any job that requires guns," he said simply.

She looked up at him. "I guess if a woman married a man who did that sort of work, she'd have to be willing to accept the fear. It's something I could never do," she added quietly. "I'd go crazy."

His thumb rubbed gently along her lower lip. "I knew a woman who didn't care if I died when I went out on a call," he said, and he looked haunted for a minute. "Angie never worried about me at all."

She winced.

He saw that, and it made him feel hot all over. It was unexpected, that they'd become so close in such a short period of time. He felt comfortable with her, safe with her. It was as if he'd known her his whole life, and it disturbed him. His headlong, growing passion for her wasn't helping the situation, either.

"You're brooding," she accused quietly.

His dark eyes met her light ones. "I don't mix well with people," he said, searching for the right words. "I'm out of step with the world at large. I keep to myself mostly, except when I socialize with the guys in my office. Only a handful of them are still married. It's a hard life for people who want families. You get moved around a lot. Or, if you are single, you get sent all over the country."

"Like you are, right now," she replied.

He nodded. "It depends on the openings and who's the best person to fill them," he said. "If you specialize in crimes against children, and there's a vacancy in a department halfway across the country, you can be transferred there." He pursed his lips and his dark eyes twinkled. "Or if you really tick off your SAC, you can get sent to a little town nobody ever heard of in Alaska, permanently."

She laughed. "Do you tick off your SAC?" she wondered.

"I never see him," he replied. "I get sent out on cases a lot. I don't have a family."

She drew in a soft breath. "Me neither."

He scowled, because it bothered him to be so comfortable with a woman he'd only just met.

"You'll hurt your brain if you keep straining it like that," she said with a smile. "What's wrong?"

"I don't know you," he said slowly. "But I know you. Right down to your bones."

"I was just thinking that, about you," she replied. "I don't get close to people. I really don't." Her gaze went over him—soft, searching. "But this feels . . ."

"It feels familiar," he said curtly. "As if we've been together forever."

She nodded.

He sighed. "This was a very bad idea."

She nodded again, and laid her cheek against his chest with a soft sigh.

His arms contracted. He sat, just holding her in the silence of the room. She was soft and warm and he loved the way it felt to cuddle her. His life had been littered with women like Angie, who weren't affectionate or nurturing. They were sexy and aggressive and they liked him in bed. That was what made this little violet so rare, he considered. She was sexy, but she wasn't cold or aggressive. And she'd feel it if he got hurt on the job.

He'd never had much nurturing. His parents had worked two jobs to keep food on the table for themselves and Tom and his late sister. There hadn't been any cuddling or bedtime stories. The kids had been raised mostly by the television set and whoever had time to babysit them. It had been a fraught childhood.

"What are you thinking about?" she murmured.

"Violets," he replied and a short laugh escaped him.

Her chest rose and fell against his. "I like violets." She curled closer. "Why is life so hard?"

"Ask a philosopher. I just go after the people who try to make it harder."

"I meant to ask if you heard about what happened at the Downing place today."

His heart skipped. "Another murder?"

"Not at all. But that ex-boyfriend of May's was over there to clean out gutters for Mr. Downing and he fell off the ladder, right onto the concrete. Some people should never climb ladders in the first place."

"Why would May's ex-boyfriend be working for Downing?" he asked. He'd known about the boyfriend, but he wanted to hear what she thought.

"It's not as if Mr. Downing cares about May, regardless of what people think. Alice, who works for him, is a friend of mine. She says that May runs off any good workers so she can get her friends hired. That man, Billy Turner, is one of them. She was having an affair with Billy until Mr. Downing advertised for someone to help nurse his wife." She made a face. "Word is that Billy was furious at being jilted. But I guess he forgave her if he's working where she does."

His eyes narrowed. "Is May really a nurse?"

"She's a practical nurse," she replied. "It's a fairly highly skilled position, and there are some very good practical nurses. May isn't one. I had a friend check her grades. She almost failed every subject."

"You're a gold mine of information," he said with admiration, smiling down at her.

"I like people, mostly," she said. "But I don't like people who take advantage of sick folks."

"That makes two of us."

He tilted her face up to his and searched her eyes for so long that her heartbeat went crazy. Her lips parted as she tried to breathe normally. He saw that. It lifted his chin and made him feel vaguely arrogant. She was special. In a life filled with women who were mostly as hard as the men, she was like the violet he'd called her, growing wild deep in the forest. He felt at peace with her. His turbulent life had given him little of that pleasure.

"You really shouldn't encourage me," she said in a husky little voice.

"Encourage you to do what?" he asked.

"Go nuts over you," she said. She bit her lower lip. "You said it yourself. We're ships passing in the night. You'll walk away and never look back." She grimaced. "I'll sit here with an empty house, and maybe later on, a cat or two, mourning you."

"You'll be over me and after some other man in three weeks." He laughed with cynicism.

"Do you really think so?" she asked softly, searching his eyes.

"I have to think so," he said, forcing coldness into his tone. "I mean it. I have no desire whatsoever to spend the rest of my life with a woman, married or not."

She studied him. "Because if you get close to somebody, really close, you couldn't bear to lose them. Have you lost somebody along the way, besides the woman you wanted to marry?"

He averted his eyes.

Her small hand flattened over his shirt, under the suit jacket. "I never gossip," she said.

"Bull," he shot right back, and his eyes were accusing. "You've been telling me all about the people in the Downing household."

"Yes, because that's your business and you needed to know. I don't gossip about people's private lives, though. Not ever."

His broad, muscular chest rose and fell. His thumb went to her lower lip and rubbed softly against it. "It isn't so much what I lost, as what I never had." He drew in a breath. "My parents never touched each other, much less my late sister and me. I grew up in a household without human contact, without love. We were dependents on the tax returns when we were small. Later, we were free labor."

"It would have been that way for me, except for my mother," she said quietly. She shook her head. "People shouldn't have kids unless both parents want them. It's unfair to everybody."

The mention of children made him uncomfortable, and he didn't know why. Children had never been part of his life. His colleagues had kids, of course, and they brought them to the few social events sponsored by his office. But he avoided them mostly.

"I'm not good with kids," he said. "I haven't been around many, except casually."

Her face grew soft with emotion. "I adore them," she said. "I spent six of the happiest months of my life work- ing on the children's medical ward at my hospital. I like working emergency," she added, "but if I had a choice, it wouldn't be the emergency room."

"Can't you choose?" he asked.

She shook her head. "No openings on the children's ward. People who work there stay forever." She laughed. "I guess I would, too. It's the next best thing to having a baby of my own."

"No woman I ever dated wanted one," he pointed out.

"Let me guess," she said amusedly. "They wanted dining and dancing and hot sex."

"Please!" he muttered.

"I'm a nurse. We've seen everything."

"I'm in law enforcement. So have I," he shot back.

"If you wanted to marry your girlfriend, you must have had feelings for her."

He averted his eyes. "I wanted her. We spent most of our time apart, and that suited us. She had a high-powered sales job and was mostly on the road."

What an empty life, she was thinking. He was a man who wanted love, needed a family, but he'd convinced himself that it was impossible.

"That's not why you didn't want kids," she said, as if she knew.

His big, warm hand came down over her small one where it was resting on his chest. "My father used a leather strap on me when I misbehaved," he said curtly. "He laughed while he did it. He used it on my sister, too. The books all say that abused children grow up to be abusers."

She let her head fall back against his shoulder and looked up at him. "I can name you four kids in this very community who had similar childhoods and grew up to be exceptionally kind people. One of them is our own sheriff," she added with a smile.

"Ralston," he recalled. "I met him. He's a nice guy."

"His father drank and beat him and his mother. He said it was why he went into law enforcement."

He smiled. "That happened to a friend of mine when I was living in Delaware. It's why I went into it, too," he confessed.

She touched his hard, chiseled mouth. "I wonder if anybody has that sweet, wholesome upbringing they write fairy tales about."

"I seriously doubt it." He drew in a long breath and his eyes sketched her face. "I have to go."

"Are you sure? Couldn't you take a personal day and we could go fishing?"

He burst out laughing. "Now how did you know that I fish?"

"Because you probably get enough shooting on the job that you don't want to consider it for recreation."

"And you like to fish, do you?" he teased.

She nodded. "But with a cane pole." She made a face. "I don't do well with more technical things."

He smoothed back her soft hair. It was coming loose from its scrunchy. "I love your hair."

"It's just ordinary," she said.

"No, it's sexy." His dark eyes narrowed. They ran down her body to her breasts, which had little hard peaks on them.

He stared at them long enough that they began to feel uncomfortable. She swallowed, hard.

"You know why they get like that, don't you?" he asked gently, indicating her breasts.

"I'm a nurse."

The smile grew. "I noticed. Pity about the pole dancing."

"Now, look here, just because I work nights . . . !"

His mouth eased down over hers in a slow, sweet pressure that very quickly made all the throbbing and breathlessness much worse. Her nails caught at his shoulders as the pleasure worked its way down from her mouth, making her moan softly.

He turned her in his arms and his mouth grew insistent, slow and ardent. She held on for dear life. This was the stuff of dreams, this gorgeous man holding her and kissing her as if he wanted her.

He lifted his mouth away a breath. His dark eyes glittered with desire and frustration. "I'm not living in the wilds of Colorado."

"And I'm not living in the wilds of Chicago," she managed.

"So it's a good thing that we're not getting involved," he continued. While he was saying it, his big hand was working its way under her blouse and up to the frilly, brief little bra she was wearing.

She caught his wrist halfheartedly.

"Coward," he drawled, but with pure affection. "Don't you want to know how it feels?"

"Of course I want to know," she returned sharply. "But the less we do together, the easier it will be to forget when you leave."

"I'm not leaving yet," he murmured, and his mouth closed her eyes and moved tenderly all over her flushed face. While he was doing that, his hand was under her arm, not in any intimate way, but in such a way that she wanted it to be. She shivered and twisted involuntarily toward him.

"It's like shooting fish in a barrel," he murmured as his mouth found hers. "I should be ashamed of myself."

Her arms slid up around his neck and she lifted herself, just enough that his hand smoothed up over her firm breast.

"Oh . . . glory," she ground out.

"And that was your first mistake," he whispered roughly. "Come here!"

The kiss was no longer teasing. It was hungry and hard and full of frustrated passion that made her sob.

His hand was at the base of her spine now, turning her hips into his so that she felt immediately what was happening to him.

He groaned. It had been such a long time since he'd felt passion. Angie didn't really inspire it. She liked it hot and fast and over, so he got used to it that way. But this woman was delicate and fragile, and he wanted to treat her like porcelain. She invited tenderness. She invited a hunger that was unlike anything he'd ever felt in his life.

She knew she couldn't save herself by protesting physically. He was getting in over his head. So she looked into his eyes, with her face flushed and her breath coming in gasps.

"I hope you want a baby right away," she stammered, "because I don't have anything to take and it would embarrass me to tears to go to my elderly doctor and ask him for birth control."

He stopped at once, half shocked, half amused at the desperation in her voice.

He looked down at her with affection, despite the ache she'd given him. "I could go with you and explain why we want it," he offered.

She hit his chest with a little fist. "That wasn't nice."

He wrinkled his nose and grinned at her. "We'd be good together."

She drew in a shaky breath. "I know."

"But a child shouldn't be born because two people lost their heads."

She nodded.

"Or because one of them was too shy to ask for a prescription."

She nodded again. It was easier than trying to think up something witty to say.

He smiled tenderly and bent to brush a shivery soft kiss against her warm, swollen lips.

"There's also the excuse that I'm too tired. And it isn't really an excuse. I didn't sleep last night," he murmured.

"Why?" she asked curiously.

"I tend to dwell on things when I lie down and cut off the lights. Things . . . bother me."

She cocked her head. "Things that happened to you, or things you did?"

"Both." And he was suddenly businesslike and abrupt. He got up, bringing her with him. He stood up. "Thanks for folding my clothes," he said, and he couldn't keep the affection out of his deep voice as he looked at her, seeing the visible evidence of his passion. She looked good with her hair disheveled by his fingers, her mouth swollen from his kisses.

"You're welcome." She smiled up at him. "It's very . . . unusual, isn't it?" she added and became somber. "I mean, someone seeming so familiar, someone you've never met before."

He nodded. "Very unusual. That's why we both have to do our best to ignore it."

"Because you won't live in the wilds of Colorado," she agreed, and her pale eyes twinkled.

He chuckled. "Something like that. And I've got a murder to solve. Stay out of trouble with the law," he added as he headed for the door.

"You're the law."

"Exactly." He stopped, turned, and bent to kiss the tip of her nose. "Sleep well."

She laughed, full of joy and not really understanding why. "Don't get shot."

"First lesson I learned on the firing range in the Army. How to duck." He gave her a grin as he picked up his clean shirts, pants, and the rest of his stuff in the bag, and closed the door behind him.

She went to bed, certain that she'd never be able to sleep after their heated interlude. To her amazement, she fell asleep the minute her head hit the pillow.

Tom forced Annalisa to the back of his mind as he started conducting interviews with people who'd seen the victim hours before her death. He had May Strickland and Billy

Turner squarely in his sights, but the sheriff mentioned that a local beautician had seen Julie on the day she'd vanished. So he went to the beauty parlor in town first.

The hairdresser who'd given Julie a permanent the morning of the day that she vanished was named Hazel. She was friendly and cooperative.

"I always liked Julie," she recalled. "She had her moods, but she was usually happy when she came in for me to do her hair. She loved trying new hairstyles and buying pretty things to go in her hair."

"Did she seem disturbed the last time she came here?" Tom asked.

"Yes. She was really upset," Hazel replied. "She said that her mother's new caregiver was paying far more attention to her stepfather than she was to her mother. Mrs. Downing would be wet all over, and May wouldn't even bother to clean her up. Julie had all the work."

"Didn't she tell her stepfather?"

"Well, that's the thing," Hazel replied. "She said that her father, rather her stepfather, didn't want to put that burden of all nursing on Julie. May had convinced him that she knew how to take care of sickly people. When he was around, she made sure that Mrs. Downing was cleaned up and had everything she needed. Julie said he'd been away on business a lot just lately," she added. "Not that he wanted to be. He loved his wife, but she owned a lot of real estate and a business and he had to keep an eye on those. He told Julie it was like pulling teeth to have to leave his wife at all. But that's why he didn't know what May was really doing."

"Couldn't Mrs. Downing tell him what was going on?"

Hazel shook her head. "She was very weak. Julie wanted to call in hospice. They have specially trained nurses, you know, but May said it would just be a big hassle with half a dozen strange people in the house all the time, and Mr.

Downing likes his privacy. She convinced him that it would be a mistake. Mrs. Downing was on heavy sedation because May told the doctor that Mrs. Downing was complaining about the pain. She didn't really know what was going on around her."

Tom was taking notes. "They said Julie didn't like her stepfather."

"She didn't like most people," Hazel said. "She was very jealous of her stepfather and afraid of losing her mother. They were very close. She was an only child and her mother had always taken care of her. She'd have resented anybody who came between them. But she did say that last afternoon that she guessed her stepfather wasn't so bad after all."

Tom let out a breath. "Too little, too late, I guess," Hazel said. "I don't think he killed Julie, but a lot of people do. Granger Downing's not a nice person, on the surface. But underneath all those stinging nettles is a man who'd give the last crumb he had to a starving man."

"I've heard that from other people," Tom told her. "In fact, I met him myself. He isn't so bad."

"He can be. Some man was making lewd comments around his wife when they first got married, and Granger slugged him." Hazel chuckled. "Almost ended up in jail, but Mrs. Downing stepped in and smoothed over things."

Tom was reflecting that a man who was that protective of his wife was unlikely to want her dead.

"But that May Strickland," Hazel continued, shaking her head. "She's bad news, any way you look at it. She isn't from here, you know. She came from Denver. She's only been in Raven Springs for a short time."

"How about her ex-boyfriend?"

"Billy Turner," Hazel replied, shaking her head. "He's local. He was accused of assault last year, but his dad managed to talk the victim out of prosecuting him."

"Do you know the reason for the assault?"

"Well, it was old man Riley Barnes," she told him. "He'd just come from the bank with a pocketful of cash that he was going to spend at the cattle auction. Billy swore the old man had said something that made him angry enough to swing on him. I never believed that. I think Billy had robbery in mind and got cold feet when the victim yelled for help and the police came." She laughed. "He got a good lecture from Sheriff Ralston and a warning. Jeff didn't want to let him off, but Mr. Barnes refused to prosecute."

"People who assault senior citizens should be prosecuted," Tom said icily.

"That's exactly what I think," Hazel said, and her expression was as hard as Tom's. "It started local folks thinking. There was a murder here about two years ago that was never solved. It involved another old man, a rich one, who lived alone. He was found on the floor of his office, stone-cold dead with the door to his office locked, from the inside."

"I'm sure they checked the windows."

"No windows," she said, surprising him. "French doors. And they were locked from the inside, too. Sheriff Ralston has been working that cold case every spare minute he has. The victim was his godfather."

"Tough," Tom said. "Can you think of anything else that might be helpful?" he added.

Hazel studied him for a minute. "Emus kick forward, not backwards."

He stared at her without blinking.

"Oh, you mean helpful about the case," she replied, with a grin. "Sorry. We have an emu farm outside town. One of the emus got loose once and our former local vet went to try and catch him. He walked up to the emu and got kicked in a very bad place because he didn't realize their legs work the opposite of ours."

He grimaced. "A lesson he didn't forget, I imagine."

"He packed his bags and went back to Los Angeles the very next day." Hazel chuckled. "He said he wasn't suited to the outback."

Tom chuckled. "It certainly sounds like it. I've never seen a live emu; only on nature programs on TV. Not much of that, either. I work long hours."

"I imagine you do. I hope you catch whoever killed Julie," she added with narrow eyes. "She was a sweet, kind girl, despite her mood swings. Nobody should be left to freeze to death, not even a rabid animal!"

"We'll find out who did it," Tom assured her. "The investigator was very thorough. We need enough evidence to convict, if we can connect it to anyone local."

"Really hurts to think our community could harbor somebody like that," she said sadly. "We're kind people for the most part. We may gossip about our citizens, but it's not malicious. It's because we care."

"I live in Chicago," he replied, "where it's a good idea to mind your own business and not have much to do with your neighbors."

She frowned. "That's a sad way to live. Do you have family there, at least?"

He shook his head. "My whole family is dead."

"But who takes care of you, if you get sick?" she wanted to know.

That question was so disturbing that he pretended not to hear it. He stood up, smiling politely. "Thank you very much for your time. If I have any follow-up questions, I'll be in touch, if that's okay."

"It certainly is," Hazel assured him. "I want that person caught, too. It gives our town a bad name to have an unsolved murder in it."

He nodded.

* * *

He went out for a late lunch, stopping by the local café. Jeff Ralston was there having lunch alone. He motioned for Tom, who had a hamburger and fries and coffee on a tray, to join him.

"Do you always eat alone?" he asked Jeff as he put his plate and mug on the table and slid the tray onto Jeff's empty one before he sat down.

Jeff sighed. "Story of my life. I was involved with an ex-girlfriend, but she went back to Denver and got married. So, yes, I eat alone, unless one of my deputies is free at the same time I am. Not likely this time of year, with snow and ice alternating weeks, and wrecks by the half dozen."

Tom chuckled as he started on his hamburger. "Sounds like Chicago in winter. We always get a few people from warmer climates who move in and don't know how to drive in ice and snow. Sometimes that ends tragically."

"Tell me about it," Jeff said with a grimace. "So, how's the investigation going?"

"I'm learning a lot about Raven Springs," Tom said. "And about the murder victim."

Jeff sipped coffee. "Learning a lot about Annalisa Davis, too, we hear," Jeff added abruptly, and with a broad smile.

Chapter Four

Tom's hamburger was suspended in midair as he stared at Jeff, surprised by the unexpected comment.

"Don't worry, it's not malicious gossip," Jeff assured him. "We take an interest in anybody who lives or works here. Annalisa is special," he added quietly and with a smile. "She had a bad time with her dad. A lot of cops drink, you know, but he was usually over the limit. Everybody protected him."

"Why?"

"He had to kill his best friend."

Tom's breath caught. "Excuse me?"

"There was a shooting downtown, the first one we ever had in Raven Springs. Two men got into an argument and one of them pulled a gun. Sam Davis was police chief here, and he was closer than any of his men to the scene of the disturbance. He got out of his squad car and only saw the back of the man with the gun. He yelled for the man to put the gun down and put his hands over his head. Except the man, who was on drugs, whirled and started to fire at Sam. He returned fire and he was an expert shot." He grimaced. "The man turned out to be his best friend. Sam knew that he smoked an occasional joint, but he didn't realize that his friend had gone on to hard drugs. Never used them around Sam, so Sam didn't know. They had to tranquillize

Sam afterwards, and he stayed drunk for a week. He never got over it. He started drinking and then he couldn't stop."

"Well, it doesn't excuse him, but it does explain him," Tom had to admit. "I've seen guys like that on the job in law enforcement. Some get into situations where they're forced to kill friends or even family. Some become suicidal, some drink.

"Most professions that require guns sometimes require you to use them," Tom finished quietly.

"I've been lucky," Ralston said. "I wounded a man once or twice. Never had to kill one. Although my deputy did. Perp had me by the throat after I pumped a nine-millimeter pistol into him. My deputy came along with his .45 just in the nick of time. Saved my life." He sighed. "Then he got drunk for a week, but I went out to see him, and the Methodist minister and I talked him down. He's sober as a judge these days and a hell of an investigator."

Tom didn't reply. He'd killed men in combat. It wasn't something he liked to remember. And then there was the one man he'd shot in Chicago, who later died. That one had soured him on life. He was still trying to get past the memory. It had been a homeless man, a Vietnam veteran, trying to hold up a convenience store with a toy gun—but it hadn't looked like a toy gun. He'd turned and pointed it at Tom and Tom had fired. The man, when Tom got to him and realized what he'd done, was forgiving even then. He was tired of living, he managed to say as they waited for the ambulance. He had no family, nobody who cared about him, no money, no job, no nothing. Dying wasn't the horror people thought it was. His whole squad had died in Vietnam except for him. He drank to forget. He couldn't stop. He told Tom not to be sorry, it was an honest mistake. He told the investigating officers the same thing. Tom stayed with him in the hospital until he died. It had torn him up. He considered how Annalisa would have behaved had she been there. She'd have crawled into his lap and kissed him and cuddled him and tried to remind him that life had a purpose and a plan, and some things that happened were not under anyone's control.

"Those are real homemade french fries," Ralston said, breaking into Tom's thoughts and indicating the untouched portion of his companion's plate. "Nothing frozen or fast food about them."

"Really?" Tom picked one up and bit into it. "Oh, my," he said and sighed.

"Great, aren't they? It's why we eat here. Oh, and there's fresh catfish on Friday, grilled or fried."

"That's about my favorite food," he replied. "I like cat-fish. I used to go out on the river late in the afternoon when I was a kid. Best time to catch them is late in the day," he recalled with a smile.

"In Chicago?"

He shook his head. "I moved there when I went with the Bureau. I was born in a little town just south of Wilmington, Delaware," he recalled. "Good fishing in the state park nearby, and plenty of tourist attractions, including the largest formal French gardens in North America at the Nemours Estate."

"Did you live there a long time?" Ralston asked conversationally.

"Until I was twelve," he replied. "Then our parents moved to a town outside Chicago."

"You have siblings?"

"I had a sister but she was killed in a car wreck," Tom told him. He studied Ralston. "Have you traveled much?"

"Just to Denver on cases," was the bland reply. "I've never been out of my state since I was born." He chuckled.

"Good Lord," Tom said, shocked.

"I guess you FBI guys travel a lot."

"Yes," Tom replied. "Maybe too much. I didn't worry about it when I was younger, but you don't put down roots when you're on the road all the time." He studied the dregs of his coffee. "It's a lonely life."

"I know that feeling," the other man said with a sigh. "I always thought I'd marry a hometown girl and settle down, but most of the women around here are married or involved or too young or too old." He chuckled.

Tom just smiled.

He stopped by Downing's house after phoning first. He wanted to talk to May Strickland. She was about to leave the house when he got there, and she looked flushed and guilty when he asked to speak with her.

"But I don't know anything about how Julie died," she blurted out.

"That's not why I want to speak to you," he said pleasantly. "I want to know about the late Mrs. Downing. You nursed her until her death, I believe?"

"Oh!" She calmed down. "Well, yes, I did. I'm a practical nurse."

"Is there someplace we can sit?" he asked.

"Certainly. Mr. Downing went to Denver today to talk to some people about a new investment. We can speak in the living room." She led him into the house. "Alice, the FBI man is here, could we have coffee, please?" she asked the maid as they passed.

Alice gave her a nasty look that she didn't see, but she smiled at Tom. "Of course. Coming right up," she said cheerfully.

Tom followed May into the living room and sat in one of the cushy armchairs beside the marble coffee table. May lounged on the sofa. She wasn't bad looking for a woman her age, he considered, but she had eyes like a shark. Dark and cold and predatory.

"Are you married, Agent Jones?" she asked with a coy glance.

"Married to my job," he replied. "What can you tell me about Mrs. Downing?"

She blinked, as if she hadn't expected the sudden change of subject. "Well, she was dying of lung cancer when I was hired to look after her. Poor little thing," she said with unconvincing sympathy. "I did everything possible to make her comfortable."

"Odd. I was told that Julie did most of the cleaning up," he said suddenly, and pinned her with his dark eyes.

"Well, Julie did help," she conceded, and her face flushed. She looked like a trapped animal.

"Have you been in the employ of any local citizens, before you came here?" he asked.

"No. Not here."

"You worked someplace else?" His voice was deep and slow and precise. But the cold stare that went with the words backed down anything May might have said in defense of her own position here.

"I, uh, I worked farther north," she said.

"Where?"

"I . . . c-can't remember at the moment," she stammered.

Alice came in with coffee, giving May time to get herself back in order. She didn't bother to thank Alice. Tom did.

He picked up the cup of black coffee May poured for him, declining any condiments. "This is good," he remarked.

"Mr. Downing only has the best," May said. "He prefers Jamaican Blue Mountain coffee. It's one of the most expensive coffees in the world," she added.

And she'd know, he said to himself. "How was Mr. Downing around his wife?" Tom asked after a minute.

"Well, he was sad, of course. We all knew she was dying and that nothing could be done for her. The doctor came out twice a day, just at the last."

"Don't they have hospice here?" he asked.

She hesitated. "Of course they do. It's just that Mr. Downing values his privacy. He doesn't like strangers around."

His dark eyes were steady on her face. She actually squirmed in her chair.

His gaze went back to his smartphone and the notes application he'd pulled up. "Julie was found in the evening, but preliminary reports from the crime lab put the time of death anywhere from six to eight hours before the ransom was paid." He looked up at her. "In other words, Julie was dead before the ransom was ready to be delivered."

She cleared her throat. "I guess the kidnapper wanted a long head start, don't you think?"

"That would be my guess. Although it would take a hard-hearted criminal to leave a young woman out in the cold to freeze to death. It's a particularly unpleasant way to die."

"I imagine so." She smiled at him.

He thought how inappropriate that smile was, and that he needed to do a lot of digging into May Strickland's background before he asked her any more questions.

He put away the smartphone, finished his coffee, and got to his feet. He glanced at May. "Thanks for your cooperation," he said. "I may have a question or two later, but I think that's all for now."

She stood up, relaxed now. "No problem," she said. "Any time."

He nodded and went out of the room and into the kitchen, where Alice was working on a cake.

She turned as he entered and smiled. "Did you find the

barbeque place all right?" she asked brightly, just as May came to the door.

"I'm going out, just for a few minutes, Alice," May said, and nodded toward the two people in the kitchen as she went quickly out the front door.

"I'll bet she fed you a lot of bull," Alice scoffed.

"Enough. What's she still doing here, now that Mrs. Downing is deceased?" He knew the answer, but wanted to have Alice corroborate it.

"She's convinced Mr. Downing that he needs someone to keep a watch on his blood pressure." She rolled her eyes. "As if he couldn't drive to the doctor's office every day if he needed to. She's like a tick. She's attached herself to him, and he's having trouble getting her loose."

He chuckled in spite of himself. "Does he find her attractive?"

"Well, I heard him tell an old friend that if he had to choose between May and a mule, he'd take the mule!"

He had to stifle a laugh. "She seems to think she's irresistible."

"She's the only one. Maybe that ex-boyfriend thought she was," she added. "She was holding the ladder for him when he fell." She glanced his way while she worked. "Anybody can stand on a ladder, unless they're pushed."

"You think she pushed him?"

"He's been conspicuous around here since Julie died, and he makes May very nervous. If anybody was involved in that, it's those two. Wouldn't surprise me if he knew something he shouldn't and May's afraid he might talk."

"Hence the falling ladder," he mused.

"Exactly. And here's a piece of free advice. If you ever get on a ladder at this house, make sure May isn't holding it for you!"

"That's one promise I can make and keep," he assured her.

He asked several other questions, mostly about Downing's daily habits and May's background, but Alice was stumped when it came to the nurse.

"Nobody knows anything much about her locally," Alice told him. "She came here from Denver." She shook her head. "I heard that Annalisa checked out her grades and they were almost all just shy of failing."

His eyebrows went up. "Do you know everything about other people here?"

She laughed. "It's a small-town thing. You get used to it."

"I'm afraid I never would," he replied.

Alice just smiled at him.

He went back to the motel much later, dragging himself out of the car with a long sigh. He noticed that Annalisa's car was also under the carport.

The porch light came on as he closed and locked the car door.

"Hungry?" Annalisa asked from the doorway.

"I had a hamburger about"—he checked his watch—"ten hours ago."

"I made meat loaf and mashed potatoes," she said. "And apple pie."

He drew in a breath. "If that's an invitation, I'll accept it. I'm too tired to go out and try to find food at this hour."

She grinned. "I've got an hour before I have to be at work. I can't bear to go on the job with an empty stomach."

He laughed softly. "I would have imagined the opposite."

She held the door open for him. "It depends on what we get and how bad it is," she said. "I threw up one time, when I'd just started training." She made a face. "I never did it again. The orderlies ran me ragged about it. And everybody knew. I guess it's sort of an initiation."

"We have them in law enforcement as well. You never show weakness in front of your unit. It's always a mistake."

"I can imagine. Sit down. Want coffee?"

"Oh, yes," he said, leaning back in the chair with a sigh.

"Long day?"

"Very long. Murder investigations are the worst. I've got a prime suspect, but I can't make an arrest without concrete proof. It's frustrating."

She put a dish of meat loaf and one of mashed potatoes and one of steamed cabbage on the table, which was already set with thin porcelain plates that had a floral pattern. The silverware all matched, too.

"You look surprised," she commented.

"Yes. Your silverware matches," he added, picking up a fork and studying it. "No two of mine back in my apartment are alike, and most of my plates are chipped," he added.

"Poor man," she teased.

He laughed. "Well, what I have is functional, at least."

"I like pretty things," she said, offering him the plate of meat loaf.

"So do I," he said, but he was looking at her with blatant affection.

She flushed. He put meat loaf on his plate and then mashed potatoes.

She hesitated with the bowl of steamed cabbage. "Don't feel you have to eat this just because I cooked it," she said. "My father loathed steamed cabbage."

"It's one of my favorite dishes," he replied softly.

She brightened. "Oh." And she handed him the bowl.

They ate in a comfortable silence. It didn't take long to get to the pie. He was hungry.

"You're a wonderful cook," he remarked.

"Only to a starving man," she teased. "Didn't anybody offer to feed you?"

He shook his head. "I had a hamburger with your sheriff at lunch, but he didn't buy it for me. No worries," he said, when she looked disturbed. "The Bureau gives us a meal allowance."

"Thank goodness. You have to have regular meals or your health suffers, especially in a stressful line of work."

"I usually grab a candy bar or a protein bar when I'm working. I don't have time to cook at home and I get tired of takeout."

She glanced at him. "That's why I cook. I don't like take-out."

"The pie is awesome."

She grinned. "It won a prize at the county fair last summer," she said proudly.

"County fair? People still have those?" he exclaimed.

"It's a small community," she reminded him. "You might have noticed all the different Christmas decorations and the displays in the windows? Everything in cities these days is generic. Not in Raven Springs. We're traditional. We even have Christmas carolers who go door to door and get invited inside to drink hot chocolate!"

"Oh, good Lord, it's like stepping back into a 1950s holiday black-and-white movie," he groaned.

"Go ahead and say it," she chided. "Come on. 'Bah, humbug!'"

He laughed deeply as he finished his pie. "I'm not much on holidays."

"You get off from work for holidays, don't you?" she asked.

"I usually volunteer to work on them, so the men and

women who have kids can stay home on Christmas, especially."

"I knew you were a nice man," she said demurely.

He cocked his head and studied her. She wore on his heart day by day. He'd never felt such an attraction to anyone. He felt safe when he was with her, as if he belonged. It had been a very long time since he'd wanted to belong anywhere. This lovely little violet worried about him, loved to cuddle with him, but she was fiery and she had a temper as well. He laughed inwardly remembering their introduction when she'd demanded that he move his car out of her driveway.

"Why are you grinning like that?" she wanted to know.

And she never missed the changing expressions on his face, he mused to himself. "I was remembering the night I met you," he explained.

She laughed. "I guess I was pretty over-the-top."

"I noticed."

"It's just that people at this motel have been using my private driveway for years."

"Pity the motel doesn't have enough parking spots for its visitors," he pointed out.

"I've told them that often enough. The manager says he's sorry, but nothing ever gets done. In fact, you were the first person who ever apologized about parking there. The others, mostly men, got belligerent because I insist that they move their cars so I can get out."

"I imagine that's frustrating," he agreed, surprised that he was angry about it. She was a sweet woman. Stupid men, to rage at a kindhearted woman when they themselves were in the wrong.

"You look really tired, Tom," she said quietly.

His heart jumped at the sound of his name on her lips. He

glanced at her and smiled. "I am. A lot of my job is verbal, but it's still wearing."

She nodded. "I understand."

"How did you know about May Strickland's grades?" he asked suddenly. "And if you searched them out, then you must know where she went to school also, right?"

She grinned. "You're sharp!"

He chuckled. "Goes with the badge. Tell me."

"I have a friend who works in Denver," she confided. "She has access to information that I'd have to pay for. She found out for me, and told me what May's grades were like. She went to a nursing school in Aspen Lodge, just outside Denver. My friend said May worked for a nursing home there just briefly."

He was taking notes. He looked up. "Did she quit or was she fired?" he asked.

"Make that *very* sharp," she mused, studying him with warm affection. "She was invited to leave. They hesitated to fire a young nurse at her first assignment. She was messing around with an intern while an old lady she was supposed to be bathing had a stroke."

His dark eyes flickered. "She should have been fired, and that information should have gone on her permanent record."

"According to my friend, there were extenuating circumstances."

Both heavy eyebrows lifted, and he waited.

"May has mental issues," she replied. "We don't like to label them these days. Politically incorrect. But she's bipolar. She's normal on some days, and about twenty degrees off-center on others."

"She has no damned business working around sick people," he said flatly.

"Well, she was diagnosed and medicated. The problem is that she won't take her medication. She did take it at her next job, probably because she realized that some employers would press the issue."

"Where was the next job?"

She sipped coffee. "At a private nursing home, La Chalet," she said, "also in Aspen Lodge. I believe she and the owner had a, well, relationship. He was an older man and May was supposedly very pretty when she was younger."

"Do you know anything at all about what went on while she was there?"

"Besides sleeping with the owner until his wife caught them, you mean?" she asked whimsically.

He chuckled. "Yeah. Besides that."

"Not really. My friend left nursing to become a skip tracer in Denver. Her husband has a detective agency that's affiliated with a big detective agency in Houston, Texas. She's very good at what she does."

"I've worked with detective agencies in Texas," he remarked, still putting notes into his smartphone. "Sorry I can't tell you more."

He looked up, affection and soft wonder in his expression. "Honey, I work for the best law enforcement agency in the world. I can take it from here. I need to make use of my very expensive training."

She grinned. "I guess so."

He smiled at her. "What is there to do in this town at night?" he asked.

She shrugged. "Not much. We don't have pole dancing or amusement parks," she teased. "There's a movie theater and an ice-skating rink. That's about all, unless someone wants to drive all the way to Denver."

He pursed his sensual lips. "There's a lot to do in Denver," he said.

She sighed. "I know. But it's a very long drive. My car wouldn't make it halfway."

"My car would."

Her heart jumped. Was he suggesting . . . ?

"I'll have to go to Denver to check this out. I can't do this much detective work online. So when's your next day off?"

The world became a wonderland, just that quickly. Her silver eyes brightened with joy. "I'm off tomorrow and the next two days," she said. "We work four days on, fifteen hours a day, and then we get three days off."

He grimaced. "You're on your feet a lot."

"You get used to it." She smiled. "What do you have in mind?"

"Just a day trip, but I'd enjoy the company."

Her face lit up. "Me, too," she said softly.

His chest expanded with pure delight. "Okay, then. You'll have to get up early."

"I'll just stay up, when I get off my shift," she said simply. "I can sleep when we get back."

He frowned, hesitating.

"I've done it before," she told him, and smiled. "I have sleep issues. Every few nights, I can't sleep at all."

He sighed. "I have those, too."

"Mine are from stress on the job," she said. She studied his face. "I expect yours are from more than stress."

He didn't speak at all.

One of her small hands slid over his that was resting on the table. "I'm not going to propose marriage," she said drolly. "I was just making a comment."

He laughed. "Is that how I looked?"

She nodded. "Pretty much." Her eyes slid over him. "I know you aren't going to settle down in the wilds of Colorado, if that helps."

His hand turned over and his fingers curled into hers. "Life is different since I met you," he said after a minute, making her heart jump. "I'm not used to women who nurture. If you want the truth, I only seem to attract the sort that step over you on the way to another man."

Now it was her turn not to speak. She was thinking that she could never do that, not for any reason. In a very short space of time, he'd become part of her day-to-day life. She frowned a little, because she didn't understand why.

"Have you ever been in love?" he wanted to know.

She laughed. "I don't think so," she confessed. "I've had crushes on doctors and once, even, on another nurse—a male one," she clarified. "But the sort of love they describe in novels, no, I don't think so." She looked up. "You?"

He made a face and drew in a long breath. "I had a crush on my next-door neighbor when I was ten. She moved away. There were a few casual things after I grew up. Angie was the closest I came to love. But that was a physical thing."

"My grandparents were best friends," she said after a minute. "They went everywhere together. They liked the same sort of things, kept to themselves, played video games together," she added, laughing softly in memory. "When he died of a heart attack, she didn't last six months. She said it was like her soul went with him, and her body just felt empty. They were married almost fifty years."

"I don't know that I want to feel anything like that," he mused.

"Me either," she confessed.

He played with her fingers idly while he thought. "There's a big ice rink in Denver," he said. "It's open late." He looked up. "I'm not much on movies out. I like to watch them in my living room, so I can get up and grab a sandwich or a beer if I want to."

She burst out laughing. "That's me," she replied. "I hate crowded places, especially now."

"So, we could go skating. If you don't know how, I'll teach you."

"I've been skating since I was five," she told him. "I love the ice. I even have my own skates."

"I'll have to rent some, but it might be fun. And there's a place near the rink that serves some of the best sushi . . ."

"I love sushi!" she exclaimed. "We had a nurse who worked with us who lived in Denver. One day when she was on day shift, she brought in a cooler full of it for us to have for lunch. I thought I'd died and gone to heaven!"

His hand contracted. "I got hooked on it in Chicago," he said. "One of the guys was crazy about it. He took me with him to this little Japanese place on a back street. I was sure I wouldn't like what I called 'fish bait,' but after the first bite, I was truly hooked. I have it every week back home."

Her eyes were full of delight. He studied her, feeling his heart lift. So many things in common, he thought, and his hand became caressing. Then, suddenly, his face went taut and he let go of her hand.

"What is it?" she asked.

"Years," he replied somberly, his eyes searching hers.

It took her a minute to understand what he was referring to. "Oh."

"When you were born, I was eleven," he pointed out.

"Well, it isn't as if you're exactly over-the-hill," she replied. "And it wouldn't matter if you were. I don't mind polishing wheelchairs."

That took a minute. He chuckled. "I'll get shot before I end up like that," he said with some conviction.

She made a face and now she was looking overly thoughtful.

"What?" he asked.

"Dangerous professions," she replied. He just nodded. "Age and job."

"Exactly."

"But we're going to be just friends, so none of that matters," he replied coolly. "We can have a day out together while I investigate a suspect. We'll have fun. And besides, there will be sushi."

That brought the smile back. He loved the way she looked when she smiled. It made her pretty face even prettier.

"If we leave early, we can get back home before you get sleepy," he said. "What time do you get off?"

"Seven, but I have to give the report to the day nurses first, and it takes a few minutes to drive home."

He was thinking. "We could leave at eight. That would give us plenty of time."

She nodded.

"Wear something warm," he added. "They're predicting snow tomorrow."

She looked crestfallen. "We might not be able to go," she said.

"Woman, I can drive in three feet of 'snow and ice,'" he pointed out. "I live in Chicago."

Her eyes twinkled. "Why, so you do! Okay. I'm game if you are!"

"I'm game, all right." He checked his watch. "I'm going over to the hospital to see that ex-boyfriend of May Strickland's. He might give me some answers."

"He's on the second floor," she told him, standing up when he did. "My friend Mary is the charge nurse. I'll phone and tell her you're coming." She sized him up with her eyes. "I'll make sure she knows you're off-limits, too."

His eyebrows lifted. "Look here, kid, I'm not property."

"Oh, yes, you are," she teased. She went close, reached up with her arms, and tugged his face down. "Private property, no trespassing . . ."

The last word went into his hard mouth as it came down over her lips. She caught her breath at the raw passion in the kiss. He lifted her against him, holding her close, feeling her warm body cling to his. He was sure that he didn't want to get seriously involved with her. His body had other ideas.

He groaned. "Hospital. Suspect. Interrogation," he managed.

She didn't say a word. Her arms tightened around his neck.

It was a long, sweet time before he finally set her back on her feet. He was breathing heavily and his heartbeat had been almost shaking her.

He was irritated, because he thought she was being coy, playing with him. But when he looked down at her, he saw the helpless hunger there, the warm affection that she couldn't hide. No, he told himself. She wasn't playing. She was as incapable of stopping what was happening as he was.

"Skates. Denver. Sushi," he said after a minute. "First thing tomorrow morning."

She nodded, her heart in her eyes. "I'll be ready."

He bent and kissed just the tip of her nose. "Sleep tight."

She smiled. "You, too," she whispered.

He turned at the door. "I knew you were trouble the minute I saw you."

She laughed.

He shook his head and closed the door behind him.

Chapter Five

Billy Turner wasn't happy to have the FBI in his hospital room at all. "I don't have to talk to you without an attorney," he said belligerently.

Tom sat down in the chair beside his bed. "You won't like the way that plays out," he said easily. "I'm interrogating you in reference to a murder investigation. If you need an attorney, I'll begin to see you as a suspect." He smiled.

Billy averted his eyes. "I never killed nobody," he said curtly.

"Then you shouldn't mind answering some questions about your girlfriend."

The man's eyes popped. "About May?" he exclaimed.

Tom nodded. He pulled out the notes application on his cell phone.

"Surely you don't think she killed the girl?" Billy asked shortly.

"I don't know who killed Julie," he said. "But I'm going to find out," he added, and he didn't blink. His dark eyes could look intimidating. They did now. "Whatever it takes."

Billy shifted in the bed and winced. Tom had had a talk with his doctor, who was making rounds on the floor when he came in. Billy had two broken ribs and a crack in his pelvis that would probably require orthopedic surgery. "You were lucky your injuries weren't worse," Tom said. "From all accounts it was a bad fall." He sat back in the chair. "Hasn't your girlfriend been to see you?"

"She's not my girlfriend. Not anymore, anyway," he said, and sounded torn. "She's after bigger game than me. Old Downing's rich, you know, and she thinks if she swans around him he'll marry her. But he won't," he added shortly.

"Are you sure about that?"

Billy looked smug all of a sudden. "I'm real sure."

"How long have you known her?"

"I grew up here in Raven Springs. I met May in a diner in Denver. My dad was well-to-do," he added. "He had investments and things. When he died, I took May out and bought her some really pretty clothes and a car and some diamonds. She moved down here to be near me, or so she said. I used up all the money," he said irritably. "So then I had to get odd jobs, just to keep up my dad's house. May got me on with Mr. Downing, after she went to work for him. I did yard work and such. He didn't know about May and me, but it didn't matter. He was crazy over his wife. I felt sorry for him when she died. He lost it. May was going to make a play for him then, but he left to go to his sister's house and stayed for a month. So much for that great plan of hers," he muttered.

"She sounds mercenary," Tom said deliberately.

"She's worse than that. She'll do anything for money." His eyes were haunted for a minute. "My mama raised me to be kind to other people. But I fell hard for May and I forgot my upbringing. Women can make you crazy for them," he said almost to himself.

"I guess so," Tom replied.

"So when Mr. Downing came back, I was still doing work for him and May stayed on because she convinced him that he needed a nurse to watch over his blood pressure. I didn't have any money. May dropped me like a hot rock. But Mr.

Downing was rich and she started thinking up ways of getting him to marry her." He glanced at Tom. "He lives high, and he's used to being around people with money. May lived in a small town outside Denver in a shack with a father who deserted her and a mother who was always one jump ahead of the law. She doesn't know how to behave in high society. It's a way of life. Not something you can just pick up. I tried to tell her that. She won't listen. She's off her meds and sure that she can get Mr. Downing to the altar." His jaw tautened. "She can't. And if she doesn't straighten up, she's going to have more problems than she can deal with." He glanced at Tom. "I know things about her. Things she doesn't want other people to know."

Tom was making notes. He was certain that the man had something on May. He might be blackmailing her. It was even more important now to find out about May's background. He was going to have to do a lot of digging in a short time.

"Was that an accident?" Tom asked abruptly, indicating the young man's leg in traction.

Billy shifted restlessly in the bed. "Sure it was," he said, but he'd hesitated and he wouldn't look Tom in the eye when he said it. "I just fell."

"Well, I hope you get better soon. I may have a follow-up question or two, but that's about all." He even smiled. "Thanks for your help."

"Sure," Billy said, looking relieved. "No problem."

Tom went out into the hall. On his way to the front door, he ran into Annalisa's friend, Mary. She was a tall brunette with black eyes and a pretty face. "If you're not doing anything later, when I get off, I make really good coffee," she said in a coaxing tone.

Tom smiled. "Sorry." And he kept walking. Maybe, he told himself, he was property after all!

* * *

He and Annalisa made an early start. She didn't seem
sleep-starved at all. She was bright and happy.

"You're cheerful this morning," he remarked.

She grinned at him. "Mary said you walked right past her
out the door last night," she replied.

He chuckled. "I did. She's very pretty," he remarked.

She made a face at him. "Thanks for noticing!"

"Now, now, if I'd been interested, I'd have taken her up on
the offer of coffee." He reached for her hand and tangled his
fingers with hers. "I thought you said she was your friend."

"Oh, yes. That's why I asked her to flirt with you."

His lips pursed.

She thought about what she'd blurted out and flushed to
the roots of her hair.

He started laughing and almost had to pull the car to the
side of the road. "Women!" he said.

She was still too embarrassed to say anything.

He pressed her fingers with his. "In all my life, I've never
met anyone quite like you."

"That could be a compliment, you know," she said.

"It is a compliment," he replied, his voice deep and soft.

She sighed, smiling now.

She was possessive of him. She'd wanted to know if he
was the sort of man who'd pretend interest in one woman
and fall into the arms of the next one he met. Which meant,
he considered, that she was very interested in him. It was
mutual. He thought about going back to Chicago without her
and it disturbed him. Amazing that a woman he barely knew
could get such a hold on him. He wasn't sure he liked it.

"I'm sorry," she said after they passed through the inter-
section of a small town along the way where a snowplow
was working. "It was a rotten thing to do."

He shrugged. "Pretty flattering, though," he replied, and his dark eyes twinkled as they met hers briefly.

"Really?"

He sighed. "Really. Angie wouldn't have cared if I'd flirted with other women. I found out that she'd been two-timing me with the man she ran off with to New York and married."

"That must have hurt."

"Hurt my pride," he confessed. "Not much else." He watched the road ahead. "I don't think I know much about real relationships."

"And I don't know anything about them."

"So I suppose we're learning together," he commented.

She smiled. "Except that you think you're too old for me, and I'm worried that you might get shot doing your job."

He whistled. "We'd better let that lie for a while," he commented with a glance. "That's serious business."

"It is?"

He nodded. "That's the sort of discussion you have when you can't bear to think of leaving the other person behind."

Her heart was doing the hula in her chest. She didn't dare look at him. She didn't speak either because she knew her voice would sound choked.

His fingers contracted. "So, for the meantime, you're a nurse in a local hospital and I'm over here investigating a murder."

She nodded. "Okay." Her voice sounded strangled. He was thinking ahead. She wanted nothing more than to consider him part of her future. But he was right. They had to take it slow. For now, at least.

"And there's Denver," he said, nodding toward the horizon.

* * *

He settled her in a coffee shop next to a building where he had an appointment with another agent.

"I'd take you with me, but I have to have a clear mind and you're distracting."

"I am?" she asked, surprised.

He smiled down at her. "Very. And no flirting with other men," he added under his breath.

"I heard that," she said.

He just chuckled.

By the time he was through speaking to Dan Parsons, the other agent, he had more than enough information on May Strickland. She really did have issues. She'd been under the care of a clinical psychologist her first weeks as a nursing student because of inappropriate behavior. The file was sealed, and he could have made an issue of it and gotten a warrant, but the information wasn't going anywhere. He could get access to it later if it was needed. What he was interested in was May's inclination to go after rich men when she worked in the nursing home. Dan had been out to do an interview with the owner's wife, Jean, who gave him a lot of information about May's tactics. Jean didn't like May at all. She said May had tried to tell tales, to break up Jean's marriage, to get her husband to divorce Jean and marry her. At least, until May understood, finally, that Jean had all the money and property. Her husband ran the nursing home, but only had a salary from the profits. May had stopped flirting with him that very day.

But there had been a very rich old man whose indifferent children had placed him in the nursing home. By promising to get him out, and playing up to him, May had managed to get some very nice gifts. When she was discovered badgering him for a check, she was invited to ply her trade somewhere else. The old man wouldn't press charges, his children didn't care, so May got away with it. About that time, she met Billy Turner, who was in Denver on an errand for his father. They met at a diner, and they hit it off at once. Billy had money at the time, and his father was very ill, so May followed him back to Raven Springs.

"I can't remember a case like this in recent times," Tom told Dan. "This woman is truly messed up."

"Greedy," came the quiet reply. "Very greedy. And there was some discussion that the old man she was trying to pump money out of had some sudden health issues. There was a suspicion by at least one coworker that May was trying to get him to sign over his estate to her and then she planned an accident. Food poisoning? Something similar?"

"Not playing with a full deck," Tom mused.

"Luckily for us. You'd better have a talk with your Mr. Downing. If he gets involved with her, he may be looking at a similar fate."

"I'll make sure he knows. Thanks for the legwork."

"Any time. But you owe me." The other man chuckled as they rose to shake hands.

"I won't forget. See you."

Tom picked Annalisa up at the coffee shop and drove to the skating rink. It was in a huge building, with seats for people who just wanted to drink coffee and watch the skaters, and a DJ to call out couple dances and free dances and the like.

"You look very smug," she told Tom.

He nodded. "I'm armed with some pertinent informa-tion." He smiled at her. "Let's get our skates on. I could use the exercise. I miss my gym."

His gym in Chicago, he meant. She smiled and sat down

to pull her skates out of her bag and put them on. She'd thought he might reconsider living in a small town. But that was unrealistic, like the hope that he might give up a profession he loved for her. However, she thought, she had today. She was going to live every second of it. It would be something to carry her through lonely cold winter nights for the rest of her life.

They skated, lazily circling the rink, holding hands. It was cold, but they were laughing as they went around and around the huge oval. It was tiring exercise. Annalisa had forgotten how much work it was to skate. By the time she took off her skates and packed them up, and he returned his rentals, they were both rosy cheeked and laughing.

"That was so much fun," she told him. "I haven't skated for a long time."

"It was fun. And now," he said with twinkling eyes, "for sushi!"

He took her to the little Japanese restaurant he'd found and they ate sushi and drank hot jasmine tea while he talked to her about his life in Chicago.

"It sounds lonely," she said involuntarily, when he got to the part about what he did on Sundays, which was to lie around and read the Sunday paper and watch movies on Amazon Prime.

"It is lonely," he confessed after a minute. His dark eyes lifted to her light ones. "I have no one to talk to. I'm pretty much a loner, even when I'm with the guys at work. They're talking about kids and baseball games and amusement parks with their families. I'm talking about a case I'm working on."

"It's that way with me, too," she confessed. "I don't get out much. I like to watch movies or the Weather Channel or the History Channel."

He smiled. "Another weather geek," he teased.

"Hey, weather is interesting," she protested.

He pulled out his smartphone, turned it on, and handed it to her. He had about a dozen weather apps. She laughed with pure delight as she handed it back.

"I should show you mine, I guess. Turnabout's fair play." She handed it over. Along with the half dozen weather apps, she had language apps, including Chinese.

"Chinese?" he exclaimed, returning the phone to her.

"It's a beautiful language," she protested. "I found this app by accident and then I just sort of fell into doing it every day. I've been at it for two years. I don't think I'll ever get the tones just right because there are four and they're very specific, but I can read some of it."

He laughed. "I speak Russian and German," he replied.

"Isn't it a small world?" she asked.

"Small, indeed." He glanced at his watch and grimaced. "We'd better get back before you fall down and go to sleep," he said. "You've been up all night."

"I wouldn't have missed it for the world," she said, her face coloring faintly.

He drew in a breath. "Honey, neither would I," he said, his deep voice soft with feeling.

They stared at each other for a long moment. He managed to pull his eyes away. "We'd better get going," he said.

It was dark when they got back to Raven Springs.

"It was one of the best days of my life," she said when he left her at her door under the carport, leaving his car there as well.

"One of mine, too," he replied. He hesitated. It was uncharacteristic. "I have to go back and talk to Billy Turner tomorrow. But what are you doing after lunch?"

"Not much," she began.

"Do you like to walk?"

She nodded.

"Me, too. Is there a park?"

She laughed. "A nice one, with footpaths. Lots of people walk there, even in snowy weather. And it will have lighted decorations everywhere, for Christmas. I'm going to put my tree up tomorrow night."

"Do you cut one?" he asked.

She grimaced. "I'm allergic to fir. I have an artificial one. It's too big, really, but I get one of the orderlies to come help me set it up . . ."

"I'll do that."

She smiled. "Okay." She searched his eyes. "Going to help me decorate it? You're tall enough to put the star on top."

"I guess it won't kill me," he said. He smiled back. "Okay. I'll see you in the morning."

"Have a good night," she said.

"You, too."

She turned to go in.

"Where are you going?" he asked.

She turned back. "Inside . . . ?"

"I took you all the way to Denver, took you skating, bought you sushi, and you're just going to walk away and close the door, shutting me out all by myself alone in the dark? I could get eaten by a bear or something."

She laughed delightedly. She walked back to him. "What would you like, then?"

"Funny, you should ask . . ."

He pulled her close and kissed her. It wasn't like the hungry, passionate kisses that had come before. It was slow and sweet and tender. The sort of kiss you'd give someone you really cared about. He moved back, and he didn't smile. He looked down at her quietly. He touched her cheek, then smiled briefly, and walked away.

She watched him all the way to the motel before she turned and went inside.

He had a list of questions to ask Billy Turner when he stopped by the hospital early the next morning. But he didn't get to ask a single one.

"He died in the early hours of the morning," one of the doctors told him.

"Died? But he didn't have internal injuries, did he?" Tom asked, stunned.

"Not at all. We're not sure what caused it. Maybe there was something that the surgeon missed."

"Did he have any visitors after I was here?" Tom persisted.

"Just one. A girlfriend. She brought him some food and tea she said he liked. He seemed really happy to see her, according to the nurse on duty," the doctor added.

Tea. Tea. He reached back into his mind for a reference and found it. May Strickland had taken Mrs. Downing a cup of ginger tea just before she died, unexpectedly according to Alice. "Do something for me," Tom replied. "Run a drug panel for poison."

"Poison?" The doctor was shocked.

Tom nodded. "I'm here investigating a murder. She's a person of interest. I won't go into my suspicions, but I think there's probable cause. I can get a warrant if I need it."

"That won't be necessary, Agent Jones," the doctor said. "We all know what goes on in our community. I'll get an order to the lab right away."

"And I'll go talk to the sheriff," Tom replied.

"Good idea. Jeff's a fine man."

Tom smiled. "Yes, he is. And a good investigator. I'll be back in touch."

* * *

Sheriff Ralston invited him into a chair on the other side of his desk. "They're running a drug panel for poison?" he asked when Tom explained what was going on.

Tom nodded. "May Strickland went to see him last night with food and tea," he explained. "I'd spoken to Billy shortly before. He was smug about May. He said that he knew things about her that could cause her some problems. If he told me, I'm sure he told her as well. And I remembered something else—Alice, who works for the Downings, told me that May had given a cup of ginger tea to Mrs. Downing just before she died."

"Poison. Well, frankly, it wouldn't be much of a surprise. May doesn't hit on all six cylinders, if you know what I mean, and it's no secret that she wants Downing to marry her. Lots of local people wondered why Mrs. Downing went downhill so fast. Lung cancer can be treated, even brought under control when it's in the early stages, as hers was." He grimaced. "If May poisoned Mrs. Downing, it will take ten men guarding the detention center to keep Downing from going over there and strangling the life out of her."

"Billy said that she'd hoped to get Mr. Downing to a minister just after his wife died. She planned on comforting him, he said, but Downing went to stay with his sister for a month and ruined all her plans."

"So then Downing's wife died, rather advantageously for May, and his stepdaughter was apparently looking for ways to get May fired. That was about the time Julie went missing, right?" Ralston asked.

"Just about. But from what I learned from the crime lab, Julie was a hefty young woman and May is smaller and older." Tom's eyes narrowed. "It would take a big man to lift someone that size, if she'd been incapacitated before she was abducted. Remember, there was a report by a man who lived near the deserted cabin where she was found that he saw a man carrying a big rug over his shoulder. What if it wasn't a rug at all?"

Ralston nodded slowly. "And if it was Julie, what if Billy did the dirty work? May spent all his money. He was jobless and without funds. What if May saw a way to marry Downing and set them both up in style, but Julie was in the way?"

"That's a lot of supposition," Tom remarked.

"Yes, but it makes sense. Billy was crazy about May. He'd have done anything she asked him to. He didn't really have much of a conscience and he'd been in trouble with the law before on an assault charge."

"I need to talk to May. But I want to wait on Billy's autopsy first. And I need to call Alice at Downing's house."

Alice was whispering. Apparently May was home and spying on her.

"Yes, I can do that. No, I haven't done anything with it. She's too lazy to do it herself. Yes, I'll do that right now. Of course."

"Alice, who's that on the phone?" May called from the next room.

"It's the dry cleaners, about one of Mr. Downing's suits," Alice called back. "Do you know anything about a tear in one of his jackets?"

"Yes, he caught it on a nail outside."

"Okay, I'll tell them to go ahead and fix it," Alice called back.

"That's fine," May responded in a bored tone.

"A good story, Alice, but is it true? We don't want May to get suspicious," Tom said.

"Yes," Alice whispered, "I spoke to them half an hour

ago, but she won't know. I'll keep it for you. Sure thing." She hung up, excited to be part of an investigation.

They held hands while they walked. Tom had to slow his pace a little for Annalisa, who only came up to his chin.

"Shrimp," he teased, but affectionately.

"You're very tall," she remarked.

"I'm not. You're very short," he replied.

She moved closer to him. "This is nice. I haven't gone walking in a long time."

"Neither have I."

"How's your investigation coming?" she asked.

"Well. In fact, I may wrap it up in the next few days."

There was a long silence on her part. She was thinking that he'd solve his case, go back to Chicago, and she'd never see him again. It would be the worst day of her life. The very worst. She hadn't realized until that moment that she was in love with him.

He stopped walking and turned to her. His dark eyes were puzzled as he looked down into her drawn, pale face. "You don't want me to go," he said very quietly.

She took a deep breath. "No. I don't. But you have a life in Chicago and a job you do that gives you purpose," she said, her pale eyes meeting his reluctantly. "It's like my job. We're both involved in careers that help other people." She forced a smile. "But I'll never forget you," she added with a forced smile.

"I'll never forget you, either," he replied. His fingers tangled with hers. "I'm too old for you, and I do a job that requires a gun." He smiled sadly. "Two different worlds, Annalisa."

It was the first time he'd spoken her name. She loved the way it sounded in his deep, soft voice. She flushed.

He drew in a long breath of his own and his fingers tightened on hers. "Maybe we should keep walking," he suggested, when it was the last thing he wanted to do. He wanted to take her back to her house and spend an hour just holding her. Odd, he thought to himself as they walked. All his life it had been a strictly physical thing, with women. But this woman made him hungry for more than just physical contact. Sex with her would be all fireworks, he knew that already. And it would be a commitment that he couldn't push to one side and forget about. He thought about Annalisa with a baby in her arms, and he went hot all over. He wondered which one of them it would look like. His dark eyes glanced to one side and studied her unobtrusively. She was pretty. Her child might be blond, like her, with his dark eyes. Or dark-headed, like him, with her pale silver eyes.

He recalled that she loved children. He smiled to himself. Maybe a family wouldn't be the terror he'd once thought.

They went back to her house after the brisk walk and after answering a phone call, which he did by going outside when he saw the caller ID, he helped her assemble the tall artificial tree. He set it up in the living room while she turned on the gas logs in the fireplace and put on Christmas music on one of the satellite stations on her television.

"Just to help get you in the Christmas spirit," she teased, smiling up at him. She was wearing a cream-colored turtle-neck sweater with her jeans, and her feet were clad only in fuzzy blue socks. He was wearing a sweater, too, a V-necked red one with a white shirt under it and brown slacks.

"You look nice," he commented to her as he placed the angel ornament on the very top of the tree.

She laughed. "So do you." She glanced at him. "But you're . . . I don't know. Subdued?"

"They found Billy Turner dead in his hospital bed this morning."

"Billy? How? Were his injuries that bad?" she wanted to know.

He smiled. "They'll all know at the hospital, so it's no secret. I think he was poisoned. They're running a panel to . . ."

His cell phone rang. He'd given the number to the doctor who was on Billy's case. "Jones," he said. He nodded. "Yes, that's what I suspected. I'll pick it up myself and notify the appropriate people. Thanks." He hung up, smiling. "Poison. Just what I suspected."

"Poison? In a hospital?" Annalisa exclaimed. "In my hospital?"

He nodded. "And that takes a disturbed person, let me tell you. I think Billy knew something that another person was afraid he might spill to someone."

"Like, for instance, who killed Julie?" she asked.

"Exactly."

"You think May did it," she murmured.

"I think May was the mastermind behind the kidnapping," he replied. "And that's privileged communication."

She just smiled. "You know me," she said simply.

He paused with an ornament in his big hand and stood just staring at her until she flushed under the intensity of his gaze. "I do know you," he said, very softly. He put the ornament on a tree branch, turned and picked her up in his arms. "I know you to your very bones. And it's going to be like pulling teeth to go home."

Her arms slid around his neck and she forced a smile. "But you can't live in the wilds of Colorado," she said on a sigh. "I remember."

"I might get eaten by bears," he murmured as he bent to her mouth. He smiled as it met his halfway. She clung to him, drowning in a kiss that seemed to go on forever. She kissed him back, her fingers tangling in his thick, black hair.

A romantic Christmas song was playing on the radio. It suited his mood. He wondered how he was going to do his job with her on his mind all the time, because there was no way he'd ever be able to forget her.

He groaned against her soft lips and raised his head. "No," he said huskily, and put her down. "We have to stop doing that."

"Because you don't like it?" she asked sadly.

"Because I like it too much," he bit off. His eyes swept over her trim figure as the music played on, and he could almost picture her with a big swollen stomach, craving ice cream and pickles. He thought of a child. He hadn't ever wanted one before. He wanted one now.

But she was eleven years younger than he was, and he lived in Chicago and he carried a gun.

His heavy brows drew together as he looked at her, his brain whirling with impossibilities.

"What are you thinking?" she asked.

"How you'd look pregnant," he said, and then scowled fiercely at his lapse of common sense. "It was just a stray thought," he added curtly.

But it wasn't. She could see it in his face. He wasn't thinking about a one-night stand. He was thinking about forever.

She could have danced, she was so happy. But she couldn't let it show. He was already regretting the unexpected honesty. Better to pretend it didn't matter.

"All of us have those," she said, and she smiled. "Now, how about let's finish this up. I made potato soup and fresh bread for supper."

"I haven't had potato soup in years," he said, and he smiled. "It's a favorite of mine."

"I make it with real butter. It was my mother's recipe."

She studied him hungrily. He was so handsome. She could hardly drag her eyes away. "Here. This is the last of them," she said as she brought out three Star Trek ornaments. One had the sound and light of the transporter from the old series, and the other had the *Enterprise* complete with Kirk's voice with the monologue that began every episode. The last one was the instrument that Dr. McCoy used when examining a patient—the same one Spock used when he surveyed a new organism. It had their voices on it.

"That's amazing," Tom said with a laugh. "It's one of my favorite retro shows."

"Mine, too. I love ornaments with light and sound. Oh, and then there's this one. It's not Star Trek, but it is outer-spacy."

"Outer-spacy," he repeated, chuckling, as she handed him Robbie the Robot and pressed the button on its side. Robbie's voice came from it, loud and clear.

"I love this one," he said, hanging it. "I've got the DVD somewhere. *Forbidden Planet*."

"I have it on Amazon Prime," she said.

"Damn!" he said, looking at his watch. "Honey, I've got to go pick up something. I've only got a small window of time to do it. I'll be back as soon as I can. Will the soup keep?"

Her heart lifted at the endearment. It sounded so natural. "Of course it will," she said softly. "Be careful."

He bent and kissed her gently. "I'm always careful."

He grabbed his jacket and went out the door. She turned back to the ornaments and pressed the Star Trek transporter one. It made her feel better.

Chapter Six

Tom had asked Alice to phone him when Downing and May were both out of the house. This was ideal, as she had something for him.

She handed him a paper sack at the front door. "If they ever find out . . ." she began worriedly.

He just smiled. "You're a princess, Alice. What would I do without you?" he asked gently.

She laughed. "Well, if I'm out of a job, it's going to be your task to find me a new one," she teased.

"I'll take that under advisement. You're certain that nobody's touched this except you and May?"

She nodded. "Positive." She sighed. "Is it evidence? I mean, is it going to be tainted because you don't have a search warrant?" she worried.

He pulled a paper out of his pocket and handed it to her. It was a search warrant for a brown-and-white thermos known to belong to May Strickland. "Wow," she said, looking up admiringly as she handed it back.

He chuckled. "I try to cover all my bases. If this pans out the way I expect, I'll be back with a search warrant covering a lot more territory."

"You might want to check May's closet," she mused. "She never washes anything, and she never brought me any laundry. See, she went out the day Julie disappeared." Her face set into hard lines. "I loved Julie."

"I'll catch her killer," he told her, and his expression emphasized it. "Thanks."

"Glad to be of help. Should I tell Mr. Downing and May about the thermos . . . ?"

"Oh, please do," he replied. "But not until tomorrow. Do something that keeps you busy enough that you won't think of it."

"I'll do that, too." She smiled at him. "I'll bet crooks run from you."

"Some have," he confessed. "Good night."

She nodded and went quickly back inside. Tom took the thermos by the sheriff's office to enter it into evidence, and asked the sheriff to relay it to the lab and then meet him at the county line to take it to the crime lab in Denver. He put as much a rush on it as he could. The culprit, he explained to Jeff Ralston, might decide to take a powder.

It was very late by the time he got through with his duties. He stopped by Annalisa's house on the off chance that she might still be up, and saw that the porch light was on and the Christmas tree he'd helped decorate was in the picture window facing the road.

He tapped on the door. She came running in her sock feet and opened it at once. "You're all right," she said, breathless and relieved and unable to hide it.

He felt his heart jolt in his chest. "You were worried about me," he said, as if he could barely believe it.

"Of course I was worried," she said, fighting tears. "You said you'd be right back!"

He pulled her against him and held her tight, rocking her, his face buried in the thick, soft blond hair curling around her shoulders.

"My God," he whispered reverently, and with feeling.

"Nobody ever worried about me. My parents never expressed any emotion at all toward me and my sister. We were just responsibilities and tax deductions. It didn't matter to Angie if I came home, because she was either away on business or, and I didn't know it at the time, out with another man."

"Well, I care," she muttered against his sweater, and he felt the moisture of tears. "You could have phoned," she added, hitting his broad chest with a small fist.

He drew back enough to see her face. Her eyes were red and swollen, her lips trembling. He wiped away the tears. He kissed her eyes shut and hugged her close. "I'm sorry. It just never occurred to me."

"Was it the case you're working on?"

"It was. Crucial evidence. I had to pick it up and then I had to have it relayed to Denver, to the crime lab. Unusual circumstances, but I don't want my suspect to go missing."

She smiled through the tears. "I'm sorry . . ."

"Sorry for caring about me?" he chided. "Shame on you." He smiled. "I like it. Although I don't like upsetting you." He bent and kissed her soft mouth with breathless tenderness. "Am I too late for soup? I'm starving."

Her heart lifted. She laughed. "No. I'll heat it up."

He followed her into the kitchen with its cheerful yellow curtains and red Christmas accents. "The tree looks good."

"Yes, it does. I love Christmas. It's how I get through hard times. I think ahead to holly and bows and lanterns and trees lit up like jewels in the night."

She was like a jewel herself, he thought. Bright and lovely and sparkling. He thought about leaving her as the case wound up, and it was actually painful. He couldn't get past the obstacles: his age and her distaste for his job. They seemed insurmountable. But they had these few days, he thought with quiet joy. They'd have to last him the rest of his life, so he wasn't leaving any tarnished ones behind. He wanted her passionately. But he wasn't going to compromise her. No protection was foolproof. Hell, he didn't want any protection. He wanted babies, and logs burning in the fireplace, and Annalisa waiting for him when he came in the door at night, running to him because she . . .

He stopped in his tracks, staring at her back as she stirred the soup in its red boiler. She loved him. Why else would she be in tears at the thought that something had happened to him? Then he realized something else. He was feeling the same thing. He was protective of her. How had this happened, in just a space of days, when he'd almost had to be dragged to Raven Springs to work the case? And now he didn't want to leave, because of Annalisa. Because she loved him, and he wanted to be loved.

"It's ready," she said, smiling over one shoulder as she poured the soup into a bowl, produced crackers on a saucer, and put it on the table. "Coffee, or something stronger?" she asked.

He chuckled. "I don't drink very often. Mostly a glass of white wine, if I have to go to some social venue. I like coffee, even this late."

"I made some, just in case," she said.

He sat down, caught her hand, and pulled her down into his lap. He studied her for so long and so intently that she flushed.

"I have to leave when I finish this case," he said through his teeth.

Her eyes were full of the sadness she felt. "Yes. I know."

"I'm too old for you, honey. And I don't think I could give up the work I do."

"I know all that," she replied. She touched his wide, chiseled mouth with her fingertips. "I'm making memories to live on. That's all." She had to stop, because she choked up.

He drew her face into his neck and hugged her close. "Yeah. Me, too," he whispered at her ear. "Sweet memories. And that's how they're going to stay." He pulled back and met her watery eyes with his dark ones. "Innocent. Like you."

She forced a smile. "Sorry."

"What for?" he teased, and he kissed her nose.

"I don't want to embarrass you or anything."

"I'm never embarrassed. I'll miss you," he added quietly. "It will be hard, for both of us, for a few weeks. But we'll adjust."

"We will," she said. "We both have important jobs." She got up reluctantly. "Your soup will get cold."

He smiled. "Okay." He tasted it. "Wow," he said, glancing at her. "It's awesome."

She smiled back, from ear to ear. "Mama's recipe. She was a wonderful cook."

"So are you, baby," he said softly.

She flushed again, at the endearment. "I'll just get the coffee," she blurted out, anxious to find something to do that wouldn't call attention to her embarrassment. She didn't want him to feel sorry for her because he was leaving. But it broke her heart. He might get over it in a few weeks. She knew that she never would.

He finished his soup, kissed her gently, and forced himself to go back to the motel. He really wanted to stay. He was being woven into the fabric of her life and he loved it. But there were just too many obstacles.

The next morning, thanks to a phone call from an acquaintance of his who was high up in politics, and who had pulled a few strings for him, Tom had the results of the thermos test. There was, indeed, poison in the tea May had taken to Billy Turner. He had concrete evidence that she'd killed the man, and he called in Jeff Ralston and a deputy to accompany him to the Downing home.

Alice opened the door, smiled, and ushered them in.

"I need to see May," Tom told her.

"She's in the living room trying to talk Mr. Downing into buying her a new couture dress," she said, tongue-in-cheek.

"Oh, I'm going to make sure she has a nice new orange jumpsuit, the latest in fashion," he returned. He walked on into the living room.

Downing was glaring at May. ". . . not about to spend that amount of money on—" he was saying. He stopped when he saw the delegation enter the room. "Hello," he said, rising. "Can I help you?"

"We're here for Miss Strickland," Tom said. "She's a material witness in a murder and kidnapping investigation."

The deputy turned May around, handcuffed her neatly, and turned her back again.

"I didn't kill Julie!" she exclaimed red-faced. "It was Billy Turner!"

Tom glanced around. Plenty of witnesses to that statement, including Alice. "But you helped him, Miss Strickland," he replied, holding back his ace card.

"I just . . . just . . ." She stopped. She looked at Tom with cold eyes. "That's not what you're arresting me for," she said suddenly.

"No, it isn't," Tom replied. "I'm arresting you for the murder of Billy Turner."

She started to speak and then just slumped. "He ran out of money, and then he tried to blackmail me about Julie. We never meant to kill her," she added curtly. "We left her in that cabin with the heat on. We couldn't know there would be a power failure when we tied her up. She was supposed to be alive. We wore disguises. She didn't even recognize us!"

That did make the case a little less brutal. Intent was

everything. "Your guilt or innocence is something for a jury to decide. You were party to a kidnapping and murder, and you poisoned your ex-boyfriend," Tom added. "I'm sorry to tell you that you're under arrest. The deputy will read you your rights."

While the deputy did that, Tom spoke to a distraught Downing. He didn't mention his suspicion that she might have poisoned his wife as well. That would be another case if and when the district attorney decided to prosecute it.

"It helps a little that they didn't mean to kill Julie," Downing said curtly, "but I can't forget the way she looked. Frozen to death. Poor thing. It was heartless."

Tom nodded.

"I never liked May. She convinced me that Julie wasn't doing what was needed for my wife. I loved my wife," he added with grief in his very posture. "After she . . . passed, nothing much mattered anymore. I should have paid more attention to what was going on. I knew Julie didn't like May and that it was mutual. May said my blood pressure was very high and needed careful monitoring." He grimaced. "Maybe I just liked being fussed over. I missed my wife. She was always watching out for me, taking care of me until, at the end, I took care of her. Now Julie's gone, too." He sighed and looked at Tom. "Sometimes, life is so damned unbearable."

Tom was thinking that, too. He'd be leaving soon, but his heart would live on in Raven Springs, in Annalisa Davis's house.

May was taken to the detention center, unprotestingly and morose, then booked. Tom contacted his superiors to let them know what was going on. He left the sheriff's office, and drove back to the motel and parked his car under Annalisa's carport and tapped on the door.

She came running, her face brilliant with delight. His heart felt lighter than air. That expression on her face made him feel like a giant. He smiled and held out his arms. She ran into them. He hugged her close for a minute, then he tightened his grip, as if to prepare her for what was coming.

"I solved the case and made an arrest," he told her.

He felt her whole body stiffen, as if she'd taken a blow. "Oh," she said, putting all her misery into the one word.

He drew back and winced when he saw her eyes.

"Who did it?" she wanted to know.

"Billy Turner, with some help from May. She poisoned him, right in his bed in the hospital, with some tea in a thermos."

"Gosh! Didn't she have sense enough to clean it up?"

"Not really."

"But if you got it from the house . . ."

"I took a search warrant with me, and Alice handed it to me in a paper sack. Criminals always make one stupid decision. Her own laziness was her downfall. She didn't like to get her hands dirty, which is why Julie was doing most of the nursing while her mother was alive. It's also why the thermos wasn't washed, which gave us a great case. That's where I was when I came over here late, after we decorated the tree," he explained. "I had to take the thermos to Sheriff Ralston and he had it relayed to Denver. We had the results from the crime lab very promptly."

"How did you manage that?" she wanted to know.

"Somebody pulled a few political strings," he said with a grin.

"Want some coffee?" she asked.

He drew in a long breath and put his big, warm hands on her shoulders. "I do. But I won't stay. I'm leaving town in the morning, Annalisa. I have to get back to work."

She stood very still and schooled her face to lie for her,

to look placid. "I knew you would," was all she said. She searched his dark eyes. "You really are gorgeous, you know," she said, trying to make a joke of it.

"And you really could be a pole dancer," he teased. "But I'm very glad you aren't. I'm happy that I got to meet you."

"Oh, I could say the same thing."

He traced a path down her cheek and his dark eyes were sad. He sighed.

"If only," she said, trying not to choke on her grief.

He nodded. "If only, honey."

He bent and kissed her, just once, barely touching her lips with his. "We have memories," he whispered.

She laughed, but it sounded more like a sob. "Sweet ones."

"See you around, Nurse Davis."

"See you around, Chicago," she replied pertly. She smiled as he went out the door and closed it behind him. She locked it and turned off the porch light and went to bed. She cried for the better part of an hour. Life was never going to be the same again.

The next morning, Tom paid the motel bill and went out to put his bag in his car, still parked under Annalisa's carport.

She saw him and came to the door. "You leaving?" she asked quietly.

"Yeah." He put the bag in the car and came around it to her back door. He studied her sad face. "Why don't you come and see me off?" he asked, hating the words even as they came out of his throat. It would be agony for both of them, but leaving her at her own door was even worse.

"I'll drive my car."

"Cabs run out there." He tucked a twenty dollar bill in her coat pocket. "Get a cab home."

She bit her lower lip. "Tom, I'm not sure . . ."

He caught her hand and led her to the car, opening the door and helping her into the front seat. She didn't even argue. She just fastened her seat belt.

The airport was crowded. It was almost Christmas. So many people traveling to see families, to spend holidays abroad, to visit loved ones. The airport at Raven Springs was decorated in red and green and gold, with holly and wreaths everywhere and a huge Christmas tree in the center of the lobby.

"It looks like Christmas," he remarked to Annalisa after he checked his bag and the clerk gave him a paper ticket to replace the e-ticket he'd gotten online.

"Yes. Christmas." She looked up at him with grief. "You be careful," she said huskily. "Chicago has a lot of crime."

"I noticed." He bent and brushed his mouth against hers. But it wasn't enough. He knew in his heart that once would never be enough.

He pulled her against him and kissed her as if he was going to war and was uncertain that he would ever return. He kissed her like a starving man. She kissed him back, her eyes pouring tears, her body straining to hold the contact even when he drew slowly away and looked at her as if she was the world, the whole world.

The loudspeaker was announcing the Chicago flight. He grimaced. "I have to go, honey," he said gruffly.

"You could call me sometimes," she said. "Send me messages and stuff."

"It would be like rubbing salt in a wound."

She acknowledged that with a tiny shrug.

He took a deep breath. "So long."

Her heart was in her eyes. But she wasn't going to make it harder for him. She forced a smile. "So long, Tom."

He turned and walked away. She watched his broad back with eyes that loved him, hungered for him, would have died for him. Her life would never be the same. She'd come home every day of her life from work and expect to see his car sitting in the carport. Except that it never would be. Never!

Tom was halfway down his way to the concourse. He could do this, he told himself. He could walk away. He'd go back to his job. Nothing would change. She was a sweet interlude. Nothing more. He'd forget her.

He remembered that first meeting, when he'd told her she worked as a pole dancer. He remembered their first kiss, the way she cuddled with him, accepted anything he wanted to do to her, nurtured him. Hot soup at midnight. No real recriminations, except that she'd been afraid for him when he said he'd be right back, and he wasn't, and she was frightened something had happened to him. She'd run to him, her face covered in tears, the fear tangible as she held him to her and shivered with feeling.

She loved him. Nobody in his whole damned life had ever loved him. He was walking away from a home and a family and a wife who'd be waiting for him, forever if she needed to. He was walking away from children playing around the Christmas tree every year. He was walking away from love.

He stopped dead. His feet felt as if he were wearing steel boots. He couldn't force himself to take one more step. This was insane. It would never work. There were too many years between them. He couldn't stop being a cop. He couldn't give up the risk, the excitement.

He turned and looked back. She was still standing there, her long blond hair falling around her hunched shoulders, her face as tragic as if she'd just seen an accident with fatalities.

She looked up then, and saw him just standing there, just looking at her.

All at once, he knew he couldn't do it. No power on earth could get him on the plane. His heart was here. His life was here. He . . . loved her.

His face mirrored his own misery. He looked at her for a long moment and then he opened his arms.

Oblivious to other passengers, to amused glances, to anything else, she ran right into those open arms and was lifted up and kissed and kissed and kissed until her mouth was sore, and then she was kissed some more.

"I love you," she sobbed against his demanding lips.

"I know," he ground out. "I love you, too."

The tears flowed down around their locked mouths as he rocked her in his arms. After a few feverish minutes, he managed to let go enough to step back from her. The joy he saw in her face made the years go away, made the threat of his job go away, made everything right.

They gave the last call for Chicago. "You'll miss your flight," she said huskily and tried to smile.

"I'm not leaving," he replied, and he wasn't smiling. "I'm never leaving. I want Christmas around the fireplace, with our kids opening presents under it."

"Kids?" she whispered.

He grinned. "Kids."

"I love kids," she confessed.

He drew in a long breath and smiled down at her with a

light in his dark eyes that had never been there before. "How long does it take to get married in the wilds of Colorado?" he asked.

"I don't know. Not long."

"I'll move back into the motel for the time being. Do you want to be married in church?"

She nodded. She hesitated. "I'm Methodist."

His eyes widened and he laughed. "So am I."

"Well!"

"Talk about being evenly matched," he murmured.

She glanced toward the window. "There goes your plane," she observed. "And your suitcase."

"So I'll buy new clothes. I need to, anyway. I need a spiffy suit to get married in. And you have to have something with a veil."

"There won't be time to organize something big . . ."

"A white suit and a hat with a veil. I'll go shopping with you. We'll find something."

She beamed. "Okay."

He rubbed his nose against hers. "What's for lunch?" he asked.

"Cold cuts." She grimaced at his expression. "Well, I thought you were leaving!"

"Well, I'm back now, and I'll help you cook."

She doubted that. The look in his eyes promised a lot of interruptions in the kitchen. But she didn't mind at all. "That sounds nice," she said.

"We can buy each other matching cane fishing poles for a Christmas present," he suggested on the way out to the parking lot. "But we may have to wait for the spring thaw to use them."

"By then, I might not be able to sit on a creek bank for long," she said with demurely downcast eyes.

"Why not?"

She sighed, smiling up at him. "I'd be willing to bet that by our nice spring thaw, I'm going to look like a basketball in front."

"Oooh," he remarked dryly. "I love women who look like basketballs in front!"

She stopped by his car and kissed him softly. "I'll do my best to cooperate."

He gave her a wicked grin. "I'm counting on it. After the ceremony," he added with a chuckle.

"Really?"

"Really. We're going to go the conventional route."

"But we haven't. You didn't propose . . ."

He was down on one knee in the snow, holding her hand to his lips. "Please say you'll marry me so I won't be frozen to the ground here."

She burst out laughing. He was going to be so much fun to be married to! "I will, I will!" she promised. "Please get up before you catch a cold!"

"You wanted conventional, honey."

"So I did." She beamed up at him.

They were married and they returned to her house, in a wild and feverish sprawl that almost landed them on the floor and did result in a slight tear in Annalisa's nice wedding suit as they struggled out of too-tight clothing in her bedroom.

"I was worried, that it might hurt," she tried to explain, but she was in such a rage of hunger that she didn't think she could even feel pain as his mouth went all over her, tracing and touching and nibbling.

"Oh, it won't hurt," he promised huskily. "And even if it did, you wouldn't notice or care by the time we get that far!"

He touched her in places and ways that she'd never dreamed of being touched, and his mouth followed his hands. But by the time he eased over her, and into her, she was pulling at him with both hands and almost begging for more than hot kisses and even more intimate ways of touching.

"Impatient, that's what you are," he accused, chuckling, but he was shivering with his own need. He went into her with one stark push and she gasped and looked into his eyes as she shuddered with pleasure. Her eyes were blank with it, her breathing quick and rough. Sounds came out of her throat that didn't sound human as he took her quickly up the ladder of pleasure right into the highest clouds. It was so intense that she wept, sobbing against his mouth as she shivered and shivered in completion. His pleasure came more slowly, but he grasped the pillow on both sides of her head and groaned harshly as it lifted him over her in an agonized arch. He opened his eyes and saw her watching him and his teeth clenched as the desire ratcheted up another whole degree and he actually cried out as he convulsed with the most intense physical fulfillment he'd ever had in his life.

She lay under him afterwards, holding him, feeling the weight of his heavy, damp body.

"No," she protested when he started to lift away. "Please don't. I like to feel your weight on me. I like to feel you . . . in me," she whispered huskily.

He shuddered and she felt him swell. He lifted his head and looked down into her surprised face. He moved, very slowly, and she gasped. She was so sensitized that it only took three lazy thrusts to put her right back up where she'd been, shuddering with delight as her own body convulsed.

He brushed his mouth over hers and suddenly brought it down hard as he pushed and pushed, swelling even more in the soft silkiness of her, his big body shivering, as hers had, when he let go and felt the ecstasy take him. He groaned as if he were being tortured. The pleasure was so intense that it was almost pain. He groaned again as he reached a new high and finally collapsed again on her sated body.

She wrapped herself around him, kissing his throat, his cheek, his jaw. "I love you so much," she choked. "I thought I'd die when you walked away, at the airport."

"I thought I would, too," he confessed. He rolled over, taking her with him. They were both covered in cold sweat, faintly shivering together in the aftermath.

"I've never felt anything like this, ever," he managed.

"Neither have I," she murmured, her face nuzzling his.

"Yes, but you were a virgin." He chuckled.

She hit him.

"It was before I met you," he reminded her. "There hasn't been anybody in a long time. And there will never be anybody again."

"Women talk, you know," she mused. "Most of them said it hurt, the first time."

He laughed softly. "You were so hungry for me that you didn't notice it, you mean," he replied. "I never dreamed that two people could give each other so much pleasure."

She sighed and smiled. "Neither did I."

"Women are supposed to know," he said after a minute, and one big, warm hand covered her belly. "Are you, do you think? Because a loving that beautiful should produce a child, if there's any justice in the world."

She sighed. "I wish I did know," she replied. "But if we keep doing this, eventually we'll both know. So," she added, lifting up to look down at his handsome face, "we should do it a lot."

He chuckled. "I'm not protesting."

"Still think I'm too young?" she asked smugly.

"Not me, baby," he replied and let out a sigh of pure contentment. He smiled. "You're just right."

She snuggled closer and closed her eyes.

It was snowing, three Christmases later. Tom was holding their three-year old son, Matt, while Annalisa cuddled the baby, Tessa, only two months old. They were sitting around the brilliantly lit Christmas tree with its ornaments, two of which said Baby's First Christmas. The artificial gas logs in the fireplace were ablaze behind the iron fire screen, and there was Christmas music playing softly in the background.

Annalisa was still holding down her nursing job, and Tom was in his third year as a bank security officer. The bank president had welcomed him with open arms as chief of security for the bank. His background in law enforcement had made him the perfect choice, and coincidentally the former security chief had just quit to take a job in another city. Tom turned out to be great at cyber crime and even catching people who planned to cheat the bank. He was responsible for the firing of one loan officer who'd embezzled thousands of dollars without raising a grain of suspicion. The bank president gave him a raise that very day.

It was a long way from the hectic life Tom had lived in the FBI. But the new job was satisfying. He was still catching crooks; just in a different way. He missed the Bureau once in a while but not enough to want to go back and join up. He was forty years old and it was time for a less dangerous job. Especially now that they had kids.

"My daddy was in the FBI," Matt said importantly, having found a picture of Tom showing off his badge when he'd resigned.

The child was fascinated with the picture. He looked up at his father, whose lap he was occupying. "Daddy, can you tell me a story about the FBI?" he asked, looking up at Tom with his own dark eyes. Matt favored his dad. The second son, Garrett, who was asleep in his playpen, favored them both. The new baby girl favored Annalisa. Tom loved it that his eldest son looked just like him. But it was a delight to him that they not only had two sons, but that they'd lucked out finally and had a girl who looked like his precious wife.

"Can I tell you a story about the FBI? Hmmm." He shifted the child, gave his wife a slow smile with eyes that showed that he loved her. "Yes, I can." He looked down at the child. "There once was a lawman . . ."

Annalisa listened to his deep, soft voice as he told the little boy the story of how he'd come from Chicago to live in Raven Springs. After five years, he was still amazed at how well he fit in here, and how happy he was.

Annalisa studied him with eyes that adored him. Not so long ago, she'd watched him start to get on an airplane and felt that her life was over. Now, here he was, in her house, with their children, content to be a husband and a father and not minding a job at the local bank. It seemed like a miracle. Well, she told herself, Christmas was the time for miracles.

Her eyes went from the beautiful tree with its decorations, to her husband with his son on his lap and then to the little girl suckling at her breast in the easy chair. She sighed with happiness. Her gaze went back to Tom, who was looking at her with that warm, tender smile that still made her insides dance. And they said dreams didn't come true. She smiled back at Tom with her whole heart. There was her dream, big and tall and gorgeous, telling their son a story. Tom glanced at her from across the room. She had the oddest feeling that he knew exactly what she was thinking. Because he looked at her and smiled and winked. And she laughed, with pure, sweet, joy.

Christmas Creek Cowboy

DELORES FOSSEN

Chapter One

Sheriff Calen Jameson wasn't ready to start snarling "bah humbug," but he was darn close to it. Along with this being the first anniversary of the worst anniversary in history, there was an inflatable cowboy-Santa the size of an eighteen-wheeler lying sideways on Main Street. It had landed there after tumbling off the roof of the hardware store.

The Santa was not only blocking traffic—yes, even a small town like Christmas Creek, Texas, had traffic—it had also knocked down a row of life-size plastic Texas longhorns. The very ones the city council had insisted on displaying every year in between streetlamps that were already overly decorated. The longhorns looked creepy with their vacant staring eyes, but it was a décor argument Calen had lost a dozen times in the dozen years he'd been sheriff.

Despite the hardware store being filled with all sorts of ropes and such, the massive cowboy Santa obviously hadn't been anchored well enough. That was the reason for the fall, the traffic jam, and why he was on the way to see the store owner.

And wouldn't that be fun?

Not because the owner, Lou "Wheezer" Sommers, was a jerk but because Lou was the polar opposite of Ebenezer

Scrooge and would insist on hauling the Santa back up to the roof so that no one missed out on this seasonal delight. Wheezer would also probably forget Calen's rule about bellowing out something Calen didn't want to hear.

Merry Christmas or *happy holidays*.

Because those greetings were reminders of that worst anniversary, Calen had let it get around the gossips that it'd be best if no one uttered anything like that to him, and most people had complied. Wheezer possibly wouldn't because in his usual holiday gushing, it would be second nature to gush first and think later.

It was Wheezer's over-the-top enthusiasm that had the man insisting the inflatable Santa go back on top of the store. Since the fall could have seriously hurt someone, Calen would make sure it was done right this time. And he'd have to do that while being bombarded with the music of the season that was being piped through various speakers on Main Street.

Too bad the shop owners hadn't coordinated the tunes because as he walked from the sheriff's office, Calen heard an annoying mix of "Jingle Bells," "Little Drummer Boy," and "Grandma Got Run Over by a Reindeer."

It was only two blocks from the sheriff's office to the hardware store, and Calen kept on his serious cop's face to deter anyone from doling out unwanted greetings, complaints, and sympathetic comments about how miserable he must be over this one-year anniversary deal.

His cop's face didn't work though.

Overly cheerful people, perhaps on eggnog and sugar cookie highs, made giddy entrances and exits from the shops while calling out hellos and "Have a good day" to him. A few informed him of the cowboy Santa as if he could have missed hearing about the darn thing. And way too many mentioned the anniversary of the "incident."

Most of those mentions were muttered "Hugs," "Thinking about you today," and other such sentiments better reserved for social media posts and greeting cards. Probably because the bulk of residents didn't want to say aloud what had actually happened.

Well, not aloud to him anyway. And not within hearing distance of any kids. Because the incident wasn't for little ears.

Calen figured this anniversary was still a tasty side dish served up by gossips, especially since some of them had personally witnessed the X-rated event that'd caused him to end his engagement to his ex, Sasha Peterson. Specifically, many had seen Sasha in the elf costume she'd donned for the dress rehearsal of the annual Christmas play.

Or rather they'd seen Sasha partly in that costume.

She'd been naked from the waist down, her green tights pooled around her ankles when all sixteen members of the chorus, Calen, and several others had walked in on her with the mayor, Owen Granger, who'd been in a Santa suit.

Both Sasha and Owen had insisted their encounter was a one-time mistake. One brought on by too much alcohol during a holiday party. They'd begged for forgiveness and had sworn it wouldn't happen again, but Calen hadn't been able to erase that image of them together. He also hadn't been able to shove aside the punch-to-the-gut betrayal by the woman who'd sworn her undying love to him. An equally hard punch from Owen, Calen's friend since childhood.

Pushing the "poor pitiful Calen" looks aside, he made his way past the Yuletide Tea Shop, which had opted to pipe out "Silver Bells," as Gladys Herman, the owner, stepped out.

"Sheriff, you're looking lower than a fat penguin's butt," Gladys announced. "When you're done fixing that Santa, you ought to come into the shop for a cup of peppermint chai. It'll perk you right up."

He made a sound that could have meant anything, but Calen knew tea wouldn't fix his mood. Nothing could. He just needed to get through this day, and then he'd have the one-year anniversary under his belt. Maybe day 366 would bring an end to the gossip about his crappy personal life.

Calen reached the Santa and squeezed past the inflated cowboy hat and around a couple of the toppled longhorns, too, as he spotted one of his deputies, Mick Webster, who was calling out instructions to Wheezer and his workers. Thankfully, they were already in the process of hauling up the Santa by pulling ropes they'd attached to various parts of the inflatable.

That was the good news. The bad was that the task had drawn gawkers, and somebody could get hurt. Calen was betting the sucker weighed over a hundred pounds. It was a miracle it hadn't smashed into someone or something other than a few of the plastic longhorns.

"All of you need to back up," Calen called out to no one in particular before he turned to Mick. "You got here fast." Mick was on patrol duty so he could have been anywhere in town or the outlying areas.

"I was in Frosty's having lunch." The deputy hiked his thumb to the diner across the street where the bottom of Santa's sleigh was smashed against the door. "Had to go out through the back."

Calen could see why Mick had needed to do that. With the darn thing wedged across Main Street, Santa's sleigh was now a barricade. It blocked the front door and windows, along with smooshing the diner's Frosty the Snowman mascot against the glass. One of Frosty's arms stuck out in what looked like a "help me" gesture.

"Happy holidays, Sheriff. We got this," Wheezer called down to him. "Oops," he immediately added, obviously remembering the greeting Calen didn't want to hear.

Wheezer was wearing a Santa suit, and the man was no doubt grinning beneath his fake white beard. "Sure sorry to add this to your downer of a day. When we're done, come on into the store for some hot cider."

Calen shrugged, neither accepting or declining, but the man was right about its being a downer of a day.

"This is bad news number two," Mick reminded Calen. "First, that group of tourists at Kris Kringle's Pond and now this."

Calen was well aware of the tourists who'd walked out onto the faux icy surface to pose for pictures despite the clearly posted signs not to walk on it. The plywood surface had bobbled and toppled them into the pond. Not exactly icy but close since the temps were in the low forties. The rule-breaking morons had been rescued without injuries, and Calen had been finishing up the paperwork on that when he'd been called about the fallen Santa.

"Bad stuff comes in threes," the deputy grumbled.

Thankfully, Calen didn't believe in that superstition any more than he did Santa Claus. Or the stability of the fake ice on Kris Kringle's Pond.

"You okay?" Mick asked him.

Calen sighed, wishing his deputy hadn't gone there. "Yeah," he lied, hoping it would be the end of it. It wasn't.

"You think she's okay?" Mick pressed.

Because most of the crowd was following his orders and dispersing, Calen looked behind him, following his deputy's gaze to the one person who wasn't moving back. Instead, the tall brunette was making a beeline toward him.

Emmy Kendrick.

Calen's longtime friend and partner in this worst anniversary in the history of worst anniversaries. Because Emmy's ex-fiancé, Owen Granger, had been the naughty Santa screwing around with Sasha. Emmy's and Calen's "we got cheated on" partnership wasn't a situation they'd ever thought they'd find themselves in, but here they were.

Emmy was wearing a gold Christmas fairy outfit, complete with wings and a glittery wand, and she had her purse and a grimy gray sack hooked over her shoulder. Probably, *hopefully*, it was a costume for children's reading time at her bookstore, 'Twas the Night Before Christmas, which was just up the street. Calen hoped Emmy hadn't given in to the holiday spirit because he was in misery-loves-company mode and didn't want any more cheer.

Calen had known he'd see her today, just not this soon. He checked his watch and verified that it was only one p.m., too early for their weekly gripe session about their exes. They reserved those for after work hours.

Emmy went to him, her troubled green eyes meeting his own brown ones, and she leaned in to put her mouth close to his ear. "If one more person asks me if I'm all right, I'm going to smack them with my magic wand," she whispered.

Calen smiled. Ah, his kindred spirit and hater of holiday cheer. She wouldn't blurt out any holiday greeting.

"Don't actually make contact with the wand," Calen advised, keeping his voice low as well. "I don't want to arrest you for assault. I'm not sure those fairy wings will fit through the jail cell door."

She pulled back from him and smiled, too. Sort of. But it was very short-lived. "We have to talk," Emmy said. "About this." She pressed her hand to the dirt-splotched sack.

Calen huffed. "Please tell me there aren't presents in there for me."

"Uh, no." She stopped though, her forehead bunching up as if considering the possibility. "Well, probably not. Calen, it's bad," she tacked on.

"Bad?" Mick questioned, obviously having heard at least

part of what Emmy had said. "Is this number three? You know, like bad news coming in threes?"

"Maybe," she muttered.

Oh, man. No more bad news, not when they still had to get through the next hours leading up to their weekly griping.

"Come with me," Emmy insisted, taking hold of Calen's arm. "If anyone asks what's going on, I'll just let them think I'm having a meltdown because of our exes stomping on our hearts."

There had indeed been some heart stomping, but Emmy had never been one who'd wanted to air her hurt in public. Again, kindred spirits, and they preferred to keep their pain behind closed doors.

"Can't talk right now, sorry," Emmy answered someone who called out a *Hope everything's okay*.

She threaded Calen through the remaining gawkers, then despite the fairy wings, Emmy squeezed them around the longhorns to head toward the sheriff's office.

"Can't talk now, sorry," she repeated when Gladys said she looked lower than a fat penguin's butt and offered her tea.

Calen didn't ask Emmy what this was about because any number of people would have heard her answer. He just allowed himself to be led and pitied by onlookers, all the way into the sheriff's office.

Since Calen had both Mick and another deputy out patrolling, it was just him on office duty today, and that meant the only other person around was the dispatcher/receptionist, Junie Carson, who'd held the job for nearly fifty years. She'd been there when Calen had first pinned on a badge shortly after he'd turned twenty-one, and she'd remained for his five years as a deputy and the following decade as sheriff.

Wearing a Mrs. Santa costume that she donned most days—the woman must have owned a dozen of them—Junie perked up when they walked in. She was probably ready to dole out the merriment junk like everybody else, but Calen immediately cut her off.

"Hold my calls," he said.

He took Emmy into his office, where he shut the door. Calen studied Emmy to see if she was indeed on the verge of a meltdown. No. This wasn't the precursor to a *they did us wrong* rant.

"Okay, what the heck is this all about?" he demanded.

"I found that in the attic when I went home for lunch," she said, patting the bulging canvas sack she was carrying.

Though the explanation was short, it took Calen a couple of seconds to wrap his mind around it. She no doubt meant the attic of the house she'd purchased eighteen months ago. The house, and therefore the attic, that had belonged to Calen's father, Waylon, who'd died over two years earlier. Emmy had bought it shortly thereafter because Calen already owned a small horse ranch on the outskirts of town. Calen's mother had long since passed away.

"Is there something illegal, or dead, in that bag?" he asked.

She didn't exactly jump to answer. "Yes to the first," she finally said. "I'm not sure about the second. Maybe."

Calen groaned. Then cursed.

Hell's bells. He'd never known Waylon to use drugs, but because of his father's rotten childhood and the loss of his wife a decade earlier, the man was what everyone called a miserable old coot. Waylon had also had an extreme hatred of all things holiday related, thanks to his unhappy childhood memories. So, maybe his father had . . . what? Severed someone's finger or something when they'd gushed Yuletide cheer?

But that didn't make sense.

If any severing had happened, no way would the severee have just kept quiet.

"When I went home for lunch, I heard something scurrying around up in the attic," Emmy continued, "so I went up to check for mice. There were mouse droppings all right." She shuddered in an *ick* kind of way. "And this. It was tucked in a corner, so you must have missed it when you cleared things out right after I bought the house."

Emmy unhooked the canvas bag and dropped it onto his desk. It was larger than an average school backpack, and it landed with a thud. When Calen had a closer look at it, he realized it was an old mail bag. That made sense because Waylon had been the town's postman for most of his adult life and had continued the job right up to his death. Maybe he'd kept his old bag and used it for storage.

Calen opened the bag, peered in and saw an assortment of letters and small packages. Dozens of them. He took out some, looking at the addresses and the postmark dates. And he cursed again.

"These are from four years ago," he pointed out.

She nodded. "And it's not the only bag. There are three more, one in each of the other attic corners. I only glanced inside them because, hey, there were those mice droppings, but some postmarks go back more than twenty years. There are dozens of them, Calen. Maybe hundreds."

Calen opened his mouth to curse again but realized there was no profanity harsh enough for this. Instead, he continued to sort through the mail and spotted what the letters and packages had in common.

Christmas.

There were holiday-themed stamps, stickers and such on each of the items. He went through more than two dozen and didn't see a bill or any junk mail in the mix. Nope. These were obviously Christmas cards and gifts that his father hadn't delivered.

The question was why?

"Yep," Emmy verified when Calen finally came up with a single curse word that seemed to fit the situation. "There's more," she went on, pulling out an envelope from her purse. "This was on top of the pile in one of the other bags. As you can see, the corner of it has been gnawed off, but the to and from addresses are still readable."

Everything inside Calen went still when he recognized the look she gave him. Because he'd been on the receiving end of it for the past year.

Sympathy.

Steeling himself up to face, well, whatever crap he was about to face, he took the envelope and saw the postmark was from eighteen years ago. December twenty-second. There was no name on the return address, but the street was listed. It had come from San Antonio, about a half hour's drive away, and it had been written in a child's scrawl. He recognized the address the letter had been sent to.

There was a name, too.

Daddy.

Well, hell in a big-assed handbasket. Calen knew bad news when he was looking at it, and this was *bad*.

Chapter Two

When Emmy had planned Calen's and her weekly get-together to bad-mouth their cheating exes, she certainly hadn't had this in mind. Of course, she also hadn't planned on noises in the attic, mouse droppings, or discovering two decades' worth of old letters and packages. That included the one letter that had caused Calen to look as if someone had punched him.

The one sent to his father's address.

Calen had yet to open or discuss it, but he would eventually have to do both. Emmy didn't want to think about the laws Calen's father had broken by not delivering all this mail, but she was certain that would have to come up. Especially since Calen would have to report the omission to the postal service.

For now though, Emmy just focused on the immediate problem of what the heck they were going to do about the piles of mail that were now on her living room floor. A place they'd brought them shortly after Calen had retrieved the other three bags from the attic. Considering he'd cursed his way through a good portion of that retrieval, they'd both decided they needed privacy. No way would he have gotten that privacy in his office.

While Calen had started the counting and sorting, Emmy had changed out of the fairy costume. Iridescent gossamer wings were great for playing mystical woodland creatures, but they sucked for pretty much everything else. She needed to sit down to get through this.

Once she'd returned from changing into jeans and her favorite Harry Potter T-shirt, Emmy poured Calen a drink, grabbed a Pepsi for herself, and located pen and paper to make notes.

"Sixty-eight letters and cards in this one," Calen announced after he'd finished counting the contents of bag number four. "And four small packages."

Emmy jotted that down and did a quick total. The four bags had contained two hundred and twelve letters and cards and thirteen packages.

Well, that total was almost true.

Emmy wasn't counting the letter she'd removed from the bag before she had ever taken sack number one into Calen's office. It'd been a shock to see it. The kind of shock that made a person say bad words and get weak in the knees. Both of which had happened. Because the letter had been from her.

And sent to Calen.

Seventeen years ago.

So much angst and agony had gone into the writing of that particular correspondence when she'd been eighteen. She had nearly chickened out many times before she had finally dropped it into the box outside the post office, certain it would end up in Calen's hands. Clearly, it hadn't, because it'd been sitting in an old mail bag in Waylon's attic all this time. Seeing it there had certainly clarified a few things.

Like why Calen had never mentioned her letter.

Like why he'd continued to treat her as the friend she had always been to him.

Since she was now in possession of some 20/20 hindsight, Emmy realized it was a good thing he'd never gotten the letter. Because if he had, everything between them would have changed. They might not even be friends now, and after the heart crushing she'd taken over Owen's cheating, she desperately needed Calen's friendship. Then again, if Calen had read the letter, maybe she wouldn't have gotten involved with Owen in the first place.

Apparently, hindsight was a gift that kept on giving, and in this case, it was doling out plenty of doubts and what-ifs for her.

Calen was no doubt going through his own what-ifs, and while he'd spent the first hour of this visit just going through each bag and counting so they'd have a total, Emmy knew him. Knew that one letter he'd put in the center was gnawing away at him. Heck, it was gnawing away at her, too, but she refused to play what-if with this one. Best to treat it like the emotional keg of dynamite that it almost certainly was.

Because it was addressed to Daddy.

Emmy had no doubt that Calen had done the math on this one, too, and he knew the letter had been sent when he was eighteen. Ironically, it'd been postmarked the same day Emmy had sent her own letter to Calen.

"It can't be meant for me," Calen muttered after he took yet another shot of the whiskey she'd poured for him.

Even though the counting was done, Calen continued to sit on the floor and stare at the red envelope with the ho-ho-ho-ing Santa stamp and the child's drawing of a snowman. Correction—a possible snowman. It could have also been a white poop emoji, but considering the holiday theme, it likely wasn't the latter.

One thing for certain was that Calen hadn't been the one to send it. At eighteen, he'd been long past the point of childhood drawings and such. So that meant someone else, a child, had mailed it to someone he or she thought of as Daddy.

Again, that meant it wasn't for Calen, unless he'd knocked up someone when he was twelve or so. When Emmy looked at him consideringly, he gave her a scowl.

"No, just no," he insisted. "I didn't have sex until I was fifteen."

She knew that. Knew, too, that overly perky cheerleader Mandy Tarkington had been the one. After that, it was a string of girls who'd obviously seen that Calen was the hottest guy in Christmas Creek. Emmy had seen it as well, but she'd never managed to catch him at the right time when both had been available. Then they'd ended up dating best friends Owen and Sasha, so Calen and she had become best friends as well.

Of course, Owen and Sasha had stretched their bestie status when they'd screwed around with each other, but that was a whine best saved for later. For now, she contemplated the Daddy letter while she chugged not booze but more Pepsi. Emmy had learned the hard way over the years that it was best to keep a clear head when dealing with stuff she couldn't wrap her mind around.

"It's like looking at multiple hornets' nests," Calen remarked. Sighing, he eyed the stacks and bundles as if they were indeed insects ready to swarm.

And he wasn't far off in that opinion.

Even if she disregarded the child's letter and the one she'd tucked away in her purse, Emmy could see plenty of possible bombshells. Like the one addressed to Dillon Mercer from his sister's college roommate, Elise, who'd visited Christmas Creek several times. The handwriting on the letter looked awfully flowery, and according to the postmark, it would have been sent while Dillon was still married.

Then, there was the one from Gladys Herman to Clive Dunbar, both of whom were well into their seventies. Neither of them had ever married, nor had they appeared to show any interest in each other. Probably because Gladys was a straightlaced business owner from one of the town's premier families, and Clive, well, wasn't any of those things. He was an occasionally employed artist whose claim to fame was that he'd been at Woodstock. A surprise to absolutely no one because he still dressed as if he were living in that decade.

Not a perfect match on paper.

But there it was, the letter/Christmas card from five years ago, and Gladys had let the "s" in her name curl into a little heart. Such a small thing, but it would fire up gossip and speculation if it got out. Which made Emmy wonder why Elise and Gladys had taken such risks.

Of course, she'd risked bunches herself when she'd written to Calen.

Emmy blamed her risky behavior on youth and the fact that the holidays made you think all things were possible. Movies like *It's a Wonderful Life* and *A Christmas Carol* egged you on. Once January reality set in though, most of those holiday possibilities just seemed like pipe dreams.

Or in her case, a Texas-sized mistake.

Calen took a deep breath and reached for the daddy letter just as his phone dinged. Because Emmy was sitting right next to him with her back against the sofa, she saw the name on the screen. Deputy Mick Webster.

Mick would be manning the sheriff's office, so maybe something else had gone wrong. Or maybe the deputy just wanted an update since Calen had told him about the mail bag before he'd left the office.

"Tell me bad news didn't come in fours," Calen snarled when he took the call. Even though he didn't put Mick on speaker, Emmy heard the deputy speak.

"Yeah, it did. Or rather fives," he said, causing Calen to groan. "But I guess you could say the fourth one is just a continuation of bad news number three about all those letters and such your dad didn't deliver. How many more did you find?"

"Too many." Calen was still snarling. Now, he put the call on speaker and began to put the small packages in a separate pile. "What's wrong?"

"Word's out about the mail," Mick said, and this time it was Emmy who groaned. Well, that hadn't taken long, less than two hours since she'd shown up at Calen's office.

"How the hell did that happen?" Calen demanded.

Mick readily supplied the name of the dispatcher. "Junie. She has better hearing than she lets on. Anyway, she claims she only told one person, but it's all over town. Folks have been dropping by and calling. I'm surprised you haven't gotten any calls about it yet."

The words had barely left Mick's mouth when Calen's phone dinged with another call. "Sasha," Calen grumbled when he saw the caller's name. He didn't answer it but rather stayed on the line with Mick.

"Folks are curious about the letters," Mick went on. "And pissed off Waylon did something like this. I suspect some are worried, too, because there might be some secrets and such in those letters and packages."

"Secrets and such," Calen repeated, eyeing the daddy letter again. "Yeah, there could be." He dragged in a long breath. "What's bad news number five?"

"There was a problem with the mistletoe ball," Mick said.

That caused Emmy to frown. The Mistletoe Ball was *the* holiday party in a town jammed with parties and other seasonal celebrations. But despite her sour mood over the cheating anniversary, the ball was important since it raised money for her favorite cause, children's literacy.

Thanks to the proceeds, the town library would be able to add dozens of books to the children's reading area. Some might think that'd be competition a bookstore owner wouldn't endorse, but Emmy just wanted the kids to read, whether they got the books from her or elsewhere.

"Not a problem with the party but the actual ball," Mick went on. "The big mirrored disco one that hangs over the dance floor. It fell, probably because of all the lights and mistletoe that had been strung on it."

"Did anyone get hurt?" Calen asked.

"Just minor stuff. Pieces of the ball flew off and nicked a few people. Including the mayor," Mick added, a smirk in his voice. "He was bent over at the time picking up something he dropped, and a sharp bit of the ball smacked him in the butt. Tore right through his pants and nicked his left ass cheek."

Even though her ex, Owen, had remained as mayor, his name was pretty much mud, and folks were not expecting him to be reelected the following year. It was petty of Emmy to be happy about that, happy about the butt nick as well, but she had earned some petty points after what Owen had done.

"You need me down at the civic center?" Calen asked.

"Nope. I've got it. You just keep dealing with the mail. Oh, and when you do come across secrets and scandals, give me the details," Mick added with an amused chuckle.

Calen, who was clearly the opposite of amused, made a noncommittal sound and ended the call. He also ignored the next incoming call after grumbling, "It's Sasha, again."

Emmy didn't want to know why his ex-fiancée was calling, but it was possibly to complain about Owen's butt injury. Maybe Sasha thought Calen could have prevented it.

Or had arranged for it to happen. There was plenty of bad blood among the four of them, but Calen wouldn't have done that. Emmy wouldn't have arranged it either, but she would have had a good belly laugh since Owen had exposed that very butt cheek on the same night he'd been caught cheating with Sasha.

Calen's phone continued to ding with more calls and texts. Emmy didn't see who these were from, and Calen didn't respond. He just sat there eyeing the letters, no doubt considering the firestorm their discovery was causing in the community. The firestorm it was causing in him, too, because although Waylon hadn't been the friendliest sort, she'd never known him to break the law.

She glanced at Calen, trying to figure out how she could help him. Hurting for him, too. Of course, Emmy was also worrying about the daddy letter and the one she'd taken from the mail bag before Calen had even gotten a chance to see it.

Did that mean she, too, was breaking the law?

Maybe. After all, once she'd put the letter in the mailbox, it was no longer hers but rather the property of the post office until it reached its destination. And that destination was the house where Calen had lived.

"What's wrong?" he asked, drawing her attention back to him. Calen was studying her. "I mean other than the obvious."

A whole boatload of words came to mind: *liar*, *thief*, and *interferer with a police investigation*. Which she technically was. She cursed the guilty conscience that was already nibbling away at her.

"Have you ever played what-if?" she asked.

Clearly, he hadn't been expecting that response because Calen's forehead bunched up. "Is this about the daddy letter?"

"No. Maybe," she amended when she realized the can of worms she was about to open. "It's just . . . I was thinking about finding out information that might possibly change . . . everything."

She saw confusion in his eyes. Because of that whole kindred-spirits connection Calen and she had, he probably thought she was talking about Owen and Sasha. That was no doubt why he sighed, moved closer to her and offered her some of his whiskey. She refused the booze but accepted the arm Calen slipped around her.

Of course, it wasn't the first time he'd offered her his shoulder, and it wouldn't be the first time she'd latched on to the comfort he so willingly gave her. But it wasn't only comfort she felt. Nope. For the past year when she'd used his shoulder, she had felt the stirrings of the heat that had started stirring way back in high school.

The stirrings that had prompted her to send him that letter.

The heat had come and gone over the years, never totally cooling. It was always there, her own secret crush. Or rather secret lust. But lately, since the Owen/Sasha debacle, Emmy had thought Calen might be experiencing something similar.

Like now, for instance.

When he looked at her and their eyes met. Then, *wham*. The heat definitely sizzled. In fact, she was surprised there weren't little cartoon lightning bolts striking between them. Bolts that warmed her from head to toe, concentrating in the center of her body.

They had never acted on the bolts or the heat. Had never even shared a pity kiss during their weekly gripe parties. But, mercy, those warm parts of her wished she could put her mouth on his and see just how hot this could get. Probably hot enough to lead them straight to the bedroom, where she figured there'd be something even hotter and better than lightning bolts.

Of course, if that happened, they'd be risking their friendship. Yes, the very friendship that had gotten them both through crappy times, including the deaths of their parents, the ups and downs of their careers, and their lying, cheating mates. Because if things could fire up enough to lead to sex, they could also fizzle out and spell the end of their friendship.

And that's the reason Emmy didn't move in on Calen's mouth.

Perhaps it was the reason he also inched away from her and quit staring into her eyes. Then again, his eyes had plenty of other things to occupy him. His attention immediately went back to the letter in the center of the piles.

After some snail-crawling moments of silence, he tipped his head to the letter. "My mom passed away the year before that was postmarked."

Maintaining her own silence, Emmy knew there was no need for Calen to fill in the blanks. A one-year-old baby couldn't address an envelope, so that meant the child had been conceived while Waylon was still married to Calen's mother.

"Maybe the sender got the address wrong," Emmy pointed out. "Maybe it was meant for some other daddy."

He looked at her again, this time without the heat, but rather with a dismissal. That was okay. She'd already dismissed her suggestion, too.

"The simplest answer is usually the right one," he muttered.

On a heavy sigh, Calen picked up the envelope and opened it. Not a letter but rather a Christmas card, a home-made one with a glittery dancing snowman that was the companion to the hand-drawn one on the envelope. There was no greeting on the front of the card, but when Calen opened it, he saw the same block writing that was on the envelope.

And there it was. That word again. *Daddy*, followed by a message.

"Daddy," Calen read aloud. "I hope you like my card. I made it just for you, but Mama helped. I love you. I hope one day me and my big brother, Calen, can be friends and that Mama and me can live with you and him. Love, Vanessa."

More snail-paced moments of silence followed, no doubt while Calen reread the message. Emmy was doing the same and trying to wrap her mind around the crotchety Waylon fathering a secret child, one who could pour out such love. One who was also aware that she had a big brother.

"I'm guessing you didn't have a clue about this," Emmy said.

"None," Calen verified.

"All right," Emmy continued, going into best friend, comfort mode, "maybe Waylon met the child's mother after your mom died, and this Vanessa isn't his bio-child. He could have kept the relationship from you because he thought you might not want him seeing someone."

Calen didn't latch on to this possibility with "take it and run with it" approval, but he seemed to be at least considering it. Considering it and making another connection.

He got up, went to pile number three and rifled through until he came up with another card. No childish scrawl or snowman on this one. It was addressed to Waylon, and the sender was Vanessa Bozeman.

"This one was from six years ago," Calen said, opening it. Out dropped a picture of an attractive teenager wearing a maroon graduation outfit.

Emmy immediately checked to see if there was any resemblance between Calen and her. There was. They had the same dark brown hair and same coloring. Emmy was about to point out that could be a coincidence, but then she saw the writing inside the card itself.

Thinking of you, Dad. Merry Christmas.
Love, Vanessa.

"Well, hell," Calen muttered.

Emmy gave him a couple of minutes to try to absorb the new message. Even if this woman wasn't his bio-sibling, it was obvious she felt a connection to Waylon. Not enough of a connection though to come forward after Waylon's death. Then again, maybe she didn't know he'd died.

"Are there any other letters from her?" Emmy asked.

"I'm not sure."

That sent them scrambling to the three additional piles to start going through them, but they'd barely started the task when there was a knock at her door. Emmy hadn't heard a car pull up, but it could be someone who'd just walked, since the house was in town.

"Calen?" someone called out after another quick knock.

Both Emmy and Calen cursed. Because it was Sasha.

"Calen, I went by your office and Junie said you were here," Sasha went on. "I need to talk to you."

Crap. What the heck did she want?

After more mutters and cursing, Calen went to the door. Emmy was right behind him. In fact, when he opened the door, she stood side by side with him, forming a human barrier just in case Sasha thought she was going to be invited in. She wouldn't be. It wasn't possible for Emmy to totally avoid her former friend, not when they lived in the same town, but she saw the woman seldom enough to feel a jolt at the sight of Sasha on the porch.

"Oh," Sasha said, her blue eyes widening a bit, maybe because Emmy was giving her a world class glare. "Oh," she repeated, shifting her attention to Calen. "I need to talk to you."

"So you said. Talk," he snarled. Apparently, he was doing some glaring, too. "If this is about the disco ball, then Mick is handling that."

Sasha shook her head, her long auburn hair swishing with the movement. "No. Uh, it's about the letters you found. The ones your father didn't deliver." She paused again, nibbled on her bottom lip, which today was coated in Christmas red. Probably to coordinate with her body-hugging sweater and pants. "One of those letters might be mine. It was sent to me, but I never got it."

Well, that got Emmy's attention, and she played a quick connect the dots. Some of those letters obviously contained secrets. Emmy should know because her own love letter to Calen had been in the mix. But what kind of letter was causing Sasha's lip nibbling?

"The letters will be turned over to the US Postal Service," Calen informed her.

"No!" Sasha gasped and then glanced over her shoulder as if to make sure no one was listening. No one was. "You have to let me go through those letters, Calen. For old time's sake."

Emmy figured the look Calen gave Sasha went past the mere glare stage. This was more like one of the deeper-levels-of-hell looks. "For old time's sake?" he repeated.

"Yes." Sasha squared her shoulders and was probably trying to appear as if she had the power here. She didn't. "Please," she added. "It'll cost you nothing to give me my letter."

"And what's in this letter?" Emmy asked.

Sasha flicked her an annoyed glance then returned her pleading eyes to Calen. "Please," the woman repeated. "You don't have anything to lose if what's in any of those letters comes to light, but I do."

Interesting, and Emmy couldn't wait to go through the piles to see what she could find. For now though, she stayed put because Sasha was moving in on Calen. As brazen as brazen could get, she reached out and took Calen's hand. Not for long though. Calen pulled back, and when he brushed against Emmy, he caught her hand instead.

Sasha noticed.

She looked at the hand lock before her narrowed gaze met Emmy's. "You can't possibly be involved with each other. Is this so you can get back at Owen and me?"

Oh, that was the wrong thing to say, and Emmy was in no mood to explain a little friendly hand-holding between, well, friends. Nope. She wasn't bothering with that explanation at all.

Emmy looked Sasha right in her narrowed eyes. "I think you're interrupting my afternoon with Calen, that's what. And it's time for you to leave."

A wiser woman probably would have just shut the door in her face, but Emmy's anger wouldn't let things stay that wise or simple. She turned to Calen and did what she'd thought about doing earlier.

Emmy pulled Calen to her and kissed him.

She wasn't sure who was more surprised by the lip-lock, but Emmy thought maybe Calen won that particular award. He made a sound of surprise, the kind a person made if they stepped barefooted onto something sharp. He also went stiff.

But that didn't last.

The next sound he made was a husky groan, and as if they'd been doing this for years, he took hold of the back of her head and brought her even closer to him. And with that maneuver, he fulfilled a whole lot of fantasies. Confirmed some things, too.

For instance, he tasted as good as he looked.

Another for instance, he was really good at this.

His mouth moved over hers, taking, taking, and taking until reality must have set in and given him a knock upside the head because he stopped and eased back. Emmy saw the heat in his eyes. Felt it. But she also saw and felt something else.

The instant *what the heck did we just do?* regret.

Chapter Three

"Well, hell," Calen grumbled as he sat in his home office and debated if he should call the number he'd jotted down.

He repeated his grumble even as he was very much aware he'd been saying that phrase a lot in the past twenty or so hours. However, he figured there'd be at least a few more *well, hell*s before this situation finally ended.

Or rather these *situations*.

Because it wasn't just one thing on his plate now.

At least he didn't have to go into work this morning, where he'd have to deal with a flood of calls from those worried about the mail. Instead, he was home, where he was ignoring the flood of calls and trying to decide if he should make a call of his own.

The toppled cowboy Santa, wet tourists, downed disco balls, and a mayor's injured butt now seemed like annoying specks in the grand scheme of things. There was no way for such bad news specks to compete with Emmy kissing him or finding two hundred and twelve letters and cards and thirteen packages that his father should have but didn't deliver.

Yes, Emmy's kiss definitely ranked high up in the breaking news of the past twenty hours.

Not a bad thing, exactly, but not good either. After all, she hadn't kissed him because of the relentless heat that they generated anytime they were together but because she'd been pissed at Sasha.

Too bad his body hadn't gotten the memo that it was a kiss all for show, because certain parts of him had reacted. The brainless part of him behind the zipper of his jeans had thought it was the best idea ever and had urged him to dive back in for more kisses. He hadn't, thank goodness. He hadn't jumped headfirst right into that stupid pool and kissed Emmy as if there was no tomorrow.

Because there was a tomorrow.

And he was darn sure he was going to need his best friend to get through all the stuff that was going on. The stuff that included him making this call and dealing with the cards that Vanessa Bozeman had sent Waylon.

Or rather, sent to *Daddy*.

There were twelve of them, and from what Calen had been able to tell by the postmarks and the occasional enclosed pictures, Vanessa had sent the first one when she'd been about six. The last had come two years ago, right before Waylon had died from a heart attack.

Calen wasn't sure it was technically legal for him to open his father's mail, but he'd justified it because he was Waylon's next of kin. He'd also justified running a background check on Vanessa since she, too, might be next of kin. He'd discovered she was twenty-four, twelve years younger than he, and that she lived in San Antonio, where she worked in a bakery. She was also a widow, having lost her husband in a construction accident six months earlier.

Before Calen could disgust himself with any more debates, he pressed in the number he'd gotten from Vanessa's background check. It was nine in the morning, so he figured she'd be up and about.

His gut tightened while he waited. And waited. And

waited. After six rings, the call went to voicemail, and he heard the recorded greeting.

"Hi, this is Nessa. I can't take your call right now because I'm probably mixing up some sugary sweet goodies that'll double the size of your thighs and make you say *mmm*. Leave a message, and I'll get back to you. Happy holidays."

The entire message was coated with plenty of glee, but the last two words were especially glee-filled. So, this woman who was possibly his sister was a holiday lover. Strange, since she had to be going through her own crap anniversary. This was the first Christmas since her husband's death.

He settled for saying, "Uh, this is Calen Jameson. Call me if you want to talk," and clicked off.

Calen frowned, added another *well, hell*, but he didn't have time to dwell on the call because there was a knock on the door. A frantic one. Since he didn't live in town but rather on the outskirts, it meant someone had driven out to his horse ranch, no doubt to ask him about the blasted unde-livered mail. Cursing his father and everything else going on, he went to the door, prepared to tell whoever it was to get the hell off his porch.

But it was Emmy.

Emmy wearing snug dark jeans, boots, and a red sweater beneath her equally Christmassy-colored coat. Colors not chosen because of her fondness for the holiday but because the tourists preferred to buy books from someone who looked the part in 'Twas the Night Before Christmas.

Bringing in the cold morning wind with her, she rushed in the moment he opened the door and then quickly closed it behind her. She peered out one of the sidelight windows.

"Someone might have followed me," she muttered, shrug-ging off her coat.

That gave him a jolt of alarm. "Who?" And because he

was a cop, his brain went straight to a worst-case scenario. Not logical. Because Christmas Creek wasn't a haven for serial killers or stalkers.

"Any one of the three-dozen people who've come to my house to ask about the blasted letters," she snarled. "It's been nonstop since you left yesterday, and it started again at eight this morning. You haven't gotten anyone out here?"

"Calls, texts, and emails but no visitors." That probably had something to do with folks not wanting to make the drive out to his ranch when they could just pester Emmy. After all, she was the one who'd found the letters, and some probably figured she'd be more likely to talk about them than he would be. "I'm sorry," Calen added.

She waved his apology off, but she was clearly annoyed when she turned to face him. Well, temporarily annoyed anyway. He saw her mood quickly morph to include something he didn't want to see on his best friend's face. Wariness.

Hell, this was about that blasted kiss.

Since he was feeling some wariness of his own, along with a whole crapload of guilt for having such dirty thoughts about Emmy, Calen decided to deflect and fill her in on the past hours since he'd left her house.

"I worked my way through the hierarchy of the U.S. Postal Service and reported the undelivered mail. They'll investigate the situation right away and come up with a solution. The most obvious one is that the mail will simply be delivered to the addressees or returned to sender if the recipient is no longer alive."

Emmy stayed quiet a moment. "And will they press charges against your father?"

He shook his head. "No need since he's not around to be arrested, but there'll be an investigation to see if anyone else in the post office here was complicit in what happened. I don't believe anyone else was involved, and that's what I put in my official statement," Calen added. "I think this was just Waylon being Waylon."

Of course, the USPS probably wouldn't just accept that nutshell explanation, but if they dug even a little, they'd learn that Waylon had loathed Christmas. That loathing went all the way back to childhood when Waylon was just six and his mother had run out on him and his father at Christmastime. After that, his father, Calen's grandfather, had apparently turned into a mean drunk who'd banned all things Christmas so the holiday wouldn't remind him of his wife's exit.

Calen could understand Christmas stuff being a trigger for bad memories. After all, he was dealing with that himself, but if he'd had a six-year-old son, he would have tried hard to put his own baggage aside and give the kid some semblance of holiday joy. Waylon's father hadn't done that for him.

And Waylon hadn't done it for Calen.

The result was that Calen had never had a Christmas tree until he'd moved out of Waylon's house and bought a place of his own. That year, Calen had gone all out, tinseling and lighting just as folks did in town. The thought of having to do all that decorating now was just plain depressing, and since he didn't have a kid around, he'd probably skip the whole holiday deal for a while.

"I'm sorry," Emmy muttered, drawing his attention back to her. She wasn't a mind reader, but she was a face reader. His face anyway. And she no doubt knew where his thoughts had gone.

He dismissed her apology as she'd done his. "Anyway, I should have an answer from the postal inspector soon. Maybe before Christmas. Maybe," he emphasized.

It would be somewhat of a miracle if it happened, but

Calen had proposed the mail and packages could be handed out tomorrow night at the Mistletoe Ball, which was always held on December twenty-third. A very short turnaround but doable in a holiday miracle sort of way. He really didn't want to have to hang on to the stuff any longer than necessary.

"I called Vanessa Bozeman before you got here," Calen continued. "She didn't answer so I left a message. FYI, she goes by Nessa."

That got Emmy studying his face again, no doubt to see how he was coping. "I don't know how I feel about it," he confessed. "It's hard to believe Waylon cheated and kept a child secret, but then again, he kept all of this secret." Calen motioned to the mail bags that were now sitting on his dining room table.

She made a sound of agreement. "But I wonder why he didn't open the cards from Nessa. I mean, if she knew him well enough to call him Daddy, then why wouldn't he want to open them?"

"Unfortunately, that might fall under one of those *secrets for the ages* deals. Well, unless Nessa can fill in some of the blanks. At this point, I don't even know for sure if she is Waylon's child. The daddy label could have been just a term of endearment."

Except that didn't mesh with what Nessa had written in the first card he'd opened.

I hope one day me and my big brother, Calen, can be friends and that Mama and me can live with you and him.

The sentiment of a child who not only believed Waylon was her father and Calen was her brother but that she had a mother she hoped one day would be with *Daddy*.

Yeah, Calen was counting on Nessa having some answers. If she returned his call. It was entirely possible she'd washed her hands of Waylon and his son.

"Did Sasha pester you again about her letter?" Emmy asked.

"Not yet, but she probably will. Whatever's in that letter must be very important to her."

The interest sparked in Emmy's eyes. "You found it?"

"I did. It was in the stash from two years ago." He walked to the table and pointed to it. Easy to see since he'd set it in the center of the bags.

"Hmmm." Emmy leaned in, studying it. "No name for the sender, just the address on Belmont Street. That's been a rental house for years with tenants always moving in and out."

Oh, yeah. Calen had noticed all of that and had wondered why the contents of that envelope would be so important to his ex. He'd also speculated about the identity of the person renting that house at the time the letter had been sent. It probably wouldn't be hard to learn that if he asked around.

"The postmark date is about a year after Sasha and you got engaged," Emmy pointed out, and even though she didn't voice her thoughts right away, she was no doubt speculating whether the letter was from another man.

Perhaps Owen.

"Sasha and Owen said their hookup was a one-time thing," she added reluctantly, "but do you think it could have been going on for a year or more before they were caught?"

"That's occurred to me. It's also occurred to me that Owen wouldn't want a love letter to his friend's then fiancée to get out. He's already going to have to fight to win reelection, and this might sour even more folks."

Emmy made a sound of agreement. "Sasha wouldn't want a letter like that to get out either because she's painting herself as the poor pitiful discarded ex who made a one-off mistake. People might not be willing to shop at her antique store if they find out she was a longtime cheater."

The moment she finished saying that, her eyes widened. Then she sighed. "Sorry. Sometimes I let the anger take hold of my mouth, and I forget you might not want to think of just how long the cheating had been going on."

No, he didn't want to think about it, but that didn't stop him from doing it. Emmy was no doubt doing the same because, after all, they were both in this nasty mess. When each had become engaged, neither of them knew they were pledging themselves to potential cheaters. It hadn't even been on their radar.

"Wait," Calen said, motioning for her to follow him into the kitchen so she could help herself to a drink from the fridge. "Sasha didn't go to your house again, did she?" he asked, scowling over that possibility.

Emmy shook her head, and then she followed it up with a shrug. "Actually, I quit going to the door, and I got Terry to cover me at the bookstore because she said folks were showing up there, looking for me."

Terry Webster. Along with being one of Emmy's assistants, she was also married to Calen's deputy, Mick. It'd been a wise decision to have her cover for Emmy because Terry wasn't the sort to let anyone bully her into divulging info about the letters. Info that she might possibly have now because Mick could have told her. Mick hadn't actually gone through the letters, but Calen had given him the highlights. What Calen had held back was any mention of the Daddy cards or the letter that Sasha was so obviously worried about.

Emmy opened the fridge and snagged one of the Pepsis he always kept on hand for her. Calen went with water, figuring his four, maybe five, cups of coffee were enough caffeine. He didn't want to deal with jitters around Emmy because

now that the silence had settled in around them, so had the
wariness in her eyes.

"All right, I'm just going to come out and say it," she
started. "About that kiss. I'm sorry—"

Without thinking, something he should have done, Calen
leaned in and kissed her. He didn't make it deep or scalding,
though that was something the brainless part of him wanted
to do. Nope. It was more of a *there, we're even*, which of course
was nonsense. Because even a tame *there, we're even* kiss
with Emmy packed a punch. He could have sworn the heat
and the need doubled his body temp.

She blinked as he pulled back, and when she met his
gaze, the wariness was gone. That was the good news. The
bad news was that she was almost certainly feeling some
scalp to toes heat, too.

Hell's bells.

Talk about opening Pandora's box. Suddenly, he was
craving another kiss. Something long, deep, and hot. But
there was no way it'd stay just a kiss. Nope. They were both
still in control of their lust, but Calen was betting that control wasn't strong enough to survive more kissing. And that's
why he started talking. If he talked, he couldn't use his mouth
and tongue for other things.

"I don't want to lose your friendship," Calen reminded
her. Reminded himself, too.

"Neither do I," Emmy readily agreed. "You're the first
person I want to talk to if something goes wrong. Or if it
goes right."

He was totally with her. It had been that way as long as
Calen could remember. Their closeness probably had to do
with their both having had difficult childhoods. They'd lost
their moms when they were thirteen—Calen's mom had died
from breast cancer, and Emmy's mother had been killed in a
car accident. Those losses left them to be raised by less than

stellar fathers. Unlike Waylon though, Emmy's dad had left town shortly after Emmy started college, and he hadn't ever returned; she'd learned years later that he'd drowned during a fishing trip.

She paused, staring at him. "Just how strong do you think our friendship is?"

Everything inside Calen went still. "Strong," he assured her, though that was a partial lie. He wasn't sure it could survive a sexual relationship if said relationship went south.

"How strong?" she pressed, but then she huffed and waved the question off. "I'm just going to assume it's very, very strong and give you this."

At first, he thought Emmy was going to kiss him again, probably because he was still dwelling on her mouth. But no kiss. Instead, she pulled something from the back pocket of her jeans and thrust it at him.

He eyed the envelope that she unfolded. Eyed her. And when she didn't offer an explanation, his attention landed on the writing. It was addressed to him.

Specifically, to him from Emmy.

Still puzzled, he glanced at the postmark. Then, he growled out another, "Well, hell." Because the date was from seventeen years ago when Emmy and he had been eighteen.

"The letter was in the first bag I found," she explained. "In fact, it was sitting on top."

As explanations went, it was a little thin. "And you took it?"

She nodded.

Again, not much of an explanation. "Why?" he pressed.

Emmy leveled her eyes on him. "Read it, and you'll know why."

Calen was reasonably sure he'd rather read a four-thousand-page treatise on the life cycle of a flea, but that was only because it wouldn't turn his life upside down. He suspected whatever was in this letter might do just that. Still, he couldn't just blow off her request, not when the letter was obviously troubling Emmy enough to take it from the bag and then bring it to him.

Wishing it wasn't too early for a shot of the whiskey he might need, Calen opened the envelope and took out the single-page handwritten letter. Even though his voice suddenly felt a little unsteady, he read it aloud.

"*Calen, I didn't want to ring in another new year without telling you how much you mean to me. You're probably going to be shocked to hear this, but I'm in love with you.*"

He stopped. Had to. And he dragged in a fast breath. He didn't look at Emmy. Calen just focused on getting through the rest of the letter. Then, he'd deal with the five words that were flashing in his mind like a big-ass neon sign.

I'm in love with you.

Powerful words indeed, but he reminded himself that Emmy had written them when she was eighteen. Technically an adult, but still very young. It was possible she hadn't known what she was saying. Possible, too, that she no longer felt the same way.

"*I'm guessing my confession surprises you,*" he continued to read, "*but I don't want you to say anything right away. Please think about it for a day or two and then call me. Of course, if you decide not to mention it at all, I'll understand. If that's what you decide, I will still always love you in secret while forever and always being your best friend.*"

She'd signed it *Love, Emmy*. Simple. Straightforward. And like a blasted arrow to his heart. Crap. What was he supposed to say now? What was he to think, especially with that whole "love you in secret" clause?

He cleared his throat, hoping the right words would magically spout from his mouth. They didn't. Thankfully though, he came up with something rather than just standing there, looking as if she'd sucker punched him.

"Why didn't you give this to me in person seventeen years ago?" he asked. "And why give it to me now?"

"Because it twisted me up to lie to you. We've both been with liars, and I didn't want to be a member of that particular club."

Well, he couldn't fault her for that. They had indeed had enough lies to last them a couple of lifetimes, and the one thing he'd always been certain of was that he'd get the truth from Emmy.

Except he hadn't.

"You kept your feelings from me all this time," he said.

She nodded, paused, nodded again and downed her Pepsi like medicine. Apparently, she was also hoping for words to magically appear.

"Trust me when I say that I agonized over that letter, but I felt as if I couldn't keep my feelings to myself any longer," she explained. "However, when you didn't mention anything about it, I figured you just wanted the whole situation to go away."

"I didn't say anything about it because I didn't know this existed." Calen held up the letter. "I sure as hell didn't know that you believed you were in love with me back then."

He waited for her to spell out to him whether she still felt that way, whether she'd been hiding her true feelings for him all this time. But she didn't volunteer any information. Maybe because the "in love" part was long gone. That made sense because after all, she had gotten engaged to Owen.

Calen released a long, slow breath that was definitely one of relief. Emmy wasn't in love with him, and showing him this old letter was just about coming clean. That was good.

He wondered why it didn't feel as good as it should have.

"I'm okay," she assured him. "I'm not going to break into a million little pieces."

But he could guess how she'd reacted seventeen years ago. "How much did you cry when I didn't say anything about the letter?" he asked.

The corner of her mouth lifted into a not so smiley smile. "Loads." She paused. "But after a while, I was just thankful that you went on as if the letter hadn't happened. Which, of course, it hadn't as far as you were concerned because you never read it."

No, he hadn't read it because Waylon hadn't delivered it to him. His father had stuffed it in an attic until it'd come to light after all this time. And that caused the what-ifs to start spinning.

Calen wasn't sure what he would have done if he'd read this letter when he was eighteen. He wouldn't have been able to respond, "I'm in love with you." He loved her, yes, but in those days, he hadn't noticed her tasty mouth.

All right, he had.

But he'd shoved his attraction to her aside because he hadn't wanted to lose her. In those days, he had a lousy track record with romance. Hell, he still did. And he wouldn't have wanted to risk hurting her by jumping in headfirst, only to have things cool between them. Or worse, completely ice over. Again, with his track record, he didn't want to take the risk.

A risk like that earlier kiss had been.

"Yes, it's scary to dive into something that could change everything between us," Emmy said, obviously sharing his risks and doubts.

Unfortunately, she shared this scorching heat, too, and despite his lingering worry, he didn't step back when she moved toward him. In fact, he stepped closer to her.

They met in the middle of his kitchen.

So did their mouths. His lips on Emmy's. Her body landing against his. This time, it wasn't a kiss for show or one to balance the scales. Nope. This was the real deal. The kind of kiss that happened for only one reason. Because that scorching heat had finally spilled over and made them stupid enough to throw all caution to the wind.

She tasted like Pepsi and really good sex. Especially the sex. And that was the problem with an amazing kiss and having Emmy's breasts pressed against him. His mind was doing huge jumps, imagining just how much better this could get. Calen forced himself to focus on the here and now.

Here and now with the taste of Emmy sliding through him. Here and now with her making a silky sound of pleasure while she slid her fingers into his hair. Calen did some sliding, too, by hooking his arm around her waist and drawing her even closer. So close that he could feel her heartbeat.

This was all new territory to him but familiar, too, because Emmy and he had actually talked about sex. Not fine point specifics, but he'd heard her voice disapproval over a guy groping at her. So, Calen didn't grope. He just kept kissing her, kept applying the pressure of his body to hers and waited to see what would happen.

Emmy was the one who started groping. Well, more or less. She slid her hand down his back until it reached his butt, and she gave him a little nudge in the right direction. Enough of a nudge that Calen was pretty sure his eyes crossed.

And sex thoughts came again.

He was trying to put another chokehold on that overwhelming urge when he heard the knocking. At first, he thought the sound was in his head, but when Emmy pulled back, he realized someone was at the door.

Someone he was going to get rid of.

Steeling himself as best he could, Calen went to the door and threw it open, prepared to give his visitor one very sour unwelcome, but he froze when he saw the smiling woman on his porch. Not someone from Christmas Creek but someone he recognized from her DMV photo.

Nessa Bozeman.

She obviously recognized him, too, because her smile widened. "Calen," she said, laughing with delight. "Finally, I get to meet my big brother."

Calen silently muttered another *well, hell* that he couldn't voice aloud because it felt as if all the air had been knocked out of him. Maybe it was some kind of cosmic genetic connection, or the realization that he'd just looked into eyes that were a DNA copy of his own.

Either way, Calen knew this woman was truly his sister.

"Oh, I suspect you have a lot of questions," Nessa said, pulling him into a hug. Well, as much of a hug as she could manage considering her hugely pregnant belly. "I'll see if I can answer them."

Chapter Four

Emmy stood frozen in the doorway, and beside her, Calen wasn't moving either. But his visitor was. Nessa continued to hug Calen. Continued to laugh as if this were the best day of her life.

And maybe it was.

Emmy hadn't read all the cards and letters from her, but it was obvious Nessa was more than happy to see her brother.

Since the icy wind was taking swipes at them, Emmy moved back so the embracing siblings could come inside. She shut the door just as Nessa finally stopped the hug, and the woman stepped back, studying Calen.

Now that Calen and Nessa were face-to-face, Emmy thought the woman looked familiar. She could also see a resemblance to Calen. Of course, DNA could be tricky, but Emmy figured Calen didn't have any doubts that Nessa and he shared the same father.

"I got your voicemail," Nessa said, uncoiling a chunky holly green scarf. "And I was already in Christmas Creek to do some shopping. I stopped by the sheriff's office, and one of your deputies said you wouldn't be in until this afternoon."

There was a lot to process in that handful of sentences,

which was probably why it took Calen a while to reply. "You knew where I live?" he asked.

Nessa smiled again. "Yes. I'll confess I've sort of stalked you over the years. You, too," she added to Emmy as she took off her coat and that scarf. "I've seen a lot of pictures of Calen and you on social media and know that you're close friends. I've even bought some books from your store. I was there last Christmas and again about three months ago."

So that's why she looked familiar. "I remember you." And Emmy picked back through her memories. "You bought cookbooks."

Nessa's smile went up a notch. "That's right. I manage a bakery in San Antonio, but what do I do on my days off? I bake," she answered with a chuckle. "I love your bookstore and all the shops in Christmas Creek. The Yuletide Tea Shop is one of my favorites and, oh, the Candy Cane Bakery. That's where I was heading when I got your message," she added to Calen. "I was craving one of those white chocolate cranberry muffins. Then I was going to Santa's Workshop to get a holiday mobile for the baby's nursery."

So, Nessa had planned on being in town for a while, which meant she now had time to catch up with Calen. That was Emmy's cue to leave.

"I'll just be going," Emmy said, fluttering her fingers toward the door.

"No," Calen and Nessa said in unison. Calen's tone had an edge of desperation to it while Nessa's was more of a *please stay*.

Emmy volleyed some glances at them to make sure it wasn't lip service. It wasn't. So she nodded, and that caused Nessa to smile again.

"From everything I've heard, you and Calen are very close," Nessa said. "I suspect he could use his best friend right about now."

Calen made a sound of agreement and met Emmy's eyes. Yes, he could use a best friend. He didn't want to put distance between them despite that kissing session they'd just had in his kitchen. Good. Maybe it meant he wasn't having any regrets about it. And since she was feeling hopeful, Emmy added that maybe the regrets wouldn't come at all.

She certainly wasn't feeling regretful about those kisses.

Just the opposite. She was trying to wrap her mind around how she could convince Calen that kissing, and maybe doing a whole lot more, were very good things. For now though, she just needed to help get him past this visit and the aftermath.

When Nessa rubbed her hand over her hugely pregnant belly, Calen seemed to yank himself out of his stunned trance. "Why don't you come and sit down." He took her by the arm and gently led her into the living room. "Can I get you something to drink?"

"No, thanks. I had some herbal tea at the Yuletide, and Gladys topped off my cup a couple of times while we chatted. It must be amazing to live in a town that feels so happy." She paused, and the smile faded. "Well, maybe not always happy," she added in a murmur.

So, Nessa obviously knew about their broken engagements. Of course, she did. If she'd visited Gladys, Nessa would have heard all about it.

"I've never told Gladys or anyone else in Christmas Creek that I'm Waylon's daughter," Nessa went on as she sat in one of the chairs across from the couch. Emmy and Calen took the sofa. "I figured if you'd wanted people to know, you would have told them."

"I didn't know about you," Calen immediately said. "Not until yesterday."

"Ah, yes. You found out when you went through the mail that Dad didn't deliver. Gladys," Nessa added, and no further explanation was needed. "He didn't open the cards I sent to him." Her smile went south again. "Since he never responded, I guessed as much."

Emmy groaned and wanted to throttle Waylon. It was bad enough that he'd withheld the mail, period, but he'd compounded that bad by not even responding to his own daughter.

Or maybe he hadn't known Nessa was his child.

"Waylon knew about you?" Emmy came out and asked.

Nessa's nod was quick. "He came to visit my mom and me two or three times a year." She stopped again. "And here's where I should go back to the beginning. Well, the beginning as I know it anyway. My mom, Miranda, and Dad met as kids when he visited his grandparents in San Antonio."

"His grandparents," Calen repeated. "That was his mom's folks."

Nessa nodded. "Apparently, Dad's father sent him there most summers, and Mom said he hated it almost as much as he hated being home. That he also resented his own mom for abandoning him, and her folks put all the blame for that on Dad's father."

"I recall Waylon mentioning his grandparents," Calen said, "but I didn't know he'd had any contact with them. I never met them because they died shortly after I was born." He paused. "So, Waylon met your mother when they were kids and they . . . kept in touch?"

Another nod from Nessa. "They dated on and off through high school, but it was hard for them to visit after my mom started college in Austin. According to my mom, they drifted apart but ran into each other twenty-five years ago." Now, it was Nessa who paused. "Yes, while he was still married to your mother."

The silence settled in for a few uncomfortable moments.

"They had an affair," Calen concluded.

"No. Again, according to my mom, it was a one-time deal. Your mother had gotten the news that she wasn't going to make it, that the cancer had spread, and Dad didn't take that well. He showed up at Mom's apartment, and one thing led to another . . ."

Well, crap. Emmy immediately looked at Calen to see how he was handling this. His jaw was set, and it was possible he was doing a whole lot of silent cursing.

"I'm so sorry," Nessa went on. "This is one of the reasons I never contacted you. I figured it would bring back horrible memories just to see me, to know that I even exist." She started to get up. "I'll be going."

"No, stay," Calen said, and he reached out to take her hand, urging her to remain seated. "My mother's death was a hard blow, but I don't connect you to that." He dragged in a long breath. "But I'm sorry Waylon didn't do better by you. What reason did he give your mom for not marrying her after he was a widower?"

Nessa lifted her shoulder. "My mom has never said. She got married two years ago and moved to Florida, so I'm hoping one day she'll spill all. For now, I'll just accept what I have. And I have so very much," she added, pressing her hand to her stomach again. "I've done a family tree for the baby. Of course, it's all just names and dates, but I'm hoping to get pictures for her."

So, a daughter. Calen would be getting a niece.

"I can maybe help with that," Emmy offered. "There are still some boxes with old photos in the attic of the house I bought from Waylon."

"Oh, that'd be wonderful. If it's okay with you?" Nessa asked, directing her question to Calen.

"It's okay," he assured her. "When are you due?"

Nessa beamed again. "In about three weeks. Of course,

it'll be bittersweet because her dad won't be there for her delivery, but I'm focusing on the sweet. I might have lost my wonderful husband, David, but I'll always have a part of him with our baby girl."

Mercy, Nessa had really been through the wringer. A wringer that would have squeezed the joy out of most. Apparently not her though.

"I'm sorry about your husband," Calen murmured.

"Yes, that was soul-crushing." Tears filled her eyes, causing Calen to groan.

"I'm sorry I brought it up," he quickly added.

Nessa waved off his apology and blinked back tears. "I nearly called you a dozen times over the past six months since I lost him. My mother was a good shoulder to cry on, but sometimes I just thought I'd like to talk to you. To both of you," she added. "I'd look at the pictures of you two and knew you were going through some tough times, and I thought maybe we could have all helped each other."

Yes, tough times, but Emmy thought Calen's and her ordeal with the cheaters felt like a tiny drop in the bucket compared to Nessa's pain.

"I wish you had called. I mean that," Calen assured her when Nessa's head whipped up, and her eyes widened.

Nessa smiled again and glanced at them. "See, just looking at the two of you gives me hope. You survived a terrible ordeal, and you both lost your moms when you were so young. Yet you're obviously happy. I swear, you were both practically glowing when you answered the door."

Emmy thought maybe her glowing moved on to a blush. Because her pink face was a result of kissing, not because they were *obviously happy*. Then again, those kisses *had* improved her mood and made her feel a lot more hopeful than she'd been in months. Of course, a lot of that hope was tied to her searing attraction for Calen, but, hey, hope was hope.

"Oh, and before I forget, I thought you might want this." She took out an envelope and handed it to Calen. "It's a copy of my birth certificate with Dad's name on it and DNA test results for Dad and me."

Calen took the envelope but kept his attention on Nessa. "Why DNA tests? Did Waylon ask for that?"

"No. My mom's the one who insisted on it. She wanted me to know who my father was. She wanted me to know you," she tacked on. "And now that we've met, I hope you won't mind me stopping by the next time I'm in town." Her smile widened when Calen nodded. "The same for you," she said to Emmy. "I'll definitely want to buy some books for the baby, and maybe we can chat."

"I'd like that," Emmy assured her. And she made a mental note to buy a whole bunch of those board books for infants.

Nessa stood. "Well, I'll be going then. I want to walk through town and see the decorations. And get that muffin." She chuckled. "I really am craving it."

"Why don't I go with you?" Emmy asked, standing as well. "The sidewalks might be a little slippery since the temps are right at freezing. The weather forecast is calling for snow tomorrow."

"Oh, I heard that. A white Christmas." Nessa's eyes lit up. "Wouldn't that be amazing?"

Well, Emmy hadn't thought *amazing* was the right word because she'd been worrying about icy roads, but since white Christmases were rare, it might indeed be a special treat.

And her mind began to spin in a different direction.

Maybe Calen and she could spend that white Christmas snuggled up together. Cuddling and talking about how this sister revelation was affecting him. Maybe sharing some of the day, too, with his sister.

"But I don't want to trouble you," Nessa insisted a moment later. "I suspect you both have work to do. I can go into town alone."

"No trouble," Emmy and Calen said in unison as he also stood. "I can take a little more time before going in to the bookstore," Emmy added.

"And I don't have to go in to the office for another hour or two," Calen explained. "I can drive, and then Emmy and I can show you around. Or we can follow you into town. Maybe show you some of the shops you might've missed on your other visits."

Nessa's smile was tentative now. "But what if people ask who I am?" she said.

"Then, I'll tell them you're my sister," Calen assured her. "Are you ready to start tongues wagging about that?"

The woman's bright smile returned. "Oh, yes. Let the tongue wagging begin."

Calen figured plenty of tongues were already getting a workout. A workout that'd started within minutes of their arrival in town, when they'd all parked in the lot next to the sheriff's office.

Because Christmas Creek was crowded with tourists, shoppers, and locals who just liked being part of the holiday buzz, Main Street was jammed, and he saw plenty of long, questioning looks. Saw behind-the-hand whispers. Of course, some of the merchants might recognize Nessa from her previous shopping trips, but there'd be much speculation as to why she was with Emmy and him.

Calen saw that speculation in the Candy Cane Bakery when the owner, Tandy Roberts, rang up Nessa's muffin and coffee to-go cups for Emmy and him. Tandy didn't come out and ask why Nessa was with them, but that was probably because the store was packed, and she had customers waiting.

"This is one of my favorites," Nessa said, eating the muffin while they stopped at the window of Santa's Workshop, one of the town's four toy stores.

As usual, the front window was set up with a display of a toy train choo-chooing and chugging its way through a mock-up of the town. Calen had seen it so many times that it was like white noise to him. In fact, the entire town had become holiday white noise, but he stopped because Nessa did. He looked in.

And frowned.

"Is that me?" He pointed to the tiny figure standing outside the sheriff's office. The hair color matched his, but the figure was skinny enough to be one of those waving blow-up characters outside a car dealer.

"It is," Emmy verified. "And that's me." She pointed to the equally weirdly shaped figure standing by the front of the bookstore. "Herman ordered the figures online and sent the artist photos of us." She put *artist* in air quotes. "They used to have a Waylon figure by the post office, but they replaced it with Wheezer's Dalmatian, which often takes naps there."

Calen had some vague memories of folks talking about that, but he'd never paid attention to the display. It was sort of, well, touching in a small-town kind of way to be immortalized in, well, a small-town kind of way.

They got more stares and whispers when they went in so Nessa could make use of the bathroom and pick up the mobile she'd ordered. The clerk, Hanna Tarver, who was one of the town's biggest holiday lovers, beamed a smile at them, and she opened her mouth, no doubt to issue that happy holidays/merry Christmas greeting. But Calen's hard look stopped her. His mood had significantly improved, but he still wasn't ready to hear it.

Instead, Hanna focused her efforts on getting the mobile for Nessa, and much to Calen's surprise, it wasn't a traditional mobile. This one featured first responder vehicles. A cop car, fire truck, an ambulance, and a rescue helicopter.

"I figured my daughter would get enough girl stuff," Nessa said when she saw Calen eyeing the mobile. "But I thought it wouldn't hurt if she had a reminder of what you did. What you are," she added, pointing to the little wooden cop behind the wheel of the cruiser.

Again, he was touched, but it also made him feel more than a little lousy. Here, all these years Nessa had wanted to meet him, had wanted him to be part of her life, and he hadn't known squat about it. About her. Of course, he could thank Waylon for that, but it still felt as if he should have figured it out sooner.

Neither Hanna nor any of the other clerks questioned who Nessa was or why she was with Emmy and him, but Calen suspected lots of questions would be asked to try to figure out this visitor.

With the mobile in a shopping bag, they went back out onto the sidewalk. "I want to thank both of you for doing this with me. A huge thank-you," Nessa emphasized. "I need to get back to the bakery, but I want to see you—"

Nessa didn't get to finish her sentence because they practically ran right into Owen. Time seemed to freeze. So did everything around them, something that happened whenever he had a chance meeting with the man whose Santa suit sex-capade was still the talk of the town.

Owen wasn't alone today. A film crew from a San Antonio TV station was trailing him. So was Owen's assistant, Tate Webster. In a small town where there was often only one degree of separation, Calen knew Tate—he was Deputy

Mick Webster's brother, and Tate's sister-in-law, Terry, worked for Emmy.

"Emmy," Owen muttered, and Calen saw the guilt in the man's eyes for a split-second before he turned his politician's smile back to the cameraman. "And here are two of the town's citizens," he announced. "Christmas Creek's top cop, Sheriff Calen Jameson, and Emmy Kendrick, the owner of 'Twas the Night Before Christmas bookstore."

Calen didn't have to see Emmy's eyes to know there was no guilt in them, but they'd be narrowed. Three hundred and sixty-six days might be enough to cool some of the anger, but it wasn't enough to forgive and forget.

Owen swallowed hard, searching for anything that wasn't Emmy or the town's top cop. The mayor's attention landed on Nessa. Owen glanced back at them, and when Calen and Emmy didn't make introductions, Calen could see the man gearing up to do his *host without a checkered past* spiel.

"I'm sure the sheriff will be at the town's annual Mistle-toe Ball," Owen said, holding up a handful of flyers that announced the event the following night. He handed one to Nessa, who eyed it, then Owen.

"Oh, I know you," Nessa said. "You're the guy who got caught having sex with your friend's fiancée while you were dressed as Santa. That's taking the holiday spirit to a whole new level."

Owen didn't miss a beat. He raised his voice, talking right over Nessa. "And here's one of the many holiday visitors to our fine town. Welcome to Christmas Creek," he muttered and tried to hurry past Nessa.

"This is my sister," Calen said, cutting off Owen's escape. "Nessa Bozeman."

Owen opened his mouth, no doubt to issue one of those plastic platitudes to go along with his plastic smile, but he stopped and obviously rethought what he'd been about to say. "Your sister? I didn't know you had a sister—"

"I do," Calen assured him in a voice loud enough for any bystander to hear. There. Within five minutes, the news would be all over town.

Calen slipped his arm around Nessa and guided her back toward the parking lot where Nessa had left her car.

"Thank you for that," Nessa whispered to him.

"My pleasure," Calen assured her.

"And thank you for what you said to Owen," Emmy added. "It's fun to watch him try to snake-oil his way out of an embarrassing situation."

Nessa and she shared a chuckle, and when they reached Nessa's car, she turned and gave both Emmy and him a hug. "Thank you again," Nessa said, handing Calen the flyer that Owen had given her. "For this day, for everything."

She got in her car and lowered the window, obviously wanting to stretch out the goodbye a little longer. Apparently so did Emmy.

"If you don't have any other plans, why don't you come to Christmas dinner at my place?" Emmy invited. "It'll be just Calen and me, and you're more than welcome."

Tears sprang to Nessa's eyes again, but Calen thought these were of the happy variety. "I'd love that."

"Great. Calen has your number, so I'll get it from him and text you the time and address," Emmy explained.

Emmy and he waved goodbye and stood there, watching Nessa drive away. What a hell of a whirlwind morning this had been. It reminded him of the day before, when Mick had said that bad things came in threes.

"Maybe good things come in threes, too," Calen heard himself say. "Nessa's arrival could be the start."

Emmy looked up at him, smiled and then touched her lips to his. Okay, that could qualify as good thing number two, so Calen decided to go for broke. He held up the flyer he was still holding.

"Want to go with me to the Mistletoe Ball?" he asked.

Amusement lit in her eyes. And maybe something more. Maybe pleasure. He added to it by kissing her, and not just a touch. It was long, deep and French. Just the way he wanted all his kisses to be with Emmy.

When he eased back, he could see she approved of that type of kiss as well because she ran her tongue over her bottom lip and made an *mmm* sound.

"Let's test just how strong our friendship is," Calen added, tipping his head to the flyer. "Let's make it a date."

"A real one?" she asked with a naughty glint in her eye.

"A real one," he assured her with his own naughty glint.

Oh, this was going to be fun. And maybe, just maybe, it wouldn't screw up things six ways to Sunday.

Chapter Five

A date.

Emmy didn't even bother to try to tamp down her giddiness. She felt like a teenager on prom night. Specifically, a teenager on prom night who had a date with the hottest cowboy in Texas. Calen's hotness wasn't an exaggeration, neither was her giddiness, but since she was in her thirties, she had to add something else to this mix.

Worry.

With all the kissing Calen and she had been doing, sex was up next on the agenda. No way around it if the kissing continued. But while she was certain the sex would be amazing, it was a risk. Not just because it could ruin their friendship but because they could both get their hearts crushed again. Still, even that terrible possibility didn't stop her from treating this like the date that it was.

The prep for said date had gone on for hours. The long bubble bath, the careful application of her makeup. Then, the hair, also carefully done. Thankfully, she'd already bought a killer red dress that fit her like a second skin. It was way more risqué than the usual outfits she wore to the Mistletoe Ball, but when she'd bought it, Emmy had thought it would be some nice payback to watch Owen's tongue hit the floor when he saw her in it. Maybe though, Calen's tongue would do the same. Not for payback but to add some more flames to an already flaming fire.

Since the giddiness had caused her to get dressed too early, Emmy poured herself some wine and paced across her living room. Not the wisest thing to do in heels that had been designed for looks rather than comfort. Rather than risk blisters, she went to the window and got her own tongue-dropping surprise.

Oh, mercy.

Calen was already there. Stepping out of his truck. And he'd gone for *go head, drown in me* impact, too. Of course, he could have managed that no matter what he wore. She figured he could have especially managed it had he worn nothing at all. But for the ball, he'd gone with a Texas tuxedo. Dark jeans, a black jacket, crisp white shirt, and a black Stetson.

Emmy threw open the door and grinned at him. "You look like Mr. December on one of those hot cowboy calendars."

He grinned back and skimmed his gaze down her. Yeah, the dress worked. "You look like I'd better get you to the ball before I see if I can change your mind and make this a stay-at-home date."

Mr. December knew the right thing to say. He touched his mouth to hers, careful not to smear her lipstick, and he slipped a red rose corsage on her wrist.

"Thanks," she said, returning the kiss and smearing that lipstick after all. But when she eased back, she saw something in his eyes. "Having second thoughts?"

"No." But then he shook his head. "I don't want to have second thoughts," he amended. "They might happen though."

The disappointment came, tamping down some of her mood. "They might," she agreed, and then added, "You know how I always have your favorite beer in my fridge, and you have Pepsi for me? Well, that doesn't stop us from having other stuff in there. Like now, for instance, I have cherry cheesecake in mine."

The look he gave her wasn't exactly flat, but it was close. "Is that your way of telling me that you can have your cheesecake and eat it, too?"

"Something like that. Our friendship is the beer and Pepsi. The cheesecake is, well, whatever else our friendship becomes."

The corner of his mouth lifted in a quick, brief smile. "I just don't want the beer and Pepsi to get . . . awkward." He stopped, cursed. "Probably best if I quit speaking in metaphors."

"Straight talk works," she assured him.

He nodded. "You've texted me three times today. Once with a funny cow video, another time to tell me about the customer who wanted to buy some UFO books, and a third one to let me know you were going to wear smutty underwear tonight. I want to think we can have all three, but I'm not sure we can."

Emmy had to pick her way through that. He wanted the fun, the job chatter, and the smutty stuff. Heck, so did she, but she wasn't stupid, and she knew that sex could ruin things between friends.

"Tell you what," she said. "Let's just go on this date and see what happens. And tomorrow, I'll send you three more texts."

He took hold of her hand, threading his fingers through hers. "What about the smutty underwear? Is that still on the table?"

She winked at him. "Well, for now it's on me. Swatches of red lace that barely cover anything, hence the smutty label."

Calen groaned, the sound of a man in sexual agony, but he was laughing when he pulled her to him and brushed a kiss on the top of her head. "All right. This date and we'll see what happens. That means it's best if I don't stand here thinking about your underwear."

Probably best if she didn't think about his either, or they wouldn't make it to the party to test out these dating waters.

She eased back, noted the frown line in the center of his forehead, and rubbed it away. "Am I the reason for the rest of this worry, or is there something else?"

"Something else," he answered on a sigh. "I haven't gotten permission yet from the postal service to hand out the letters and packages. They assured me they're working around the clock until after the holidays, so they could give the okay any minute now. There'll be some disappointed people if the mail isn't handed out tonight."

Calen was obviously disappointed as well, and she didn't have to guess why. Once the undelivered mail was no longer in his possession, then people would stop bugging them about it.

"All right," she said, "so this will be a party fraught with tension, gossip, and speculation. Oh, and the added bonus of seeing our exes."

"Don't forget all the holiday greetings we'll have to hear," he added.

"Nope, let's not forget that. If things get too uncomfortable, just think of my smutty underwear."

She smiled when that got him to chuckle. Mission accomplished, and she hoped the lighter mood would stay with him throughout the night.

Calen helped her into her coat, and she locked up before they went to his truck. She had a moment of fantasy déjà vu because when they'd been in high school, she'd imagined dates just like this with Calen. Of course, she hadn't given him any signals that she was open to such dates, and if it hadn't been for her showing him the letter she'd written all those years ago, this night might not have happened either.

The fantasy continued when the snow began to fall. Big fat flakes that drifted down like little paratroopers. Since the temps were low enough for the snow to stick, the town known for its holiday celebrations might indeed get one of those rare white Christmases.

"Nessa called," Calen told her as he drove toward the civic center. "She wanted me to make sure you were truly okay with her coming over for Christmas dinner."

"I am," she assured him. "Are you?"

"I am," he verified after a short pause. "I'm still angry at Waylon for not telling me about Nessa. It was a punch in the gut to learn she existed, but it's not awkward like I thought it would be when I first tried to call her."

Emmy made a sound of agreement. It hadn't been awkward for her either. In fact, she was pretty sure Nessa and she could become fast friends.

"Despite everything Nessa's been through," Calen went on as he parked by the civic center, "she's managed to stay positive. Hopeful. I think you and I lost our hopeful outlook when Owen and Sasha were caught cheating."

She made another sound of agreement, and everything inside her went still when he looked at her. Not with the scorcher heat. No, this was something else, and if she had to put a label on it, Emmy thought it might be . . . peace. Maybe just a little anyway. If so, she was all for it since they hadn't had a lot of peace over the past year.

"Let's do this date," he said, dropping a quick kiss on her mouth. Okay, so the scorcher heat was back, and even stepping out into the cold didn't lower it.

However, stepping inside did.

That's because every eye seemingly turned in their direction, and the party chatter stopped. In fact, everything except the music stopped, making the only sound in the grand hall the band's overly cheery version of "Frosty the Snowman."

"Clearly, we've impressed them with our choice of party attire," Emmy whispered out of the corner of her mouth as they took off their coats and put them on the table by the door.

Calen laughed, and just like that, the tension eased in her chest. He helped ease it even more when he took her hand and led her into the crowd. They threaded their way to the bar, where he snagged two glasses of champagne.

As usual, the civic center was all decked out for the occasion in a way that only a small town like Christmas Creek could manage. Lots and lots of decorated trees, something that had caused spats over the years as various clubs, committees, and businesses vied to take charge of the decorations. In the end, it was decided that anyone could contribute a tree.

And any- and everyone had.

You couldn't go more than five feet before encountering one, and they varied from tabletop size all the way to the twelve-footer that the mayor's office had contributed. The bookstore's tree was next to the fireplace, and as usual her assistant, Terry, had done an amazing job, decorating it with book ornaments and glittery holly.

There was a strong scent of pine, fir, and spruce. The décor was overwhelming, too, with some of the trees lit and tinseled from top to bottom while others had gone all blue, red, or green. The only space without a tree was the dance floor. The disco ball reigned king there, so obviously someone had managed to get it fixed. She wondered, briefly, if Owen's butt was still stinging from his injury and then decided he wasn't worth a single moment of her thoughts.

Little by little the chatter started again. Emmy heard murmurs about Waylon's secret love child. More muttered remarks about how Calen and she were obviously drowning their misery with a rebound date. Still others gossiped about the letters and packages that were still in limbo.

She did a quick mental count. "Apparently, there's more talk about us than Nessa and the mail," Emmy remarked, sipping her champagne.

That caused Calen to smile again. A very short-lived one though, because Gladys quit whispering to her bestie, Junie, and made a beeline toward Calen and her.

The woman was wearing the same green wool dress that she wore most years, and she murmured greetings to them before she leaned in toward Calen. "I just wanted to offer my sympathy on Waylon not telling you about your sister. I didn't know," she assured him. "As far as I can tell, nobody in town did. He kept it quite a secret."

"Yeah, he did," Calen confirmed. "FYI, Waylon's secret wasn't Nessa's fault. I'm hoping everybody in town will remember that."

"Oh, folks won't look down their noses at her, if that's what you're worried about. Heck, most of us know her because she shops here a lot. We just didn't know she was your sister." She paused. "Junie said she thought you found out about all this in one of the letters Waylon didn't deliver."

Calen nodded but didn't offer any more.

"Uh, Junie said you took the mail to your house," Gladys went on.

There was nervousness in her voice. In her eyes, too, and Emmy thought of the letter she'd seen from Gladys to Clive Dunbar.

"I did," Calen confirmed. "I'm hoping to have permission tomorrow to go ahead and release them. If not, it could be a while."

A while because the day after tomorrow would be Christmas, and the post office would be closed.

Gladys nodded and moved in even closer. "Well, I was

wondering if any of the mail was addressed to me. Or from me."

"I recall one letter," Calen said, studying her and no doubt seeing the woman's anxiety as well. "Once it's released, it'll be delivered to the intended recipient."

Gladys's forehead bunched up. "I suppose that has to happen? It's just, I, well, I might have said some things in a letter that could sort of make someone uncomfortable."

Emmy didn't know if that discomfort would be felt by Gladys or Clive. "Maybe it'd be best to give the recipient a heads-up?" Emmy suggested.

Gladys sighed and downed her entire glass of champagne. She looked at Emmy. "Have you ever taken a risk by telling someone something they might not have ever suspected?"

"Yes." Emmy could answer without hesitation.

Perhaps it was that lack of hesitation that caused the flash of surprise in Gladys's eyes. "Then, you know it could backfire."

"Yes," Emmy confirmed. "But I also know it might not. My advice? Give the recipient a head's-up."

And just in case Gladys didn't know the immediate location of that person, Emmy motioned toward one of the food tables where Clive was standing in his green bell-bottoms and tie-dyed shirt. Clive wasn't the sort to spring for tickets, but since he painted the Christmas murals on the civic center's walls, he always got an honorary invitation.

Gladys blushed, but Emmy didn't think it was because Calen and she knew the woman's secret. Nope. This seemed more of a naughty blush, and Emmy could relate since she'd spent most of her adult life thinking naughty thoughts about Calen.

When Gladys started moseying in Clive's direction—emphasis on the moseying—it seemed to be a cue for others to start converging toward Calen and her. At least a dozen came, all talking at once. Or rather whispering at once about getting a look at the mail. That gave Emmy her own cue, and she set aside their champagne so she could lead Calen to the dance floor.

"Apparently, there are a whole bunch of secrets in Christmas Creek," she murmured to him.

"Apparently," he agreed, pulling her into his arms.

Emmy might have said more about that, might have speculated what those secrets were, but she felt the slide of his arm around her waist. Felt the sparks when Calen pulled her closer until they were body to body.

Everything else vanished.

Well, everything that wasn't Calen related anyway. Her whole being was attuned to him. To just this moment. To the fantasy of being here with him. She could see the need for her in his eyes. Oh, her best friend was still there in that need and heat, but this combination of confidant and lover was so much better.

"You're smiling," he said, and then added, "Since we've gone public by coming here on a date, you want to get folks' minds off the mail?"

He didn't wait for her to answer. Calen leaned in and gave her a kiss to remember. It was one of those long, slow ones that was no doubt a little too long and slow, considering how many eyes were on them right now. But the advantage of a great kiss was that it fuzzed her head enough that she decided not to think about that either. She just melted into the kiss, and when Calen finally ended it, she melted against him with a satisfying sigh.

"Interrupting anything?" someone asked.

There went her satisfying sigh, but Emmy bit off the groan that bubbled up in her throat because she knew the snarler was Owen.

"As the sheriff, shouldn't you be working on getting our mail released?" Owen went on. "Mail that your father hid and didn't deliver."

"It's my night off," Calen said, and though he didn't groan or snarl, it was obvious he was annoyed by the interruption.

"You're making a spectacle of yourselves," Owen accused.

Calen and she huffed in unison and turned toward the pest that she'd once agreed to marry. In hindsight, she had really dodged a bullet there. "You mean like the spectacle of you having sex with Sasha?" Emmy countered. She leaned in, narrowed her eyes. "Because you don't get to lecture me about anything. Understand? Understand?" she repeated in a louder, meaner tone when Owen didn't respond.

Okay, so she apparently still had some pent-up anger, but it wasn't about Owen's cheating. It was because he apparently thought he still had the right to inform her of his opinion. He didn't.

Emmy had to do some mental head-shaking because clearly this mean, cheating streak had been in Owen, and she'd never seen it when they'd been together. Of course, she'd known he was ambitious, and often he'd let ambition drive him to work long hours and make big plans. Owen had wanted her for his wife because she fit his image of the woman he wanted beside him as he climbed up the political ladder. But in hindsight, she had to wonder if she'd ever been truly in love with him. Had she accepted his proposal only because Calen was getting on with his own life? With someone other than her?

Her shout had caused the room to go quiet again, and Owen's assistant, Tate, moved in to take hold of his boss's arm. Always the diplomat, Tate muttered an apology to no one in particular and tried to get Owen to back away, but her ex held his ground and shifted his attention to Calen.

"Don't hurt Emmy because you're trying to get back at Sasha and me," Owen insisted.

That was just the wrong thing to say, and now it was Emmy who took hold of Calen's arm when she felt the anger rev through him. "Just remember my slutty underwear," Emmy told him. And it worked. Her words stopped Calen from moving in to punch Owen's lights out.

Emmy put her fingers on Calen's chin, turning his head to make eye contact. "This is our date, and I say that on this date Owen doesn't even exist. It's just you and me."

She didn't exactly hold her breath, but she waited anxiously for Calen's reaction. Obviously, his deputy, Mick, was concerned, too, because he set his drink aside and came closer.

"You need help?" Mick asked Calen.

"No," Calen assured him, and he gave Owen one last glance before he turned back to Emmy. "Let's finish this dance."

And that's what they did. Thankfully, Calen made some moves that put distance between Owen and them.

"I don't want any part of what Owen just said to be true," Calen stated. "I'm not here tonight to get back at—"

"I know," Emmy interrupted, and because she thought they could both use it, she brushed a kiss on his lips. "But you're still worried the hurt can happen. It can," she admitted. "But I think we're past the point of no return here, don't you?"

Calen looked her straight in the eyes. "Yes. I just don't want to lose you."

"Then we'll take it slow," she said, though Emmy immediately frowned. In some ways, they'd been on the slow route for over two decades. In other ways though, in ways that involved smutty underwear, they were going full speed ahead.

When Calen cursed, it took her a moment to realize the bad word wasn't in response to their dilemma but because his phone had buzzed. He whipped it from his pocket, and she saw his pissed-off expression fade when he glanced at the screen.

"It's Nessa," he relayed and answered the call. Since both the music and conversation were back to normal levels, he put his finger in his ear, no doubt so he could hear. "What?" he said to Nessa. "Why are you here?"

Emmy glanced around, expecting to see his sister, but she wasn't there, and Calen cursed again. The moment he finished his call, he took hold of Emmy's arm and steered her toward the door.

"Nessa wanted to see Christmas Creek in the snow," Calen explained as he grabbed their coats. "But her water broke. She wants us to go to her right away because the baby is coming."

Chapter Six

Apparently, *right away* wasn't a hard-and-fast guideline for labor and delivery. Calen was learning that firsthand. Emmy, too, as they waited for news of the baby's arrival. Something Emmy and he had been doing for more than six hours since they'd made their frantic rush to the hospital.

This was hardly the hot date night they had planned, but then Nessa probably hadn't anticipated delivering her baby three weeks early at a hospital where she didn't know any of the doctors. It was both of those things—the early labor and the unfamiliar surroundings for Nessa—that were causing Calen to pace.

And worry.

Emmy had joined in on that pacing until her party shoes had sidelined her to fidgeting in a waiting room chair. She'd also done searches on her phone to figure out the risks of Nessa delivering early, but both the Internet and the nurses on duty had assured them that all would be well. Calen hoped it wasn't just lip service.

"Christmas Eve," Emmy muttered. "That'll be your niece's birthday."

His niece. That was something he'd thought he would never hear since Calen had believed he was an only child.

But it felt right. Well, right-ish anyway, and he was going to think of his sister and her baby as sort of a Christmas gift.

His phone dinged with another text, and Calen ignored it as he had the dozens of other texts he'd gotten in the past six hours. Calen figured most were just nosey people wanting to know what was going on, but they would hear soon enough. By morning, the news would be out, and there'd be plenty of tasty topics, including Emmy's and his party kiss, their run-in with Owen, their hasty departure to the hospital, the mail, and Nessa.

Calen practically snapped to attention when he saw Dr. Abernathy making his way toward them. Since he was the only OB in Christmas Creek, Calen figured he had to be the one who'd been called in for the delivery.

"A healthy baby girl," Dr. Abernathy announced, motioning for them to follow him. "Nessa's doing great, too, and she wants to see both of you. Don't stay too long though, only a couple of minutes, because we need to run a few routine tests on the baby, and the new mother needs some rest. Six hours is a fairly short labor, but it's still exhausting."

Added to that, it was nearly two in the morning, so even without the labor, Nessa had to be ready to crash.

By the time the doctor finished filling them in, they'd reached the door of the delivery room, and when Abernathy opened it, Calen spotted Nessa on the bed. She had the baby cradled in her arms.

"Isn't she beautiful?" Nessa asked. Man, she was beaming. The woman always seemed to have a smile on her face, but this went beyond a smile. "Six pounds, twelve ounces. Twenty inches long."

Emmy and Calen went closer and peered into the blanket. The baby looked pissed off, like a riled Hobbit, but, yeah, Calen felt that tug, too. Heck, maybe it was a DNA thing that made him already feel protective of the kid.

"She's precious," Emmy said, leaning in to gently touch the baby's hair. "She looks like Calen and you."

"I thought so, too," Nessa agreed, and there were tears in her eyes. "She has David's coloring though." Her voice cracked a little.

Calen felt a punch of grief for a man he'd never known. A man who would never see his child. And that was no doubt the reason for some of those tears Nessa was fighting. She won the fight, maybe because despite her loss, Nessa knew she still had so much, and that *so much* was nestled in her arms.

"Now, I just have to come up with a name," Nessa added. "Something Christmassy. Holly, maybe. Or Noel."

"Or Eve for Christmas Eve," Emmy supplied, causing Nessa to both smile and tear up again. "Do you need us to call anyone or get anything for you?"

"I'll make some calls in the morning, but I might need someone to go to my house and get my suitcase. No hurry on that though since we won't be going home from the hospital for three days. I can get my boss or one of my friends to bring it."

Now, this was something Calen could do to help. "I've got a four-wheel drive so I can get your keys from you in the morning and drive out then. It's still snowing, but it's supposed to stop in a couple of hours."

Christmas Creek only had one snowplow, which was more than most small central Texas towns had, and the snowplow operator, Elbert Sherman, would be out and about at sunrise. Still, the roads probably wouldn't be that bad since they were only expecting two inches.

At the mention of the weather, Nessa perked right up again. "Oh, I don't want to miss seeing the snow. Maybe when they're done with the tests and such, I'll be moved to a regular room with a window."

Calen didn't mention that it probably hadn't been a wise thing for her to come to Christmas Creek to see that snow, not when she'd been so close to delivering. But all had worked out, and while this hadn't been Nessa's original plan, he was glad to have a chance to spend a little time with the baby and her.

When Nessa yawned, it was their signal to leave so she could get some rest. "Whatever you decide to name her, she's beautiful," he murmured to Nessa and brushed a kiss on her forehead.

Emmy did the same to both Nessa and the baby, and they started out, just as a nurse came in. No doubt to do those tests the doctor had mentioned. Calen gave his sister one last glance before Emmy and he left.

"Uncle Calen," Emmy remarked as they made their way down the hall. "Wow, a lot of changes in the past forty-eight hours."

"Yeah," he agreed. When those changes had started, Calen had thought they would bring only gloom and doom, but things had shifted.

"We blew right past the one-year anniversary of the cheaters," Emmy went on, and they stopped at the ER doors to put on their coats. "I'd steeled myself for a bad one."

So had he, but despite their earlier run-in with Owen, the cheaters were no longer on his radar. He probably wouldn't extend an olive branch to Sasha and Owen, but in a weird kind of way, they'd done him a favor. If the engagements and weddings had gone on, he wouldn't be having this moment now with Emmy.

And it was indeed a moment.

With Emmy warm, smiling, and snuggled against him,

they stepped out into the soft snow and the quiet. Everything, including his truck, was white and sparkling, thanks to the streetlights and those lights coiled around the lampposts. Not ordinary lights because this was Christmas Creek, but twinkling holiday ones.

He had to admit it looked magical, and Calen totally got why Nessa hadn't wanted to miss this.

"Wow," Emmy muttered. She stopped outside his truck, looked up and let the snowflakes drift onto her face.

Another moment.

Calen had always known she was beautiful, but that beauty skyrocketed tonight because it had been a long time since he'd seen her this happy. There were no shadows from the crap year they'd had. No worried looks about, well, anything. This was just Emmy looking way too good not to kiss.

So, that's what he did.

There were snowflakes on her lips, but her mouth wasn't cold. It was soft and warm, and it felt like a Texas-sized invitation for him to take more. He went with that, too. Deepening the kiss, pulling her even closer to him and sinking in. He'd already had one hell of an amazing night, but it just kept on getting better.

He didn't stop the kiss until oxygen became an issue, and when he eased back so they could take a breath, Emmy was sporting a dreamy smile. And looking at him as if she might give up breathing for another kiss. Calen was right there with her.

"It'll take me about five minutes to get to your house," he said, hoping that Emmy took his statement for the invitation it was.

She did. Her smile widened, and Emmy caught onto the front of his shirt to get him moving into the truck.

* * *

Finally!

That was the thought running through Emmy's head as Calen and she kissed their way to her front porch. Calen certainly wasn't holding back, but she worried that he might come to his senses and reconsider this.

Emmy didn't want any reconsidering. She only wanted Calen.

Somehow, she managed to fumble around enough to get her key in the lock, and because they were leaning against the door, they practically tumbled inside. Without missing a beat, Calen kicked the door shut, and in the same motion, hauled her against him. All in all, it was an amazing place to be.

The adrenaline high was still going, and that might have played into the quick escalation of their kisses, but Emmy suspected no matter what had gone on and even without the magic of the snow, the heat between them would have exploded.

Because it'd always been there.

The heat was certainly there now, and it was notching up this need she had for him. The notching was happening for Calen, too, because it didn't take long for the touching to start. An awesome next step because Calen slid his hand between them and cupped her right breast.

He swiped his thumb over her nipple, which wasn't hard to locate because it was hard with arousal beneath her barely there bra. Calen didn't let his other hand stay idle, either. That one dropped to her butt, and with one clever move, he shoved her against him, aligning them in the best possible way.

There was a problem though with best possible alignments. The heat rose even more, turning need to desperation.

The battle for clothing removal started, and time seemed to matter. She pulled at his coat, then his jacket, while he went after her own coat and the zipper on her dress. Calen was clearly a lot better at this than she was because he had her down to just her underwear and heels before she'd barely started to undo the buttons on his shirt.

And then he played dirty.

He took those dirty kisses to her throat. To her breasts. Kissing her through the thin lace until the heat rushed through her from head to toe. It gathered in the center of her body, which was where Calen and his clever mouth went next. He tongue-kissed her stomach before going even lower.

Then, lower.

Her panties were apparently less than a millimeter thick because she felt every bit of his mouth. His breath. And yes, his tongue. By the time he'd given her a few of those kisses, Emmy could take no more. She was too close to a climax, and she didn't want to take that journey without Calen.

"You'd better have a condom," she insisted while she dropped down on her knees and went after his shirt.

Now, it was his turn to fumble around to reach his wallet. Emmy didn't make that task easy for him. Nope. Turnabout was fair play, so once she had his shirt off, she ran her tongue from his throat, down his bare chest to his abs. The man was built.

Later, she intended to play around with all those amazing muscles, but for now, she settled for just one more bit of torture by kissing the parts of him that she unzipped. Like her nipples, one part of him was especially easy to locate, and she laughed when he cursed her.

Apparently, her attention jacked up his need to desperation as well because he helped her with his jeans. Then his boxers. And it didn't take long before Emmy had a fully naked Calen to play with.

Calen must have wanted fully naked as well. He went after her bra and panties, shimmying them off her. Now, he used both his mouth and hands to keep touching her, to keep kissing her until that climax was shimmering all around her.

"Condom," she repeated, dragging him to the floor.

He yanked one from his wallet, and then everything seemed to move very, very fast. He got it on in a blink, rolling on top of her.

And then into her.

Things went from very, very fast to a standstill. He stopped, just stopped, and robbed her of what breath she had with the look he gave her. Not regret. This was the hot, needy demand of a lover. It didn't last. It was gone in a blink, because the heat was a greedy little sucker that wouldn't be denied.

Calen started the strokes inside her, as slow as he could probably manage, considering that his own body had to be on fire. The strokes built. Harder, faster, deeper. And built. Until Emmy couldn't have staved off that climax even if she'd wanted. She felt her body clamp around him, felt the climax slam through her, and she made sure she took Calen right along with her.

Emmy held on to him, savoring these last moments of the frenzied ride. Savoring everything about what had just happened.

"Eighteen years in the making," she muttered. "That's how long I've been secretly lusting for you."

She smiled and let the dreamy feel of pleasure slide through her. That was how long she'd loved him, too. But thankfully, she didn't blurt that out. Even though Calen had read the letter she'd written to proclaim her love, it was best not to muddy the waters. Especially since it might not take long for Calen to have second and third thoughts about what they'd just done.

Emmy had no doubts, none. Well, not until Calen's phone dinged. Not a text or call. It sounded like the note of a piano key.

Cursing under his breath, Calen reached over to their pile of clothes and yanked his phone from his pocket. Then he cursed again when he saw the screen.

"That's an alert from my security system," he explained, already moving off her. "Someone's broken into my house."

Chapter Seven

This was not the way Calen wanted to cap off the night with Emmy. Or rather this very early morning with her. He especially didn't want to arrest someone for breaking and entering, but that was what he would end up doing if the person who'd triggered his security alarm was still in his house.

A silent alarm, which meant the intruder likely didn't know he or she had tripped anything.

The security system had come with the place when Calen had bought the ranch eight years earlier, and since it extended to the stable and barn where he kept his horses, he turned it on when he was away from the place at night. Even though the crime rate in Christmas Creek was low, it didn't mean some idiot might not try to steal equipment or one of the horses. That had never happened before, but maybe the rare snowfall and too much Christmas booze had played into the crime.

Or plain old-fashioned desperation.

He was going with door number three on this one, betting the intruder's motive would be a whopping amount of desperation.

Calen hadn't even tried to talk Emmy out of coming with

him, but he would have if he'd thought a violent altercation was about to occur. But the chances of that happening here were slim. He suspected he knew exactly what he'd find when he pulled into the driveway.

And he was right.

Sasha's car was parked next to his house. She must have seen or heard him approaching because she came scurrying onto the porch. In all his years of law enforcement, he'd never seen anyone with a guiltier expression.

"Good grief," Emmy grumbled. "What do you want to bet this is about that letter Sasha's been whining about?"

That was a sure-thing bet, and Calen wouldn't take her up on it. He also didn't have to guess how Sasha had gotten in. After their breakup, he hadn't asked for his key back because he'd believed she wouldn't be stupid enough to do something like this.

Apparently though, he'd been the stupid one, because here she was.

The key would have gotten her through the door, but her entry would have still triggered the security alarm since she wouldn't have had the code to disarm it.

Sasha froze for a couple of seconds before she turned back toward his front door as Calen and Emmy got out of the truck. He didn't catch what Sasha said, but her action clued him in that she wasn't there alone.

Hell. Did that mean Owen was inside?

Calen was so not in the mood to deal with that ass tonight.

"Let me guess," Calen said to Sasha while Emmy and he made their way to the porch. "You decided to try your hand at trespassing and burglary?"

"I just dropped by for a visit," Sasha insisted, causing Calen to roll his eyes.

"Mercy, you're a bad liar," Emmy exclaimed. "About some things anyway," she added, obviously remembering that Sasha had kept her attraction to Owen under wraps.

Sasha didn't look offended, but she volleyed glances at Emmy and him, maybe picking up on the clues that they'd just had sex. Their disheveled hair and clothes. The stubble burns on Emmy's chin from their rough kisses. And the overall sated look that might still be surrounding them. Of course, any feeling of sexual satisfaction was quickly being overwritten by anger at his ex sneaking into his house.

"FYI, stealing mail is a federal offense," Calen advised her.

His warning put some serious alarm in Sasha's eyes, and she snapped back her shoulders. "It's not stealing if it's mine."

"It's not yours," he pointed out. "Until I hear differently, it belongs to the post office."

Calen kept on scowling. Not just because of this little B and E mission, but because his past with Sasha was the reason he hadn't already given her the damn letter. The more she pushed, the more Calen dug in his heels.

When he started to step around Sasha to go inside, she shifted, apparently believing she could block him from entering his own house. Calen just lifted her up by her elbows and moved her aside. Emmy and he went in, and Calen spotted a second intruder by the stacks of mail and packages on his dining room table. Stacks that had been rummaged through.

"I told you to run," Sasha grumbled. Not to Calen or Emmy but rather to the man who was in Calen's dining room.

Tate Webster, Owen's assistant.

Obviously, the rummaging was still going on because Tate was holding several letters in his hands.

"I wouldn't run and let you take all the blame for this," Tate told Sasha, and with a heavy sigh, he put the letters back on the table. Like his partner in crime, guilt was plenty evident on his face. Calen figured it coordinated well with the surprise that was on his. "We thought you'd still be at the hospital. It's all over town that your sister's having a baby."

"Had a baby," Calen clarified. He pointed to Tate and then shifted his finger to Sasha. "So, Tate sent you a card or letter that has something written in it that would clue folks into the fact that you two had an affair." It wasn't a question, and neither of them denied it. "Judging from the postmark, the affair was going on right about the time you got engaged to me but before you had sex with Owen."

Again, no denial. And that made Calen feel like an idiot for not having seen this side of Sasha.

"Why?" Calen asked.

Sasha shrugged, and then as if her bones had dissolved, she sank down onto the floor. "The therapist I've been seeing says it's because my parents always wanted me to be perfect, and that the sex is my subconscious way of rebelling."

Calen was having trouble working up any kind of sympathy. Yes, her parents were controlling, but they were also rich and had pampered Sasha. Maybe the pampering hadn't been enough. Maybe nothing would be enough. Some part of Calen had always worried about her neediness, though he had assured himself that Sasha's good qualities outweighed the bad.

He no longer believed that.

Trust was all-important, and he never would have had

that with Sasha. Sadly, Sasha might never have it in herself if she turned to forbidden sex to solve her problems.

"So, what's in the envelope?" Emmy asked.

Slowpoke-y turtles could have won races in the time it took for them to answer. "Naked photos of me," Tate finally said.

"I sent some to Tate," Sasha added, picking up the explanation. "He got his. I never got mine because your stupid father didn't deliver the letter."

Calen let the insult go because it was hard to defend a man who had indeed done a whole bunch of stupid things. "Any reason you two didn't just text or email the pictures?"

Sasha gasped. "Do you know how many times that backfires? All the time," she said, answering her own question. "We thought the mail would be safer and sort of old-fashioned."

Emmy groaned again, repeated her, "Good grief."

Calen and she were obviously of like minds about this. There was nothing old-fashioned about sending naked pictures. Then again, maybe in Sasha's mind, there was.

"So, does Owen know about this thing you had with his assistant?" Calen asked Sasha.

"No." That answer came instantly from both Sasha and Tate.

It was Sasha who continued, "I want it to stay that way. You're supposed to take this letter and the others to the post office, right?" She waited for Calen to confirm that with a nod. "The post office where Janice Fay Merkins works."

Calen could see where Sasha was going with this. Janice Fay was one of the biggest gossips in town, and the woman would look at every letter that Waylon had failed to deliver. She would see that this one sent to Sasha had come from a renter in the house on Belmont Street, and Janice Fay would soon figure out that renter was Tate. The woman wouldn't keep that tidbit to herself. Nope. Janice Fay's blabbering would start a whole lot of speculation that would end up painting Sasha and Tate in a bad light.

"I don't want Owen to know," Sasha insisted.

"Of course, you don't." And because Calen couldn't resist, he added, "You said it was a one-off with Owen. Was it with his assistant, too?"

"Oh, what does it matter that you know the truth," Sasha spat out as she got back to her feet. "No, it wasn't. I cheated. Obviously, so did your father. And so did you."

Calen was certain he looked offended. Because he sure as hell was. "I didn't cheat."

"Sure, you did," Sasha said with the certainty of gospel. "Maybe not sexually, but you cheated with Emmy."

Emmy's sound of outrage was slightly louder than Calen's. "And in what warped fantasy world did that happen?" Emmy challenged.

Sasha sighed, and the fight drained out of her eyes. "Because Calen has been half in love with you since high school. Best friends," she added in a *yeah-right* mumble.

Both Emmy and he issued some denials, but Sasha had quit listening. She took hold of Tate's arm, and they walked out, leaving Emmy and Calen standing there to deal with what she'd just said.

Calen muttered another denial, shook his head, and would have said something he might have ended up regretting because either way he went with this, it could come back to bite him in the ass. Thankfully, he didn't have to say anything else because his phone dinged again. Of course, it'd been doing that most of the night, but now seemed like a good time to check.

"Is there a problem with Nessa?" Emmy immediately asked.

Calen shook his head and showed her the screen. Finally, he could start wrapping up some of the chaos Waylon had started.

Because the postmaster had agreed to allow the undelivered mail to be handed out at the post office today.

Chapter Eight

Emmy figured she had to be functioning on some previously unknown supply of energy because here she was at the hospital at eight in the morning when she'd gotten no sleep.

Oh, she'd gone to bed all right after Calen had driven her back to her house. He'd walked with her to her door, given her a long goodnight kiss and the assurance he'd call after he'd finished setting up the mail delivery. But she hadn't managed even a catnap because there'd been way too much going on in her head. Too much going on in her body, too.

She still had a buzz from the sex with Calen. Amazing sex. Amazing enough to become the benchmark for all future sex. And she didn't believe it'd been lip service when Calen had kissed her goodnight so he could go to work. Still, his quick departure had left her feeling that too many things had been left unfinished.

Too many things left unsaid between them.

Emmy thought of what Sasha had said about Calen being half in love with her, but Calen had neither confirmed nor dismissed it. In fact, he'd seemed relieved to be able to drop the subject because of the text he'd gotten about the mail. And it was his non-answer that spoke so loudly. He wasn't ready for anything involving the L-word. And why should he be? They'd been on one date. One incredible date but still just one. All those times they'd hung out and been there for each other didn't count.

Did they?

Mercy, Emmy wanted them to count, but she knew the last thing she should do was try to speed things along. She just had to accept that their friendship was more important than their romance. Even if it felt as if they were now mixed into one.

Shoving that thought aside, Emmy gathered her purse and gift bag and got out of her car so she could go into the hospital. It had quit snowing, and the sun was out, making everything look as if it'd been dusted with a magic fairy wand. She'd always thought Christmas Creek was a wonderful place, but today it was picture-perfect.

Emmy threaded her way through the halls to the room number that Nessa had texted her earlier. She tapped on the door, got a quick "Come in." But when she stepped into the room, she saw Calen.

Her heart skipped a beat or two.

It just wasn't fair for someone to look that amazingly hot with sleepy bedroom eyes and sexy stubble that had gone past the five o'clock shadow stage.

"Emmy," Nessa greeted.

Calen's sister was sitting up in bed, eating takeout from Frosty's diner while the baby slept in a basinet next to her bed. Nessa had gotten a room with a window, a huge one that overlooked a small park dotted with snow-covered Christmas trees.

Emmy gave Nessa a hug and smiled down at the baby before she handed Nessa the gift bag. "It's books for both the baby and you."

"Eve," Nessa supplied. "That's what I decided to name her. Eve Elizabeth Bozeman, since Elizabeth was my grandmother's name."

It fit. So did the easy vibe in the room. Emmy tried to keep the vibe going by smiling at Calen, but it was impossible to hide anything from the man who knew her so well. That meant he saw every ounce of worry in her eyes. Not regret. Not one bit of that. But worry that things would truly be different between them. Or that they wouldn't be different at all.

"Oh, thank you," Nessa gushed, going through the books. She plucked out one of the baby board books and began showing it to Eve.

The baby opened her eyes and looked at the pages. Maybe. Emmy was going to choose to believe she was doing exactly that.

"So, when are you being discharged?" Emmy asked.

Nessa sighed a little. "Not until the day after tomorrow."

Which meant Eve and she would be here in the hospital for Christmas. Emmy thought she could do something to make that a little better.

"Instead of Christmas dinner at my house, I'll just bring it here," Emmy said. Nessa opened her mouth, no doubt to say it was too much of a bother or something similar, but Emmy put a stop to that. "Glazed ham, roasted potatoes, green beans, and homemade rolls. Better than hospital food," she added. "It'll be nice to have the meal here with you and Eve."

Nessa searched her eyes as if looking for any sign that Emmy wasn't totally onboard for this. There wasn't any because she was as onboard as could be.

"All right," Nessa finally said, her eyes a little teary. "Thank you. Thank you both."

The baby began to squirm and then let out a kitten-like cry. Nessa sprang into action, setting aside the books to scoop up the baby. The little girl turned her mouth in the direction of Nessa's breast.

"Oops," Nessa said. "All this talk about food must have

made her hungry. I'll need to nurse her. I don't mind if you both stay for that—"

"Thanks, but I'll pass," Calen said so fast that it caused Nessa to chuckle. As he had shortly after the delivery, he kissed the top of Nessa's head, and this time did the same to his niece. "I'll be back later. Text me if you need anything."

"I will," she assured him.

"I'll be going, too," Emmy said, doling out kisses as Calen had done. She didn't mind being around someone breast-feeding, but Calen and she had to talk.

After saying her goodbyes, Emmy went into the hall and was thankful to find that Calen was waiting for her.

Emmy started with an easy topic. "No sleep?" she asked.

He shook his head. "After I dealt with the postal service, I drove to Nessa's to get the suitcase she'd already packed." He checked the time. "The post office will start handing out the mail in about fifteen minutes. There's already a long line. Might need crowd control," he added with a smile that didn't quite make it to his eyes.

Well, crud. Something was wrong.

"I culled out Sasha's letter before dropping off the rest at the post office, and I went by her place on my way here to give it to her," Calen explained. "No need for Janice Fay to see it and start speculating."

"That was nice of you." And Emmy was glad he'd done it. Sasha had enough in her life to work out without adding the possibility of a relationship with Tate. Plus, it would fire up the gossips even more if word got out that he'd bedded his boss's lover. That, in turn, would fire up the gossip about Sasha, Owen, Calen and her.

"I did the same for Gladys," Calen went on. "I took her the letter and then encouraged her to give it to Clive. She's considering it."

"Good. Waylon might have postponed true love, but he didn't squelch it." Emmy winced. "Sorry."

It surprised her when he smiled. "You don't have to walk on eggshells," he assured her, then took hold of her hand. "Come on. Let's walk to the post office."

She didn't object to that because any time alone with Calen was a good thing. Hopefully, she wouldn't say something stupid to spoil the mood.

And what a mood it was.

Once they were out on the sidewalk, she could see the town. At other times of the year, the decorations just looked tacky, but the snow had made them look, well, like Christmas.

They walked, the sun and the warmth of Calen's hand chasing away the cold, and an easy silence settled around them. There it was again. That word, *easy.* It was what she'd always had with Calen, and she'd been terrified of losing it. But here it was. She hadn't lost it after all, even if things weren't the same old, same old between them.

The snow had kept the tourists away and with most folks at the post office, Main Street was deserted. Only a handful of the shops had opened, including the diner and the bakery, and she caught the scent of bacon, cinnamon rolls, and coffee.

When they reached the diner, the door opened, and Sasha nearly smacked right into them. She held a to-go bag and a large cup of coffee.

"Oh," Sasha muttered. "Emmy, Calen." She paused, swallowed hard. "I want to thank you again for bringing me the letter. And for not arresting Tate and me."

"Not a problem," he said, already moving past her. "Have a good life, Sasha."

"You sound as if you mean that," Sasha muttered.

"I do," Calen said without even glancing back.

Emmy didn't need to ask if he had meant his words. He

did. The 367 days of getting over the past were done. Added to that, Waylon's hatred of all things Christmas had finally ended in bringing a lot of people a happy Christmas this year.

Of course, that left Emmy with one big question.

What now?

Apparently, part of the *what now* didn't include Calen hurrying to the post office. They continued to stroll before stopping outside the window of Santa's Workshop. Emmy intended only a cursory glance, but her glance became a stare when she spotted the figures of Calen and her. They were no longer at the sheriff's office and the bookstore but were standing together in front of the replica of Santa's Workshop.

Just as they were right now.

"When I passed by the window earlier, Hanna Tarver was adding some fake snow," he explained. "I asked her to move us closer together."

Emmy couldn't have been more surprised if the inflatable cowboy Santa had toppled onto them. "Calen," she said on a rise of breath, "that's . . . romantic."

"I have my moments." And he smiled. A real honest-to-goodness smile that made her want to kiss him. Of course, plenty of things made her want to kiss Calen.

"Maybe we can be best friends with benefits," she threw out when they started moving again.

He stopped and looked down at her. "Maybe. But I was thinking of something more."

More sounded wonderful. And a little confusing. "What could be more than friends with benefits?"

He was quiet a few seconds. "Lovers with benefits?"

Emmy chuckled. "I think lovers already get benefits."

"All right, then people in love, with benefits," he amended. Her gaze flew to his, but Emmy didn't see any trace of a joke. Nope. However, she saw something a whole lot better. The heat, the need. Maybe a dash of hope and holiday cheer.

Calen eased her closer to him. "Sasha was wrong. I'm not half in love with you. I'm all the way in love with you."

And there it was. All her best fantasies rolled into one. A happy Calen. A hot Calen. A Calen who felt the same way about her that she felt about him.

"I'm in love with you, too," she murmured.

He flashed a smile before his mouth came to hers for a long, steamy, extremely satisfying kiss. Emmy had no doubt, none, that it'd be a lot more satisfying once she got him behind closed doors.

"Am I going to spoil the moment by saying the holiday words?" Emmy asked with her mouth still against his.

"Emmy, nothing can spoil this moment," Calen assured her.

Because that was true, they said it together. "Merry Christmas."

Coming Home for Christmas

KATE PEARCE

Chapter One

Caleb Erickson gripped the steering wheel as his truck gave another death howl and veered to the side of the snowy highway as if looking for a place to die.

"Don't you fricking dare," he growled as he wrestled for control on the ice. "Just eight more miles and we're home!"

Home . . . that wasn't the right word anymore for the place he'd been born and raised, especially not since his mother had passed away. Now he was an occasional and reluctant visitor to a man who barely bothered to acknowledge his existence. He breathed a sigh of relief as the lights of the town appeared ahead of him. He could stop at the Gonzaleses' place and see if Mike could take a look at his truck and get him out to the ranch. Even as he had the thought, the engine gave a death rattle and gave up on him. Caleb steered toward the snow-banked pavement so he wasn't blocking the through street before he gave in to the inevitable. The sudden silence after the horrendous clanking of the past few miles was almost a relief. Snow fell around the cab, blurring the holiday lights strung along the shop fronts as it melted on the windscreen.

Caleb got out of the cab and tried to orientate himself in

the biting wind. Most of the shops were dark or boarded up for the winter, which wasn't encouraging. There were lights on in the coffee shop, but when he trudged over to try the door, it was locked. He got out his cell phone only to realize he'd forgotten to charge it during his all-night drive down from Seattle and it was as dead as the town.

"Dammit," Caleb muttered as he shoved it back in his pocket. Now he'd have to walk to the mechanic's shed at the end of the street and see if Mike was around. He pulled his knitted hat further down over his ears, zipped up his collar, and headed down the center of the deserted street because it was easier to walk on than the sidewalk. Even before he reached the premises, he realized he was on a fool's errand. The huge barn doors were closed, and all the lights were off. He turned a slow circle, his teeth chattering as he viewed his hometown. He had no phone so he couldn't call anyone and no truck to get anywhere anyway. He couldn't even turn and run because he'd end up dead in the snow.

His glance passed over and then came back to a familiar old-fashioned house opposite the coffee shop. It was double fronted and four stories high with a wide covered porch all the way around it. He squinted through the snow. There were lights on and it looked almost welcoming. Caleb sighed, his breath frosting in the freezing air.

He retraced his steps past the hulking shadow of his truck. There was no one else out, but that wasn't surprising. In conditions like this the best thing to do was hunker down at home and wait for the worst of it to pass. He opened the gate of the white picket fence and approached the steps up to the porch, where a lighted sign next to a brightly lit Christmas tree proclaimed:

GRANNY SMITH'S B&B
OFFERING THE COMFORTS OF HOME SINCE 1943.

Caleb grunted as he ascended the creaking steps. If Mrs. Smith had been here that long it might explain why she was always so cranky. She'd never liked the local kids and had chased them out of her yard and away from her fruit trees with a dedication and speed that had defied her age.

The front door opened just as he was about to knock, and he was confronted by a smiling vision in a ruffled pink apron covered in blobs of chocolate.

"Good evening!" she trilled. "I'm so happy you are here!"

Caleb almost took a step backward. He wasn't used to being met with such enthusiasm, being broad, well over six feet tall, and having a natural disinclination to smile.

"I was expecting Mrs. Smith," Caleb said.

Her smile dimmed. "I'm afraid she passed away last year."

"Sorry to hear that." Caleb half turned away. "And I apologize for disturbing you."

"Don't you want to come in?" He frowned as she pushed the door open even wider. "Do you need something?"

"I need somewhere with a phone so I can call Mike about my truck." He gestured behind him. "It's broken down."

"You can do that here," she offered. "I really don't mind. It's not as if I have any actual guests to look after right now."

There was something disconsolate behind the brightness of her tone, but that wasn't his problem. He needed to get to a phone and if she was willing to let him in, he'd accept her offer.

"Okay, thanks." He wiped his boots on the mat and stepped into the wide hallway. From what he could see nothing had changed in the place since he was a kid. There was a glass chandelier in the center of the ceiling and the wide planked flooring was good local redwood that was probably original to the house. The only difference was that the whole place was decked up like a Christmas wonderland with blinking lights, holly, and at least two more fully decorated trees.

She directed him toward the reception desk to the left side of the hall.

"The landline is there." She paused, her blond hair illuminated by the light from the chandelier. "Can I get you some coffee? On the house, obviously."

"That would be great." He walked over to the desk. There was a list of local numbers right beside the phone, including the one and only taxi service, the hair salon, and the mechanic's shop.

He called the number, and when no one answered he left a message about his truck and hung up. His gaze swept the ornate furnishings in the front parlor and the heavy fringed drapes that blocked the view of Main Street. It was deadly quiet inside the house, apart from the sound of someone humming as they approached his space.

Little Miss Sunshine smiled brightly as she set the mug of coffee on the desk in front of him.

"Did you get what you needed?"

Now that he thought about it, there was something naggingly familiar about her.

"Nope. My truck stopped running and I can't get hold of Mike."

She sighed. "That's terrible. How are you going to get home?"

"You know who I am?"

"Of course, I do, Caleb." She looked slightly hurt. "Didn't you remember me?"

He studied her face and frowned. "Uh, yeah, I guess . . ."

"It's nothing to worry about." Her smile dimmed. "I suppose I've changed quite a bit, although we *have* met several times over the years when you came back to visit your parents

and I was here with Gran. Obviously, I'm quite forgettable."
She drew herself up. "I'm Lucy Smith."

This wasn't quite how Lucy had envisioned meeting Caleb Erickson again. She'd had dreams—many dreams of how he'd see her walking through town, and he'd be struck dumb by her beauty, fall to his knees, and kiss her feet for being such a little shit to her when he was a teenager. Not that he'd been any worse than the other boys, she'd just cared more because she'd always had a horrendous crush on him.

"Lucy Smith?" His brow creased as he considered her. She knew exactly when he remembered her because his expression changed to one of horror. "Little Lucy?"

"I'm five foot four. Just because you're overgrown doesn't make me short."

He angled his head, his gaze dropping from her face to her toes and then back up again.

"Nice apron."

Her cheeks heated. "It's one of Gran's. I borrowed it while I was baking my holiday cookies."

In fact, she'd hoped some of her grandmother's legendary cooking magic would rub off on her while she attempted to replicate her recipes. It was Lucy's first holiday season without her gran, and she was missing her badly.

"Oh!" She pressed her hand to her cheek. "I forgot to put the timer on."

She ran back toward the kitchen, where the smell of burning already permeated the room. "Darn it!" She grabbed a towel and opened the oven door to discover she'd rolled her gingerbread too thin, and the edges had started to scorch. She set the cookie tray on the side and went to open the window.

"I've got it," Caleb said as he reached right over her head and released the catch on the frame.

"You're not supposed to be back here," Lucy pointed out as she hastily removed the failed batch of gingerbread people from the tray before they engraved themselves on the surface forever.

"I'm not a guest." Caleb was looking around the kitchen as he leaned against the sink. "Not a lot has changed in here."

"Why change things when they still work?" Lucy asked as she quickly rolled out a new batch of dough and cut the shapes. She couldn't afford to do anything to the place anyway.

He shrugged his wide shoulders, his cool gaze now on her. "I remember you at school."

"Yup, I was that annoying little kid who followed you and my brother Dan around all the time."

"Yeah, you were definitely annoying."

Lucy tried not to roll the dough too hard or accidentally throw the rolling pin in his general direction. Caleb had always been a straight talker, so why was she surprised that he spoke the truth?

"We'd do anything to get away from you."

"I remember." Lucy put the new cookies in the oven. "You tied me to a tree in the backyard with my jump rope once."

Caleb frowned. "That wasn't nice."

"No, it wasn't, especially as it started raining."

He shoved his hand through thick reddish-brown hair that matched his tight beard. "I guess I should apologize."

"It was probably Dan's idea." She offered him an out as she washed her hands.

He winced. "No, that one was all me."

"Then I accept your apology."

He'd brought his coffee through with him and sipped it as he stared at her. She considered what to say next. As a hotelier she shouldn't ask any personal questions, but as a resident of Quincy, she felt some responsibility for his personal safety— or that was what she was going to tell herself.

"Did you call your dad?"

He set his mug down by the side of the sink. "Not yet."

"Won't he be worried?"

"I didn't tell him when I planned to arrive, so he's not exactly expecting me." He hesitated as he pulled his phone out of his pocket. "My cell's out of battery."

"You can charge it right there." She pointed at the electrical outlet. "It looks like the same brand as mine."

"Thanks." He plugged it in and turned back to her.

Lucy made herself meet his gaze. "I'm sorry about your mom."

"Me, too."

"You must miss her."

"Yeah." He picked up his mug. "Is there any more coffee?"

"Help yourself." Lucy pointed at the dresser. "There's a whole pot right there."

"Thanks. You can put it on my tab."

"As I said, coffee's free," Lucy reminded him, her gaze fixed on his broad shoulders and long jeans-clad legs as he turned his back on her. He'd certainly filled out since high school. She'd seen him occasionally when he'd come into town, but she'd never had much opportunity to talk to him without blushing and stammering like a fool. It wasn't surprising he'd erased her from his memories. But it was definitely a setback when she'd given him her heart when she was nine and decided she was going to marry him.

"Stupid . . ." Lucy murmured to herself before addressing Caleb again. "Shall I see if there's a taxi available to take you out to the ranch?"

He turned to look at her, his expression guarded. "I'd rather wait for my truck to be fixed."

"You know what it's like here. That could take a while and Christmas is less than a week away."

"As I said, Dad isn't expecting me, and I'd rather have my own transport."

"I suppose that makes sense," Lucy said cautiously. "But wouldn't you rather be home than stuck here with me?"

"You don't want guests?" He raised his eyebrows.

"Of course, I do." He had no idea how much she needed them right now.

"Then you've got one." He nodded. "Is it okay if I get my stuff from my truck while you sort out a room for me?"

"Absolutely." She nodded like she was in a trance. Caleb Erickson was staying in her house. Voluntarily? And he was even willing to pay for the privilege?

"Great." He drained his mug.

She froze as he walked over and paused to look down at her. He leaned in so close she could smell the coffee on his breath and flicked her nose.

"You've got cookie dough on your cheek."

"Thanks." "I'll get going before the snow buries my truck." He nodded at the back door. "I'll come in this way, so you don't have to leave those cookies again."

A minute later he was gone, leaving Lucy gawping at the door like a fool.

The timer pinged, making her jump, and she checked the cookies, and reset it. If she hurried, she could get Caleb's room prepared and be back down to take the cookies out. With that thought she ran up the wide staircase and stood on the landing. Where to put him? She turned toward the rear of the house and selected door number three. There was a king-sized bed, and a walk-in shower big enough to accommodate his tall frame.

She considered him naked in that shower and almost tripped over her own feet.

"Be professional, Lucy," she admonished herself as she made sure the gas fire worked, that there were warm towels on the heated rack, and that all the potions and lotions for the bathroom were present and correct. She'd aired the bed on the previous day and just had to turn down the covers.

Even as she smoothed a hand over the sheets where Caleb would soon lay his head, the timer went off in the kitchen and she hurriedly descended the stairs. A blast of cold air from the opening back door heralded Caleb's return. She turned to smile at him as he set his bags on the tiled floor.

"Perfect timing."

"It's really snowing out there." Caleb took off his hat and gloves. "I'd forgotten how bad it can get."

"You don't come back very often," Lucy remarked as she transferred the cookies to a wire cooling rack.

"Maybe I don't consider it home anymore."

She looked up, saw the bleakness of his expression, and decided not to say a word.

"Seattle might be wet, but it's not so remote." He moved restlessly around the kitchen, his gaze everywhere. "The gingerbread smells like the kind my mom used to make."

"Help yourself," Lucy offered. "I'm making enough to feed a nonexistent army of guests."

He took a piece, bit into it, and chewed slowly. "This is good."

"My gran's recipe." Lucy smiled at him. "Have you eaten tonight?"

"Nope."

"I know it says bed and breakfast on the door, but I do offer dinner, and I haven't had mine yet." Lucy paused to check his expression, which didn't help much because he'd always been hard to read. "It's a chicken casserole with dumplings."

"I could go for that."

"Great!" She turned off the oven. "It's been sitting on the bottom shelf cooking away all afternoon while I baked the cookies. I checked it just before you arrived and it's ready to go." She paused. "Would you rather eat by yourself in the guest dining room, or here with me?"

He frowned. "Here."

"That makes life much easier." She found plates and silverware and put them out on the pine table along with the casserole.

"Can I help?"

She glanced at him as she went by. "What would you like to drink?"

He shrugged. "Water's fine."

"I definitely have that, and there's iced tea and lemonade in the refrigerator."

She left him opening random cupboards looking for glasses while she went into the old washroom that housed the industrial-sized freezer, backup refrigerator, and extensive pantry. She decanted lemonade into a jug, found some ironed napkins, and came back into the kitchen to find Caleb had taken off his sheepskin-lined jacket to reveal a thick black sweater over jeans.

He'd always been the ideal man for her, and nothing had changed. She finally remembered to take off her apron.

"Nice to see you getting settled in." She set the jug and napkins on the table.

"It's warm in here."

"I'm glad to hear it. We had to replace the whole heating system last year and it cost a fortune."

"I guess it would." He sat opposite her. The light brought out the red tones in his dark auburn hair. He nodded at the casserole dish. "Smells great."

Lucy helped herself and let Caleb do the same. A comfortable silence fell between them, enhanced by the ticking of the kitchen clock and the patter of hailstones on the windowpanes. It felt like they were the only two people in the world and that she was living out her most personal of fantasies. Except, in her dreams, after dinner, Caleb would sweep her off her feet and carry her up the stairs to bed.

She took another peep at his face, only to find his gray gaze trained on her.

"What is it?" She touched her nose. "Is there something else on my face?"

"I was just looking." He paused. "I'd forgotten how pretty you are."

She took a hasty sip of her lemonade and ended up choking herself so badly that Caleb had to get up and slap her on the back.

After he resumed his seat, she jumped out of hers, and started collecting the plates.

"There's apple pie and ice cream if you're still hungry?"

"Apple pie would be good, but I'm avoiding anything with the word ice in it."

"I hear ya." Lucy nodded. "I'll warm some up for you."

He grimaced. "I guess I should try and call Dad while you're doing that."

"You go ahead."

She determinedly turned her back as he held the phone to his ear and eventually started speaking.

"Dad? It's me. I should be with you by Christmas Day. Anything you want me to bring from town for you? Call me back when you get a chance."

He set the phone on the countertop and looked over at Lucy. She decided not to ask him why it would take him four days to travel the eight miles up to the ranch.

"He almost never answers his cell or landline."

"My grandma was the same. She always answered the

B&B number, but never her own phone. It's probably a generational thing."

"Did she leave you this place?"

"Yup." Lucy smoothed a hand over the scarred surface of the pine table. "I think I'm the only one in the family who loved it as much as she did."

"What about your parents?"

"Back in Seattle. Dad's working at the hospital and Mom's a tenured professor at the university."

Caleb nodded. "I hear from Dan occasionally."

"Nice." She smiled. "Probably more than I do. He's a terrible correspondent. He only calls when he's stuck somewhere and needs money."

"Sounds like Dan." Caleb started on his apple pie. "This is good."

"Thanks, I made it." Lucy cut him another slice and indulged in a little fantasy about him coming home to her every night for pie and . . . other things maybe involving whipped cream.

"Have you ever left here?"

She set down the spoon. "Yes. I went to college at Humboldt."

He half smiled. "That hardly counts."

"Maybe not to you, but I enjoyed it." Lucy deliberately ignored the many implications behind his words. "Not everyone gets into Stanford like you did."

"Did you apply to anywhere except Humboldt?"

"Of course, I did. Caleb Erickson, are you judging me? I was offered a full scholarship there."

"Hell, no." He leaned back in his chair until it started to creak. "Nothing to do with me. You just always struck me as a smart little kid."

"I'm only six years younger than you are." Lucy pointed out.

"Yeah?" He studied her again, his hand smoothing over his mouth and beard. "I thought it was more than that."

"I'm twenty-eight, and for your information I spent several years working for a multinational hotel chain before I decided to come back here and help Gran out. So, stop trying to treat me like a country hick."

His eyebrows rose. "Still as feisty as ever then."

"I had to be, growing up with Dan as a brother."

"I bet." He returned his attention to his apple pie.

Lucy waited for her temper to settle. She rarely got mad, but Dan and Caleb had worked out exactly how to yank her strings, and it seemed nothing had changed.

"Would you like some more coffee?" Lucy reverted to professional mode as she cleared the table.

"No, thanks." He stifled a yawn behind his hand. "I think I'll turn in. I drove down overnight."

"Then I'll show you to your room." Lucy washed her hands and went to help him with his luggage.

"I've got it." Caleb waved away her help and she didn't argue. She walked back through to the main hall, ascended the stairs, and stopped at the door to number three.

"We still use old-fashioned keys here." She unlocked the door and handed the key to Caleb, who went into the room. "As you're the only guest, breakfast can be anytime you want. I don't think I'll be going anywhere in this weather, so just come down to the kitchen when you're ready to eat."

He had his back to her as he set his bags down and looked around the room. She stayed where she was and pointed out various things rather than intrude on his space.

"It's a nice room." He nodded.

"You're welcome."

He came back toward the door and looked down at her. "Thanks for taking me in."

"It was my pleasure."

He leaned in and dropped a kiss on the top of her head. "Night, little Lucy."

"Night—" Before she'd even finished speaking, he shut the door in her face, leaving her standing there opening and closing her mouth like a goldfish. Eventually, she turned and went down the stairs to begin closing up for the night. Caleb Erickson was back in town for the holidays, staying in her B&B, and he'd just dropped a friendly kiss on her head like she was six . . .

Lucy sighed. Would he ever see her as an equal, or was she doomed to be his best friend's little sister forever? She had a few days to make him see her in a different light and she was determined to take advantage of them. Fate had dropped Caleb on her doorstep for a *reason*. Now all she had to do was decide what to do about her unexpected gift.

Chapter Two

Caleb breathed in the unfamiliar smell of lavender-scented sheets and slowly opened his eyes. Light filtered in through the heavy drapes, but the absence of sound was so absolute that he lay there and let it surround him. It was never quiet in the city. There was always something flashing, beeping, wailing, or adding to the background roar of crowded humanity.

He'd hated it when he'd first moved on campus at Stanford, but over the years, he'd convinced himself that it was the buzz he needed to stay alert and successful. These days it felt like a clamor he could do without sometimes, which he guessed meant he was getting old. Not that he'd ever been much of a party animal. He'd been too big, too shy, and too awkward to make many friends or belong to the right clubs. Even his love of playing football had fizzled and died when he couldn't even make it into the training squad. If it hadn't been for Dan and a couple of other guys, he wouldn't have stuck it out.

He yawned hard enough to crack his jaw and stretched his arms over his head. He had no idea what time it was, and for once he didn't care. The last couple of years had been so hectic he'd hardly had any time to make the journey down to see his parents.

His stomach rumbled and he decided to get up, take a shower, and go and see what little Lucy Smith could rustle up for him for breakfast. She'd been a cute kid with an annoying habit of attaching herself to him and Dan and refusing to be shaken off. They'd constructed elaborate plans to avoid her—some of which he now regretted . . .

Having no siblings of his own, he hadn't known how to deal with a sweet-looking girl, but Lucy's ability to thwart his and Dan's plans had shown him she wasn't averse to a bit of trickery herself. At first, he'd been gutted when she'd looked at him and cried until he'd realized she could cry at will and always deployed her ultimate weapon to get him and Dan into the worst trouble possible. So, he'd hardened his heart and followed Dan's lead in getting as far away from her as possible.

And now she was all grown-up and probably bearing a truckful of grudges against him, which she wouldn't act upon because she was a professional hotelier. At least Caleb hoped that was the case. She hadn't poisoned him last night, so he was hopeful he'd stay alive for the rest of his stay. She was still pretty cute, and she had a dry sense of humor he really appreciated.

He turned on the shower and was pleased when it ran hot and true, and he could get his broad shoulders into the space without getting stuck. There was sandalwood shower gel and shampoo that he used lavishly before drying himself off and checking his bag for a fresh set of clothing. When he opened his door, the fresh smell of cinnamon and coffee reminded him he was hungry.

He padded down the stairs in his socks and headed for the kitchen. The door was ajar, and Lucy was chatting away to someone he couldn't yet see.

"Could you just *try*? I mean I love you, and you do nothing for me in return."

Caleb frowned. What kind of loser was she dating? She deserved way better than that. He pushed the door open wider, ready to give the unknown person his most ferocious glare and realized there was no one else there.

"Oh!" Lucy spun around. She'd obviously been talking on her phone. "Caleb! I didn't hear you come in!" She rushed toward him. "Would you like breakfast?" She glanced at the clock. "Well, technically I suppose you could call it brunch now. I left the menu on the table and coffee and juice are available on the side."

He stared down at her and wondered whether to say anything. Technically she wasn't his responsibility, but years of considering her as a little sister couldn't be ignored.

"That dude you were just talking to?"

"What dude?" A crease appeared between her brows as she studied him, but he was committed now.

"The one who doesn't do shit for you?" he added, even though she knew damn well who he was talking about. "Ditch him. You deserve better."

"How do you know? I might have turned into a terrible person who breaks hearts as easily as I crack eggs for waffles."

"Somehow I doubt that." He stared into her indignant blue eyes. "I guess I'm standing in for Dan right now, okay? Because we both know he'd say the same thing."

"But he's my brother."

It was his turn to frown. "Yeah."

"And you're not." She turned away and busied herself with something in the sink. "Now what can I get you to eat?"

Even Caleb realized she wasn't going to talk to him about what had just happened, and stopped pushing. He'd keep an eye out in case the guy turned up at the B&B and maybe give him some gentle advice out of Lucy's hearing that would send the little shit running back home to his momma. He sat down and studied the menu before raising his head.

"Waffles, scrambled eggs, and bacon would be good."

She flashed him a quick smile. "Coming right up along with your coffee."

Lucy's mind scurried around like a bag of trapped mice as she cooked Caleb his breakfast. Okay, he'd totally gotten hold of the wrong end of the stick about who she was talking to, but he had come to her defense, even if it was in a brotherly way. She glanced over at the rocking chair set near the old fireplace where Colin, her grandma's cat, was ensconced on a cushion.

He weighed around twenty pounds, had the pointed ears and massive paws of a Maine coon, and the superior attitude to go with them. He'd been spoiled rotten by her grandma and barely bothered to move unless food was being offered. It had taken her six months to persuade him that canned food was an acceptable substitute for the lovingly hand-cooked fish and chicken he'd become used to. The thought of poaching fish at six in the morning made Lucy turn cold, clammy, and nauseous.

When she'd come into the kitchen earlier, two mice were playing right under Colin's nose while he regarded them with some interest, but with no desire to evict them. Lucy had been gently lecturing him all morning about his shortcomings and Caleb had obviously heard the last of her warnings and totally misunderstood what had gone down.

Why she hadn't immediately corrected him was another matter entirely. For a moment, when he'd spoken up for her, she'd thought he was finally beginning to see her as a person of interest. But no, he was merely doing big brother duty, which wasn't what she wanted at all.

She concentrated on her cooking, keeping up a flow of

bright remarks, which Caleb, who had reclaimed his charged phone, responded to with the occasional grunt. As she put the warm plate in front of him, he finally looked up.

"What's that groaning noise?"

She listened along with him. "Snow on the branches?"

"More than that." He picked up his fork. "Do you run on a generator, or are you connected to the town grid?"

"We have both."

"Sensible." He chewed slowly. "Then maybe it's your water heater?"

"I had that replaced three months ago."

"Boiler?"

Lucy paused to consider the sounds. "Maybe."

"I'll take a look at it after I'm done eating."

"You will?"

He frowned. "I grew up on a ranch. I'm still good with my hands."

"Really?" Lucy opened her eyes wide and sighed. "I *love* a man who's practically inclined."

His gaze dropped to her mouth and lingered there before he abruptly looked away.

"Do you think you'll ever come back to run your place?" Lucy asked hastily.

He shrugged. "Dad's never indicated he cared either way. In fact, whenever I ask him how things are going, he tells me not to worry my head about it, like I'm five."

"Maybe he finds it hard to let go of being the boss," Lucy suggested. "My gran was like that. It's one of the reasons none of her own kids stayed on here to manage this place."

"He doesn't think I'm capable," Caleb said bluntly. "He's never forgiven me for going away to college."

"That was sixteen years ago."

He shrugged. "He made up his mind that I was gone, and nothing I've said or done since has changed his opinion."

Lucy bit her lip as she considered him, and he raised an eyebrow.

"What?"

"Sounds like you need to sit down and talk it out."

"Like my dad believes in any of that touchy-feely stuff. If my mom couldn't persuade him to—" He stopped talking. "Anyway, he's a lost cause."

"And I think you're wrong. Every time he comes to town and your name comes up, he brightens up. He's so proud of you."

Caleb leaned back in his chair and crossed his arms, an all-too-familiar obstinate look on his face. "Funny how he never says it to me."

"Do you ever tell him you're proud of him, too?"

"Hell no!" Caleb was scowling now. "He'd probably catch on fire with embarrassment if I said anything like that, and run for the hills."

"Have you ever tried?"

"My mom tried. She wore herself out loving that man, and forgiving him, and—" He stood up. "Thanks for breakfast. I'm going to take a stroll down Main Street to get some fresh air. I'll look at the boiler on my way back in."

He picked up his coat and hat she'd left airing by the fire, stepped into his boots, nodded brusquely, and went out the back door, leaving Lucy feeling more confused than ever. Something was obviously up between him and his father. With his mom gone, was there any way of repairing the damage? Lucy wasn't sure, but if she could wish for one thing for Caleb while he was home for the holidays it would be that. And that he saw her in a new light, of course, but that was totally selfish.

To her surprise he came back quickly and popped his head in through the door.

"The wind's whipping up, it's clouding over again and there's another storm coming through. Where's the key to your outhouse?"

"You mean where I keep the boiler and all that other important stuff?" Lucy asked.

"Yup." He held out his gloved hand and she set the key in it. "Thanks."

"Tool kit is out there, too," she added. "Just in case you need anything."

Even from the kitchen she could hear the banging, thuds, and occasional curse word as Caleb worked his magic. She'd been upstairs and tidied his room, which he'd left in an acceptable state. He'd even attempted to make his bed. She'd replenished his shampoo and shower gel and brought in clean towels before dusting and vacuuming.

Now she was sitting at the kitchen table wrestling with the November accounts. She tried to ignore her worries about what the snowstorms had done to her December, which was usually one of her best months as visitors and family returned to Quincy to enjoy the holidays. She'd had nothing but a series of cancellations as the local roads and airports closed, cutting them off from civilization.

Caleb came in carrying the toolbox and stamped his feet on the mat.

"I tightened up everything I could see on the boiler and the hot water tank. Let's hope that helps."

"Thank you." Lucy leapt to her feet and poured him some coffee. "My handyman hasn't been able to get up here for weeks, so nothing's been fixed."

He gave her a considering look. "You should learn how to do that stuff for yourself."

"You're right." She held his gaze. "Thanks for the re-minder that I can't rely on anyone else when living out here."

He frowned. "That's not exactly what I meant."

"It's true though, isn't it? I mean we all need to be self-reliant. The myth of neighbors helping neighbors is long gone."

"Now you sound like my dad complaining about the good old days."

Knowing how Caleb felt about his father, Lucy didn't take his remark well. "You started it."

"I just suggested you should know how to fix your own damn house," Caleb said evenly. "That's all."

"And I agreed with you." For some reason Lucy was in an argumentative frame of mind. "If only I had the time be-tween running this 'damn house' all by myself to take a few classes or something."

"You don't have any staff?"

"Not at present."

Caleb frowned. "Your gran had at least two people work-ing with her."

"And I can't afford to do that."

He let out his breath as he set the toolbox by the door. "Things are that bad?"

She pointed at her accounts book. "The weather's been against me this year. We've had massive snowstorms and wildfires, which stops people coming up here."

"Understandably." He nodded.

"Hopefully things will perk up next year," Lucy said brightly. She didn't want him thinking she was a complete loser. She wanted his positive attention, not his sympathy. "I've got enough capital in reserve to see me through at least another season."

"That's not much." Caleb was back to frowning again.

"And it's not your problem," Lucy said firmly. "Can I get

you some coffee? Or are you planning on calling Mike down
at the shop?"

Caleb knew when he was being given the brush-off, but
he wasn't quite done. He pointed at the table.

"I could take a look for you."

She stiffened like an outraged cat. "No, thanks."

"That bad, is it?"

"Yes, and as I said, it's got nothing to do with you." She
met his gaze. "Weren't you just telling me I had to learn to
cope on my own?"

He opened his mouth to argue because, hell, he was kind
of enjoying seeing her all riled up, and then thought better
of it. He held up his hands in a placatory gesture. "Backing
off."

"Thank you." She walked over to the stove to get him
some coffee. She was wearing jeans today and a pink
sweater with some kind of lacy collar. Her hair was in pig-
tails that should've made her look about six, but somehow
made her look hot.

Caleb blinked as his gaze fell to the nicely rounded
curves of her ass. She was his best friend's annoying little
sister. He wasn't planning on being anywhere near Quincy
for the rest of his life, and he wasn't generally into super-
positive people who kept smiling through their worries.
Okay, so he might tend to go too hard the other way, and
only see the problems, but he'd been raised by a man who
never saw the good in anything, and that had kind of stuck.

He took his phone out of his pocket and thumbed through
the numbers. There was no reply from his father, but there
were six messages from his team, which he pretended he
hadn't seen. He'd told them not to bother him unless it was
an emergency, but they seemed incapable of functioning

without him being around. Once that would've made him feel needed, but now it was something of an irritant, and it was all his own fault.

His phone rang and he answered it without thinking.

"Hey, Caleb. I sent you the three options we're considering. Which one do you want us to try first?"

He let out a breath. "Vin. I'm on vacation. How about you solve that for yourselves?"

There was a long silence. "But what if we choose wrong and you get mad?"

"I won't."

"But you like to be involved in every single decision."

There was a rising note of panic in Vin's voice.

"And maybe I need to learn to be more hands-off so that I can enjoy my leave," Caleb said. "I picked you guys and I trust you, okay? If the first option doesn't work, go on to the second, wash and repeat, and send me a report when you're done."

There was an even longer pause—so long in fact that Caleb began to wonder if his deputy had passed out.

"Vin? Are you still there?"

"Yeah, I'm just . . . trying to assimilate this new information."

Caleb winced. "As I said, I trust you, okay? And don't work right through the holidays. Make sure everyone on the team takes time off."

"Okay." Vin paused. "Are you sure you're feeling all right?"

Caleb frowned. "I'm good, thanks."

"Then I'll get back to work and try not to bother you again."

"Thanks." Mindful of the incoming storm, Caleb plugged his phone into the socket to recharge and turned to find Lucy studying him intently.

"I guess I'm something of a control freak." He shrugged.

"I guess." She handed him the freshly brewed coffee.

"I'm trying not to be that person anymore."

"Sometimes it's hard to accept help, isn't it?" She sighed and looked back at the table. "Maybe I should learn that lesson myself and ask you to take a look at the books."

At first, Lucy wasn't sure what woke her up, but she sat up in bed and reached for the lamp switch. Nothing happened and she fumbled with it again, clicking it back and forth uselessly in increasing panic. Outside the wind was howling like a banshee and buffeting the walls of the house like a living thing.

She got out of bed and ran toward the door, bumping her knee against the end of her bed, and the rocking chair, before she reached her goal. The only light came from the blink of the smoke detector in the ceiling. She hammered on Caleb's door and went in without waiting for an answer.

"The power's out."

He sat up, a vaguely darker shape in the overall gloom of the room and she headed toward him.

"It's okay." He sounded hoarse. "No need to panic."

She grabbed hold of his hand like a lifeline.

"Hey, you're shaking."

His night vision was obviously much better than hers because the next minute he'd picked her up, tucked her in beside him, and put his arm around her shoulders.

She leaned in against his warm bare skin. "I hate the dark."

"Yeah?" He hugged her even closer. "The backup generator should kick in any moment now."

She shivered and placed a tentative hand on his chest.

"It should've happened immediately. There must be something wrong."

"I'll take a look at it in a minute."

"I don't want you risking your life out there," Lucy warned him.

His low chuckle resonated in his chest. "I'm not that stupid. I'm happy to wait it out until morning." He paused. "Seeing as there's no heating, why don't you stay here with me?"

"In your bed?"

"You're already in it," Caleb reminded her as he smoothed her hair like she was a cat. "It's way easier to stay here than leave and get cold and afraid again."

"I don't want to be by myself," Lucy confessed. "I get really . . . panicky when it's dark and I feel like I'm trapped."

Caleb's hand stilled in her hair. "Wait—this doesn't have anything to do with me, does it?"

"No, this one was all Dan. He locked me in the closet under the stairs, went outside to play, and forgot about me for hours."

"Shit." Caleb dropped a kiss on her head. "That's terrible."

"To be fair he was really upset when he realized what he'd done, but I've never stopped getting stressed about small, dark spaces," Lucy admitted.

"I'm not surprised."

Lucy rubbed her cheek against Caleb's chest hair and wondered how his beard would feel against her skin. She'd only just realized he was completely naked under the covers whereas she was covered neck to toe in a flannel nightdress.

"How about we lie down again?" Caleb suggested. "It's still dark. We can sleep through till it's light, and then get up, and assess the damage."

"Okay."

He eased them both lower on the pillows, keeping his arm around her. She fitted perfectly against his side, her slightly bent knee close to the jut of his hip, and her hand palm down on his chest over his steadily beating heart.

"Is this all right, or do you want me to let you go?"

"No!" She instinctively dug her fingers into his skin, and he winced. "Sorry!"

"Not a problem." He sounded even more hoarse. "I forget that even sweet little kittens have claws."

She smiled against his skin and breathed in a whole lungful of essence of Caleb Erickson, which made her feel quite giddy. Between her fear of the dark and her fascination with Caleb she wasn't sure how she was expected to sleep. The man of her dreams didn't appear to have the same problem. He gradually relaxed beside her, his breathing slowing, his grip on her shoulder easing as he fell asleep again.

Lucy sighed and closed her eyes. She'd imagined being this close to Caleb many times. She hadn't anticipated he'd be so unaware of her that she'd bore him back to sleep. Maybe it was time to admit that he felt nothing for her except friendship and stop her foolish obsession with him.

Caleb woke up to the very pleasurable sensation of someone stroking his skin. He kept his eyes closed as he tried to remember where he was. He wasn't exactly what you might call a lady's man, having something of a reputation as a grump, so a woman in his bed wasn't usual. He cautiously inhaled and caught the scent of Christmas, which didn't narrow it down much.

His eyes snapped open, and he looked down at Lucy's blond hair. Her cheek rested over his heart, and one hand covered his chest. Her nightdress had ridden up around her waist and her thigh was nestled comfortably across his groin. She was humming in her sleep, her fingernails lightly scratching his chest hair like he was a prized pet. He flexed his fingers and realized his hand was cupping her naked ass.

He reminded himself that she was his best friend's little sister, and that she had no idea that she'd curled herself around him in her sleep. It made no difference to his dick, which was enjoying the attention way too much.

"Mmm . . ." Lucy murmured as she rocked against him. "Nice."

He didn't have the nerve to ask her what exactly she was referring to. Perhaps if he kept still, she'd wake up, roll away from him, and be none the wiser about his intentions. Because, man, he had some very specific things he'd like to be doing with her right now, like kissing his way down her throat, waking her up from the inside with his nice, hard dick . . . and, where the hell had that thought come from?

Her hand slid lower, and she shifted position, easing her knee down so that she could—Caleb inhaled sharply. Sweet loving jeebus—Lucy Smith had her fingers wrapped around his shaft. His dick responded with great enthusiasm as she gently squeezed him. His hips almost came off the bed, but he tried to stay still as she gave him the most unexpected and erotic hand job of his life.

He breathed through his teeth and tried not to moan as her fingers slid through wetness and warmth, spreading it over his shaft, easing her task. She kissed his chest, her teeth settling on his nipple to torment him even more.

"Uh . . ." Caleb groaned, his hand coming to rest on her shoulder. "That's . . ."

Her fingers stopped moving. A moment later she raised her head and stared at him, her gaze horror stricken.

"Oh my God! I thought I was having a really good dream!"

He considered her for a pulsating second. "Then keep dreaming, okay?" he growled, as he drew her down to kiss her properly. "Don't you dare stop."

He explored her mouth with an urgency that surprised him, his fingers framing her face as he coaxed her into kissing him back. Her instant response made him forget everything except the tight clasp of her hand on his dick and the sweet, hot taste of her tongue.

"Let me . . ." He curved his long fingers around her ass and found her wet and waiting for his touch. "Damn . . ."

He thrust into her; his thumb pressed against her tight bud in the same rhythm she was using on him. When she came almost immediately, he felt like he'd won an award, and instantly followed suit, his hips jerking forward as he came over her still working fingers.

He lay back against the pillows, holding on to her, and let the waves of satisfaction roll over him. It was still dark enough not to be able to see her expression that clearly. He wasn't exactly sure what he was going to say when all he wanted to know was if they could do it again and move on to more.

Eventually she whispered his name. "Caleb?"

"Hmm?"

"Do I need to apologize?"

"Hell, no."

She went quiet long enough for him to almost fall back asleep.

"Are you sure?"

He opened one eye and kissed the top of her head. "It's all good."

The pause this time was even longer.

"Then, do you think we could do it again sometime?"

He came up on one elbow so that he could look at her beautiful face. "How about now? And this time I want to be inside you when you come."

Still holding Caleb's gaze, Lucy reached out her hand

and opened the drawer of the bedside cabinet. "There are condoms right here."

"Nice to see you're prepared for every eventuality." Caleb scooped up a handful and set them on the top of the cabinet. "Now, where were we?"

Lucy swallowed hard as Caleb reared over her, his expression intent, and stripped off her nightdress. He was such a big guy that he made her feel very soft and feminine. He eased her thighs apart and knelt between them. She moaned as he kissed his way down over her stomach and rubbed his bearded chin against her most sensitive flesh, making her squirm.

"Nice," he murmured, as he used his fingers and his tongue to bring her to a shuddering climax. "*Very* nice."

She grabbed for his shoulders as he straightened up and put on a condom. She wanted to see his face in the moonlight when he thrust inside her—to see if the reality was even better than her most lurid fantasies.

He leaned in and gently kissed her. "You want me?"

"Oh, yes please," she said shakily. "Very much."

His rare smile was a thing of beauty as he carefully pressed forward. She tried not to gasp at the size of him and tilted her hips to accept him even more deeply. He took his time, rocking back and forth until he was fully seated inside her.

At some point, Lucy forgot to look into his eyes because she was far too involved in the physical act of making love. If it was a dream—and her only chance of ever getting this close to Caleb—she'd give it everything she had. She held him in her arms as he shuddered through his climax and eased himself down to lie beside her, his chest still heaving.

"That was . . . awesome."

Lucy smiled and cuddled up against his side. "Exactly."

He sighed, put his arm around her, and instantly fell asleep. She was okay with that because it meant they didn't need to have any awkward conversations about what had just happened between them. Knowing Caleb, any communication might be short, to the point, and not necessarily in her favor.

Lucy slowly opened her eyes. She couldn't bear to wake up and see the dawning realization on his face that he'd had sex with his best friend's little sister. What if he started to apologize? She waited a few moments to make sure he was truly asleep and then slipped out of the bed. She needed some space to make sure she was ready to deal with any reaction he might have in the cold light of day.

Chapter Three

Caleb woke up slowly and rolled onto his side expecting to see Lucy stretched out beside him. But the bed was empty and the sheets on her side were cold. Caleb frowned and sat up, his gaze moving to the window, where cracks of light showed through the drapes. He had no idea what time it was because the electricity was still off, and he'd left his cell phone in the kitchen.

Where had she gone? He'd expected her to stay with him, although he guessed he hadn't put that thought into words before he'd fallen asleep. Maybe she'd assumed he wouldn't want her to hang around? Caleb groaned and flopped back onto the pillows. Maybe she was regretting what had happened and gone AWOL? Or, even worse, something bad had happened in the night while he was snoring away, and he'd completely missed it.

He got up, ran into the bathroom, and stepped into the shower before he realized the water was only lukewarm. He ran out almost as fast as he'd gone in and toweled himself dry before dressing in his warmest clothes. The kitchen was warm because the old gas range was humming away. There was no power and no noise from the generator, which was worrying.

"Lucy?" He called her name, but she didn't appear. The only creature around was the big old cat who barely bothered to raise his head before falling back to sleep again. Caleb put on his outdoor gear and opened the back door, almost recoiling from the ferocity of the gusting wind and the slap of ice-cold air. He turned his collar up and stomped through the snow to the rear of the property where the old outhouse held the mechanical machinery that ran the B&B.

He opened the door to find Lucy crouched in front of the generator as she read something off her cell phone.

"Hey," he said. She jumped about a foot in the air as he kneeled beside her. "What are you trying to do?"

She pointed at the small yellow unit in front of her. "This is the backup for the backup generator. It's powerful enough to run the freezers, a few lights, and my chargers. I think it's out of gas. I can't get it to work."

Caleb glanced around the shed. "Most people keep a five-gallon tank of fuel on hand in case that happens." He stood up. "I'll take a look around."

She stayed where she was and ran through a list of safety checks she'd obviously gotten from the internet or her handyman.

"I found the tank." He held it up and shook it. "It's empty."

"Dammit!" Lucy bit her lip.

"We can get gas," Caleb reminded her.

"From where, exactly? Everything is shut down. If the whole town's power is out, the pumps at the gas station won't be working either."

"True." Caleb frowned.

"Then we're screwed. And when I say we, I mean me. If you call your uncle Chip, I'm sure he'll come and get you."

Chip was the foreman out at the ranch and was considered family. Caleb had known him all his life. He was pretty sure Lucy was right and that Chip would come and pick him up, no questions asked. He glanced over at her bowed head and made a few quick decisions.

"I know where I can get the gas."

She still wouldn't look at him.

"From my truck. I'll siphon it out." He pointed at the far wall. "There's a tube there that would work, and I can use the empty tank."

He didn't wait to see if Lucy agreed with him. He grabbed the tank and the tubing and took off down the road. It was harder to find his truck than he'd anticipated, as it had disappeared under an anonymous bank of snow. After investigating all the possible lumps and bumps, he managed to get to the fuel tank and start the process of decanting the gasoline.

Once he'd got things going, the transfer went smoothly, apart from the fact that he was standing in the middle of a snowstorm freezing his nuts off. By the time he staggered back to the B&B he was shaking so hard his teeth were chattering.

Lucy looked up as he came into the outhouse.

"Oh, my goodness! You're freezing! Go into the house and warm up!"

He crouched down by the generator. "Got . . . to . . . get this working first."

"I can do that." She gave him an ungentle shove. "Go inside!"

"Not happening. Do you have a funnel?"

"Yes, it's here."

"Hold it steady, then." He carefully poured the gasoline into the tank and screwed on the cap. "Let's see if it fires up."

The sudden noise was loud in the confined space, but still gratifying. Caleb checked the power cables were properly attached. He helped Lucy roll them out into the house where a central set of power sockets had already been configured to cover the important outlets. At least his teeth had stopped chattering, but he was still grateful when she offered him a mug of coffee from the old tin pot on the gas stove.

"Thanks."

The sound of the refrigeration units powering up broke the unaccustomed silence. Caleb took a good long slug of coffee and studied his companion properly for the first time since he'd got out of bed. She was rushing around the kitchen, feeding the cat, and chatting about toasting bread or something. If he hadn't have known better, he would've thought she'd never been in his bed the previous night or that they'd had sex.

"Are you okay?" he asked.

"Yes! I'm great!" Her attempt at a smile wobbled. "I mean I can't run my business, the main generator that was supposed to be fixed isn't, and I can't even remember to fill up a five-gallon gas tank, but at least I'm alive!"

He set his mug down, walked over, and drew her into his arms. For a second, she went stiff and then she gulped in a huge breath and leaned her forehead against his chest.

"I'm sorry. I guess I'm just a bit overwhelmed . . . with everything."

He kissed the top of her head and just held her. As someone who came up with complex solutions for a living, not giving her a plan of action and telling her how to execute it was hard. He'd never been good at emotional things. The only person he'd ever confided in had been his mother, and even that had stopped because she always told his dad everything he'd said.

For a moment, he desperately wished she was still alive so that he could say sorry for cutting her off—for not telling her how he felt because he didn't want another lecture from his father. In her mind she'd been trying to bridge the gap between them in the only way she knew how. He hadn't appreciated how hard that must have been until she was gone, and now, he and his dad had nothing to say to each other at all.

"You should go to your dad." Lucy said.

"Maybe," Caleb said. "I'll give Chip a call and see whether it's possible."

She eased out of his arms and immediately rushed toward the hall. "I need to check the light on the landing is working. It's the only one connected to the small generator upstairs."

His fingers curled into his palms as he immediately missed her presence. He wasn't sure if she was just too busy reacting to the current crisis to have a conversation about what had happened between them, or if she was determined to pretend that nothing had happened at all. He wasn't okay with either of those scenarios, but as long as she was trying to save her beloved B&B, he wasn't going to make a big deal out of it.

His gaze went to the open door.

And what was he going to say to her anyway? He wasn't coming back to Quincy, she wasn't moving to Seattle anytime soon, so how could they make a relationship work? She deserved better than that—better than him. She was a good and decent person. He checked his cell, which had retained some charge, and found Chip's number. There was something he could do to help, but whether she'd go along with it or not, he couldn't yet say.

Lucy went into Caleb's bedroom and stopped dead as images of the night she'd spent in his arms rushed through her. The bed looked like they'd been in a fight, which made her blush. He'd been an amazing lover, even better than her imaginings, and she'd never forget him.

She drew the drapes and pulled up the blinds to let in what little sunlight there was, changed the linens on the bed, and refreshed the bathroom. If Caleb took her advice and called Chip, she'd almost be glad to see him go because she'd had her one perfect night and that should be enough.

"Hey."

She turned to find him observing her from the doorway. He'd been like that as a child, always quietly watching, letting others take the lead even if the initial suggestion had been his. But Stanford had changed him into a more forthright version of himself, who took control and didn't suffer fools gladly. "I called Chip."

"Oh, good!" Her stomach plummeted even as she offered him a bright smile. "Can he get here and pick you up?"

"Yeah."

"That's great. Do you need a hand with your bags?"

His frown returned. "You really want to get rid of me?"

She went to walk past him with the bundle of damp towels in her arms, but he stayed in the doorway, and gently caught hold of her elbow.

"Lucy . . ."

She had to look up at him, and the genuine concern in his gaze made her unable to look away.

"I *want* you to be safe and warm, Caleb. That's not going to happen at the B&B until I can get someone to fix the generator," she said simply.

"What about you?"

She shrugged. "I'll manage. I'm like the captain on the *Titanic*."

"Ready to go down with a sinking ship." He shook his head. "Not happening. Either you come with me, or I stay here." He gazed at her expectantly. "What's it to be?"

"I can't just . . . turn up like that!"

"Sure, you can. I bet you know Dad better than I do these days."

"But he hasn't invited me! And what about the B&B? Who's going to look after everything if I'm not here and unexpected guests turn up?"

"One, Dad will be delighted to see you, so he doesn't have to talk to me. Two, the B&B will do fine on the secondary generator. Three, no one will be turning up in this weather when the roads down to the freeway are completely blocked."

"You turned up," she pointed out.

"I'm special."

"But—"

He talked over her. "If you don't want to go, I'll stay here. I can be way more useful to you than to Dad right now, and I bet he'd agree."

"I need to put these towels in the laundry."

He stepped aside. "Go ahead. Let me know what you've decided by the time Chip gets here, okay?"

Lucy never responded well to deadlines, and Caleb's ultimatum didn't make her very happy. She stuffed the towels in the laundry basket and considered her options. Unfortunately, Caleb was right about the likelihood of guests turning up being zero. If there weren't any guests, then there was no need for Lucy to stay at the B&B.

She went to call out to Caleb, who was packing in his room.

"What about Colin?"

"Who's Colin?" he shouted back.

"The cat."

"Cats are pretty good at taking care of themselves, you know."

She thought of something else. "And what about all the prep for Christmas I've done?"

"You can bring the food with us if you like. I bet Dad didn't get much in. He always left that to Mom."

He appeared in the doorway, his bag on his shoulder. "I need to go out to my truck. I'll be back in five. Start packing."

"I'm still not sure if I'm—"

He disappeared down the stairs and the front door opened and closed.

"Coming," Lucy muttered, and glared at the closed door. She let out a frustrated breath. She'd had her one night with the man of her dreams. Should she leave it at that? There were so many things that could go wrong if she tried to make any more of it, and Caleb wasn't sticking around anyway.

But she wanted to do it all again . . . She looked up toward the attic space her grandma had converted into an apartment for the owner, and went up the stairs. Maybe if she helped Caleb and his father get on better, he'd be more likely to come back and see her, too.

She packed a small suitcase and lugged it down the two flights of stairs to the entrance hall. Caleb came in the door with another bag over his shoulder.

"Snow's easing off." He took off his beanie and set it on the reception desk, his gaze moving to her bag. "Glad to see you're coming with me." He gestured behind him. "I spoke to the Rosbergs next door. Denise said she had a spare key to this place and would be more than happy to look after Colin. Brian said he'd keep an eye on the generator, and if the repair guy turns up, he'll let him in and update you."

"You did all that?" Lucy asked.

"Yeah." He frowned at her. "What about it?"

"It's just . . . I'm not used to having anyone to take care of stuff for me anymore. It's kind of nice." She smiled at him. "Thank you."

He looked disconcerted. "It's no big deal."

"It is to me."

He turned on his heel and headed for the kitchen. "Let's check everything out before we leave. I don't want any loose connections or further power outages. Brian has spare gas for the generator if it needs it, but he reckons the power will be back on by tomorrow."

Caleb was obviously as uncomfortable being thanked as she was accepting help. She followed him down the hallway.

"I need to pack up the food. It shouldn't take long."

"You go ahead while I check out the power situation."

She was just finishing up when she heard the honk of a truck horn. An ancient Ford truck pulled up at the side of the house and an equally ancient cowboy got out. No one knew exactly how old Chip was because according to legend he'd arrived in Quincy about the same time as the redwood trees. His complexion was as rugged and brown as tree bark, and he'd lost one of his front teeth in a brawl way back when. He knocked on the back door and she went to let him in.

"Miss Lucy." He touched the brim of his hat to her. "I hear you've been putting up with young Caleb."

"His truck broke down, so he's been staying here, yes."

He stomped into the kitchen. His spurs that were stuck good and tight on his boots rang against the tiles. He looked around. "Seems wrong without your grandma here somehow."

"Tell me about it." Lucy sighed. "I miss her so much."

Caleb came in. "Chip. It's good to see you."

"Right back at ya, youngster." Chip winked at Caleb. "Your dad's been fretting for days waiting for you to turn up."

Lucy sighed as Caleb's expression shifted to his usual skeptical frown.

"I didn't get that impression. He didn't even call me back." He looked over at Lucy. "Are you good to go? I'll start loading the truck."

After Caleb took the bags out, Chip met her gaze across the kitchen table.

"Those two are as stubborn as mules." he said. "Sometimes I just want to knock their heads together."

"Caleb thinks his father doesn't want him at the ranch," Lucy said.

"And Isaiah thinks Caleb doesn't want to be there."

"Maybe we should lock them in a room together and leave them there until they work it out?" Lucy suggested.

Chip chuckled. "I'm game if you are." He nodded at the countertop. "Don't forget your phone. We've got power up at the ranch."

"Thank God for that." Caleb came back into the kitchen. "Now, if we can just load up this Christmas baking, I think we'll be good to go."

Lucy carefully locked the back door and took a long look at the house her grandmother had bequeathed to her. It looked almost magical with its snow-covered roof and dripping icicles. How terrible would it be if she lost the business less than a year after inheriting it? Her grandma would be turning in her grave and coming back to haunt her, and her parents would be vindicated that she wasn't smart enough to run anything. She looked up as her cousin Bernie, who ran the coffee shop, came running over the street.

"Are you okay? I had to throw out all my dairy as the refrigerator shorted out, but other than replacing that I'm good to reopen."

"The generator's failed." Lucy hugged her cousin. "I'm waiting on the repair guy, but as you might imagine he's quite busy right now. I'm going with Caleb to his dad's place for the night. I'll be back tomorrow."

"Caleb Erickson?" Bernie asked.

"Yup."

"Your all-time favorite crush?"

Lucy looked around to see how close Caleb was to them. "Ssh. He doesn't need to know that."

"Lucy, everyone in town knows how hard you crushed on him."

"Except Caleb."

Bernie paused. "True. He wasn't one of those guys who thought they were God's gift to womankind. He was pretty clueless."

"And let's make sure he remains that way," Lucy said firmly. "Which he will—if you don't blurt it out right in front of him, okay?"

Bernie grinned at her. "You still like him, don't you?"

Lucy didn't say anything and pretended to be checking the time.

"You do." Bernie nudged her arm. "Then why don't you do something about it?"

Lucy wasn't going to mention she already had, because Bernie's head would probably explode.

"I'm only going with him because there's no heating at the B&B."

"Like you couldn't come home with me." Bernie gave her a gentle push. "Lover boy's looking for you. Have a good time and don't forget to ask for what you really want for Christmas."

Caleb was holding the door of the truck open for her. "You look flushed."

"I'm fine, thanks." She gestured at the box of food. "I'll keep an eye on this lot on the way, but tell Chip not to drive too fast."

"He drives like a tortoise," Caleb said gloomily. "We'll probably get there around midnight."

"Now, now." Chip got in. "No need to rush. Better to get there in one piece, I say."

"And I agree," Lucy chimed in. "Caleb thinks he's still in Seattle."

"I wish," Caleb muttered as he shut the passenger door and put on his seat belt.

Lucy's smile disappeared as Chip backed carefully out of the driveway. Caleb was back into doom-and-gloom mode. She had a horrible suspicion that things would get worse the closer they got to the ranch and his father. Her optimism of helping to bring them together died in the clear light of day. She'd never succeeded in getting her own parents to understand her choice to return to Quincy, so how she'd thought she could help the Ericksons was a mystery.

"Hey." She looked up to see Caleb had turned in his seat to study her. "It'll be okay. The B&B will still be standing when you get back."

"Thanks, that wasn't what I was worrying about but now I'll add it to my list."

His smile was unexpected and warmed her soul. "You've got this, Lucy Smith."

She smiled back at him. "I absolutely do not, but I appreciate the vote of confidence."

He nodded and turned back to stare out of the window as Chip settled into a steady pace Lucy estimated at five miles an hour. She didn't care how long the trip took as long as they arrived safely. She got to stare at the back of Caleb's head and indulge in her foolish fantasies. She was fairly certain that when they got to the ranch, reality was going to come crashing back, and she'd better be prepared to deal with whatever awaited her, for Caleb's sake.

Chapter Four

After Chip opened the main gate up to the ranch, which he proudly announced was now solar powered, Caleb leaned closer to the window to take in every inch of the property his family had owned for generations. He couldn't see much thanks to the snow, but everything looked to be in good shape. It didn't surprise him. His father was a hard taskmaster and expected nothing less than perfection from his family and his employees.

Lucy's reaction to his efforts to sort out her worries had made him want to hold on to her even more. Maybe she was beginning to realize that the other loser on the phone who didn't take care of her wasn't worth keeping around. Not that he'd been thinking about her being involved with any other guy when he'd been making love with her. That had just felt *right*.

Caleb didn't realize he was holding his breath until they drew up in front of the rambling ranch house with the old red barn set at a right angle to it. The white picket fencing had been replaced with more durable metal and wire, but overall, the place looked the same as it had when he was a kid. There was no sign of his dad, which didn't surprise him. He wasn't one to stand on ceremony and was probably out working.

"Let's take your bags around the back," Chip said. "I'll go and see if Isaiah's in the barn."

"Thanks for the ride!" Lucy said from behind Caleb.

He'd almost forgotten she was here. What had he been thinking, dragging her into what might turn out to be a war zone?

He picked up the bags, leaving her with the food, and followed Chip around to the mudroom at the side of the house. He wiped his feet and waited to hear his mom's voice welcoming him home before he remembered she wasn't there anymore. The kitchen looked cold and uninviting without her at the center of it. He tried to imagine how it felt for his dad, living with that loss every day, and couldn't.

"I always loved this kitchen," Lucy said as she set her boxes on the table. She touched Caleb's arm. "Are you okay?"

"Why wouldn't I be?"

"Because this is the first time you've been here since your mom's funeral." She hesitated. "I know how hard it can be to realize that someone is not coming back."

Yeah, she got it, but it didn't mean he had to like it. Some stupid, foolish part of him had hoped it had all been a mistake—that she'd still be there.

"I know she's dead, Lucy." He turned back to the door. "I'll go and get the rest of the stuff. You stay here in the warm."

When he returned, Chip had the coffee going and was having a playful chat with Lucy about something her gran had once done or said to him. He liked seeing her in his mother's kitchen. She made him want to smile.

"Caleb."

His father appeared at the interior door; his expression as hard to read as ever. He was almost as tall as Caleb but was leaner and had the light coloring of his Scandinavian ancestors, whereas Caleb favored his Scottish mother.

"Dad." Caleb nodded at Lucy. "I hope you don't mind me bringing a guest with me."

"Not at all." His dad turned to Lucy. "I was sorry to hear about your grandmother's passing. She was a hardworking woman."

"Thank you," Lucy said. "I miss her very much. I guess you'll understand that seeing as you lost your Annie recently, too."

For a moment, his dad's face crumpled and then he blinked hard. "I'm getting along without her."

Caleb opened his mouth and then shut it again. He'd just arrived, and Lucy needed somewhere to stay the night. If he got into everything with his dad right now, they'd be ordered off the premises before they'd even unpacked their bags.

"How are things on the ranch?" Caleb asked.

"Same as ever." His dad helped himself to coffee and looked at Chip. "Haven't you got work to do?"

Chip raised his eyebrows. "Cool your jets. I'm just visiting with Miss Lucy and Caleb. I'll be done when I've finished my coffee."

"Good." Isaiah nodded at Lucy. "Make yourself at home. I'll be back for dinner around six. There's a beef casserole in the oven."

He walked past Caleb and out into the yard, leaving Lucy and Chip staring after him.

"He'll warm up," Chip said. "He's pleased you're here."

"Hard to tell when he barely spoke a dozen words to me," Caleb said. He picked up Lucy's suitcase. "I'll show you where the bathroom is, and you can get settled."

Lucy followed Caleb down the shadowed hallway, her heart hurting for him. She was occasionally at odds with her parents, but they would never have treated her as coldly as Isaiah had treated Caleb. Despite their frustrations and divisions, they all loved each other, and sometimes that was enough to get them through the hard parts. They passed the family room, where a recently cut pine tree sat forlornly in a tub beside the wood-burning stove. There were two boxes of decorations and a jumble of lights on the coffee table. Caleb noticed her looking.

"Mom used to do all that stuff. I guess Dad hasn't gotten around to it."

"I could help if it wouldn't give offense?" Lucy offered.

"He probably wouldn't even notice, so knock yourself out." Caleb opened a door to the right. "Bathroom's through here. Dad has his own in the master bedroom, so don't worry about him knocking on the door."

He went through into the room opposite. "This is my old bedroom and there's a guest room to the right of the bathroom."

Lucy took a deep breath. "Can I stay with you?" She immediately went to qualify her question. "I mean, if that's okay, but if your dad wouldn't approve, it's his house, and—"

"I'd like that," Caleb said simply. "And I don't care what he thinks."

She looked up at him. "I know this is hard for you, Caleb."

"You have no idea." He let out a frustrated breath. "How am I supposed to communicate with someone who barely bothers to acknowledge my existence?"

"Meet him on his own terms and in his own environment?"

His brows came together. "Meaning what, exactly?"

"My dad always says that he gets the best out of Dan when they work alongside each other rather than him sitting behind his desk asking questions Dan doesn't want to answer."

"You think I should get out there and help?"

She shrugged. "If you want to try and reach him it can't do any harm, can it?"

"I *want* closure," he said strongly. "I want to walk away from him knowing I did everything I could, and that he understands that."

"Then get out to that barn and make yourself useful," Lucy said. "And I'll sort out the food and the Christmas decorations."

He leaned in and kissed her gently on the mouth.

"You're full of good advice."

"Dan would say I'm bossy."

"And I'm not Dan." He kissed her again. "I'll see if I can find my old work clothes and get out there."

"I bet everything's exactly where you left it."

He smiled for the first time. "Probably."

She left him to investigate and went back into the kitchen to work out where everything was. The huge casserole was cooking gently in the oven and about ten potatoes sat on the shelf above the pot, baking away, as well. There was a large refrigerator and freezer that made it easy to store all the Christmas goodies she'd brought with her. As she worked, she kept coming across little reminders of Caleb's mother—her handwritten recipes, the labels on the spice jars in the pantry, a card from Caleb she'd kept on the pinboard.

Lucy left everything exactly where she found it. After putting a bag of cookie dough on the table to defrost, she went through to the family room and stared at the newly cut pine tree. It smelled divine but looked a little sad without lights and tinsel. When she'd set up the three Christmas trees at the B&B, she'd been reminded of her grandma so much she'd cried. She could understand why Caleb's father hadn't wanted to do the tree himself, but the place needed something to show it was Christmas, and the tree was already cut down, and just standing there looking sad . . .

It took her a while to untangle the lights and test them to see if they were working. They were the old-fashioned multicolored ones she secretly still loved. She placed them on the tree first, just as her grandma had taught her, and opened the box containing the ornaments. There was the usual selection of battered but beloved family treasures. She even recognized the things Caleb had made in school because she'd made the same ones six years later with the same teachers.

There was a battered angel to go on the top, but Lucy wasn't quite tall enough to get it up without a chair. She considered the grimy face and dress and took the doll through to her bathroom, where she gently cleaned the porcelain and sponge-washed the patches on the white skirts. The rich smell of the casserole drifted through from the kitchen, and she checked the time. She'd half been expecting Caleb to come straight back. He'd been out there for at least two hours, which had to be promising.

Didn't it?

"What do you want?" Caleb's dad looked up as he approached.

"Thought I could lend a hand." Caleb tried to sound both helpful and upbeat as he checked out the inside of the barn. It was still as clean as a barn could be, with nothing out of place except for the occasional bird's nest in the rafters his dad grudgingly allowed to stay.

"Doing what, exactly?" Isaiah asked. "Nothing complicated to fix around here."

Caleb slowly let out his breath. "I'm sure there are stalls to muck out, manure to shift, or livestock to deal with?"

"Stalls need turning out." His dad handed him a shovel. "You can start at the other end. Wheelbarrow's just outside."

Caleb put on his work gloves and walked down to the opposite end of the barn. He got the wheelbarrow, checked the occupant of the first stall, and went on in.

"Hey, Snowy. Long time, no see. How's it going?"

By the time he'd raked out the third stall he'd forgotten about the cold and was working up a sweat. Chip and his dad worked right along with him, exchanging the occasional word but otherwise keeping to themselves.

Caleb stopped near his dad. "Do the horses need feeding?"

"Not yet."

He nodded and went back to his task. The motions were so familiar that he soon got into the rhythm and was almost surprised when his father finally spoke again.

"Time to get washed up for dinner." He turned to Chip. "You're joining us, right?"

"Couldn't keep me away," Chip joked. "I saw those cookies Miss Lucy's been baking. If they're anywhere near as good as her grandmother's we're in for a treat!"

Caleb gathered up the tools and wheelbarrow and hosed everything down before replacing it in the feed room while his dad stood silently by. He shut the door and turned to face him.

"Anything else I can do before we go in?"

"Not right now." His dad whistled to his dogs. "I could do with some help later tonight."

"Okay." Caleb walked past him and headed for the house.

"Thanks, son."

Caleb didn't stop walking or acknowledge his father's comment. As far as he was concerned, that grudging attempt to converse rated around a zero. The weird thing was—he didn't care. Being in that space with his father had been remarkably soothing and familiar. He'd almost enjoyed it. Weird how different the chores he'd endlessly complained about as a teen now seemed far more important . . .

He pushed open the door to the mudroom and inhaled a lungful of Christmas. Lucy was in the kitchen making gingerbread cookies. Her hair was in a messy bun on top of her head, and one of his mom's old aprons covered her clothing. He paused to appreciate her. She had a touch of the Christmas fairy to go along with her sunny personality and she really did brighten his day.

Caleb frowned. What the hell was wrong with him? Enjoying working in the barn and smiling foolishly at his best friend's annoying little sister . . .

"What's up?" she asked, her spatula held in one hand like a wand.

"Nothing. It smells good in here."

"That's the casserole. It's nothing to do with me."

"Yeah, it is." He kept walking. "I'd kiss you, but I'm covered in horse shit."

"Eew." She wrinkled her nose and warded him off with her spatula. "Go and take a shower."

"Already on it." He winked and moved on through, his steps slowing as he neared his bedroom. When had he started winking? His team in Seattle wouldn't recognize him right now. He was the hard-driving boss, the man who made them work twenty-four-seven, without remorse.

And he was tired of being that person. Of constantly out-performing himself. He let himself into the bathroom and regarded the Spider-Man shower curtain his mom had bought for him when he was fifteen. The plumbing was better now and the water hot and plentiful, even if he did have to stand in the bath and bend his head down about a foot to get it under the spray.

He only noticed Lucy must have put shower gel and shampoo in the wire basket when he recognized the scent from the B&B. Despite her claims to be ditzy she was nothing of the sort. Now that he thought about it, her parents had always been a little dismissive of her achievements. Her decision to take over her grandma's business obviously hadn't pleased them. He soaped his hair, rinsed it off, and stepped out onto the rag rug his mom had made.

He wrapped himself in a towel and went back into his bedroom to change. He could hear the water running in his dad's part of the house, which meant dinner wouldn't be long.

"Oh!" Lucy came in and hurriedly shut the door behind her. "I didn't realize you were out of the shower."

Her gaze lowered to his bare chest and stayed at the towel knotted on his hips. "You look . . . nice."

"Nice?" He took a step toward her. "Like, how nice?"

"Like if I didn't have cookies in the oven right now and your father wasn't expecting us for dinner, I'd be unwrapping you like an early Christmas present." She licked her lips, which did all kinds of things to his anatomy.

"How long until the timer goes off?" Caleb asked hoarsely, forgetting he wasn't supposed to be totally into her.

"Five minutes."

He sighed. "That's definitely not long enough."

She came toward him, went up on tiptoe, and kissed him very slowly. "This will have to sustain me through dinner."

He patted her ass. "I'll make it up to you, I promise."

She blew him a kiss and headed back for the door. "Dinner's nearly ready, so come on out when you're dressed."

* * *

Lucy made her way back to the kitchen, her face still flushed from the amazing sight of Caleb in the flesh. She hadn't seen much of him in the dark of the previous night and he was truly spectacular. Years of working on a ranch had honed his physique and he'd obviously kept up his fitness levels. She was proud of herself for not outright drooling, falling to her knees, ripping off the towel and kissing his—

"Evening."

She jumped as Isaiah Erickson came out of the pantry carrying the salt and pepper. He set them on the table and turned to look at her.

"Hi!" she said brightly. "Thanks so much for letting me stay with you until the generator gets fixed."

He nodded and gestured toward the family room. "Did you decorate the tree?"

"Yes, I hope that's okay?" She regarded him anxiously. His poker face made Caleb's look like an amateur.

"It's fine." He paused. "It's nice to see the lights up."

"It definitely makes things more Christmassy," Lucy agreed. Her timer went off. "I'll just get these cookies out of the oven and then we can start dinner."

He sniffed the air. "Gingerbread?"

"Yup." She smiled at him. "I remember Caleb always liked it."

"He must have got that from me. Annie wasn't keen on it, but she made them for me anyway."

Lucy set the cookies to cool, and took out the baked potatoes and casserole dish. "Caleb is like you in many ways. You both have a great work ethic."

"Well, we're both stubborn. I'll give you that." He made

sure she had something to place the dish on at the table. "I'll find a spoon."

The back door opened, bringing in a blast of frigid air, and Chip came in rubbing his hands.

"Something smells good."

"It's me." Caleb arrived from the opposite direction. "I just showered."

Chip chuckled. "Bet you haven't smelled like that for a while, son."

"Nope, but mud and manure wash off much easier than the city stink." He'd put a brown sweater on over a shirt and wore jeans. His hair was still spiky and wet. Seeing him next to his father made it easier for Lucy to see the likeness between them.

"What can I do to help?" Caleb asked.

"There's beer and iced tea in the refrigerator if anyone wants it," Isaiah said. "And get the butter and sour cream for the baked potatoes."

"Will do."

It didn't take long before they were all sitting around the table with plates full of food. Lucy took the seat next to Caleb. Chip sat opposite her, and Isaiah was at right angles to his son. The empty chair where Ann had sat was a reminder of the family's loss.

For a while they all just ate. Lucy hadn't realized how hungry she was. They'd basically skipped lunch, and she'd used up a lot of calories during the previous twenty-four hours.

"I see you finally got your tree up, Isaiah," Chip said cheerfully.

"Nothing to do with me." Isaiah took a sip of beer.

"It looks fantastic," Caleb said. "Thanks for putting in all that effort, Lucy."

Isaiah cleared his throat. "There's no need to get all defensive, son. I already told her I was okay with it."

Lucy glanced at Caleb, who was also drinking beer and maybe should have gone for the tea.

"It didn't take me long." Lucy tried to lighten the atmosphere. "And I just love the holidays. I have three trees up at the B&B."

"Shame you had to close down right at peak holiday season," Isaiah commented. "I don't remember your grandma ever having to do that."

"The roads up here are closed, and there's no way any of her guests are getting here in the worst storm in living memory," Caleb said evenly. "It's hardly her fault."

"I didn't say it was, son. I was just making an observation." Isaiah's frown was so like Caleb's it almost took Lucy's breath away. "And how about you stop butting in and let the girl speak for herself?"

"She's not a girl, Dad."

Under the cover of the table, Lucy placed her hand on Caleb's muscled thigh and squeezed hard. "He knows I can stand up for myself, Mr. Erickson." Lucy smiled. "We established that when I dropped my book bag on his head when I was nine."

"He was always complaining about you tagging along with him and Dan. I guess he changed his mind about that." He paused and Lucy tensed. "You two an item now?"

"We're just good friends," Lucy said hastily.

"Good enough to share a bed but not to court?" Isaiah's gaze bored into Caleb. "Is that how I brought you up to treat women, son?"

"After the way you treated Mom, you don't get to comment." Caleb scowled right back. "Lucy and I understand each other and that's good enough for me."

Isaiah frowned. "I treated her just fine. Annie was very happy with me."

"Because she's a much better person than you will ever be," Caleb said softly. "She put up with a lot of shit."

"From you as well. How do you think she felt when you upped and left at eighteen and never came home again?"

Lucy and Chip exchanged an apprehensive glance across the table.

"I think she understood why I left."

"Because you thought you were better than us? That this place wasn't good enough anymore?"

Caleb frowned. "I *never* felt like that. I didn't come back because you made me so unwelcome, with your constant digs about me destroying family tradition, of me not caring about my birthright, about how selfish I was to want something different for myself."

Isaiah shook his head. "That's bullshit."

"That's the truth and you just don't like it." Caleb sat forward. "You made me feel like I would *never* be good enough to run this place. That even if I gave up on all my dreams and came back, I'd still never hack it because I wasn't *you*, Dad. And I'd never ever measure up."

Caleb abruptly stood up. "This is pointless." He nodded at Lucy. "Thanks for dinner. I need to make a couple of calls. There's a VC who wants to invest in my company I need to talk to. I'll be back to help clear up, okay?"

He walked out and Lucy heard the bedroom door slam down the hallway.

Isaiah crossed his arms over his chest. "I see he hasn't changed one bit."

Chip sighed. "Neither have you, my old friend."

"He doesn't listen! He just goes off on me."

Lucy took a deep breath. "I think he was trying to tell you he doesn't feel welcome in his own home, Mr. Erickson. He sounded pretty hurt to me."

"Hurt?" Isaiah snorted. "He's just mad that I'm not willing

to listen to his excuses for not being home for his mother more."

"He's right though," Chip said slowly. "You never say a nice thing about him to his face. Why would he want to come home to listen to that?"

"I don't want him getting a big head or thinking he's special or something."

"But he *is* special. He built his own tech company from scratch and made a success of it. Maybe that's not what you wanted him to do, Mr. Erickson, but he did it, and maybe he's hurt that you can't even be proud of him for that," Lucy suggested.

Isaiah scowled. "And what's a VC anyway? Why is that more important than taking the time to listen to his own father?"

"Perhaps you should ask him yourself, Isaiah," Chip said pointedly. "Show an interest."

"Like he does in the ranch?"

Chip snorted. "You shut him down whenever he tries to ask. You did it earlier."

"I . . ." Isaiah stopped talking. Chip departed. Lucy cleared the plates and stacked them in the sink while Caleb's father stared into space and occasionally sipped his coffee.

Eventually, Lucy approached him. He looked at her like he'd never seen her before.

"Annie did all the important talking with Caleb."

Lucy tried to think how to frame what she wanted to say. "But she's not here anymore. I guess you're finding it hard to communicate with Caleb."

"You've got that right." He grimaced. "I'm not one to reach out to people."

"Neither is he." She paused. "But he's your only son. Don't you think Annie would want you to make every effort to make sure Caleb feels loved?"

In other circumstances, Isaiah's horrified expression would have made her laugh, but she really wanted to help Caleb.

"I don't do that mushy, emotional stuff."

"But if you don't reach out to him," Lucy said slowly, "and his mother is no longer here to bring him home, you might never see him again. Is that what you want?"

His expression turned to stone, and he rose to his feet.

"I've got to get on. Thanks for the cookies."

He disappeared in the direction of the barn. Lucy balled up the damp tea towel and threw it at the door. The Erickson men were two of a kind, walking away when things got too hard for them. Her original idea of locking them both in a room and leaving them there until they worked it out was more and more appealing.

She retrieved the tea towel and tossed it in the laundry basket. And now she'd have to tell Caleb she'd pissed his father off even more . . . She was beginning to have a lot of sympathy with the absent Annie.

Chapter Five

Caleb ended the second call and pressed his fingers into his skull as he was hit by a raging headache. The venture capitalist was enthusiastic. He was talking about a major investment with the possibility of an IPO in eighteen months. Caleb groaned. Could he stay sane for that long? Did he even want his company to go public?

Lucy came in, her expression wary. "Is everything okay, Caleb?"

He looked at her and considered what to say. She sighed. "Man, you Ericksons are tough nuts to crack. I can see where you get it from now that I've talked to your father." She half turned back to the door. "I need to get the angel on the tree. I'll leave you to it."

"Hold up."

She looked inquiringly over her shoulder at him.

"One, you're not tall enough to get the angel up there without my help, and two, I'm trying to think what I want to say to you."

She smiled. "Then, how about we accomplish the first thing while you work on the second?"

"Sounds good to me." He rose to his feet and went to take her hand. "My mom got that angel from her Scottish granny. If you look under her skirts, she's got tartan stockings."

"I noticed." She squeezed his fingers. "I cleaned her up a little."

"Mom used to do all that stuff. Last Christmas I guess she was too exhausted to do much." He grimaced. "I wish I'd spent more than two days here with her."

"You're an entrepreneur. I'm sure she understood that." Lucy picked up the doll and fluffed out her net and satin skirts.

"I used that as an excuse not to stay." Caleb held her gaze. "With good communication networks there's no reason why I couldn't have worked from here. I just couldn't bear seeing her face when Dad and I got into it."

He set his hands around Lucy's waist and lifted her effortlessly above his head.

"High enough for you?"

"Absolutely." It took Lucy a few moments to work out how to fix the angel onto the tree and make sure she was straight. "All done."

Caleb lowered her very slowly, making sure her body slid right over his. He kept hold of her when she reached the ground and looked into her blue eyes.

"Thanks for doing this."

"The tree?" She raised her eyebrows. "You must have realized by now that I just love the holidays."

"Everything," Caleb said simply. "You just being here is making it hurt less."

Her expression softened and she cupped his bearded chin. "I'm glad to help. I know how hard it is to lose someone you love."

He nodded and drew her back along the hall to his bedroom. He checked that there was no sign of his father and shut the door behind him.

"Sit down."

She went and sat on the bed, her hands in her lap, and looked up at him expectantly.

"I have a software company. I started it right out of college, and I've been growing the business ever since."

"I know." Lucy nodded. "My parents constantly held you up as an example of how a small-town person could go onto greater things if they really made an effort."

Caleb winced. "Sorry about that."

"They did the same to Dan." She half smiled. "Didn't really work with either of us."

"The thing is—in the last year the business has grown fast, and I've been trying to micromanage everything."

Lucy pointed at herself. "This is my shocked face."

"I've been working seven days a week, pushing my team to exhaustion, and when Mom died, I . . ." He paused. "I just kept going because it was easier than dealing with her loss, you know?"

Lucy nodded, her blue gaze full of sympathy.

He sat on the chair opposite her. "And now we have the opportunity to expand the company even further, take more investor money, and aim to go public in eighteen months."

"That sounds . . . amazing."

"It is," Caleb said. "But it's not going to be easy."

"You'll get it done," Lucy said. "You're smart, capable, and so good at what you do that you can't fail. I believe in you."

Her smile was so full of her belief in him that he almost couldn't stand it. If he went ahead and committed himself to eighteen months of hell, he'd probably never have the time to see her or his father. Did that bother her, or had she already given up on him ever hanging around?

"If I go that route, it gives me a reason not to come back here," Caleb said carefully.

"I . . . kind of assumed that was a given, anyway." She looked down at her hands. "I've loved being with you,

Caleb, but I do understand that it's temporary." She finally looked up. "And I don't regret it at all."

He nodded. "Me neither."

"Then, we're good, right?" She rose to her feet with a bright smile. "I just remembered I forgot to turn the oven off after I took out the cookies."

She practically ran out of the room, leaving Caleb with a sense that something wasn't right. He started after her, his stocking feet making no sound on the wood flooring and abruptly stopped when he reached the kitchen. There was no sign of Lucy and the oven had been off for a while.

He was just about to head to the back door when he heard a stifled sniff from the pantry. The door was ajar, but he didn't need to go in to realize Lucy was crying. The sound hit him hard in the gut. Was she crying over him? He didn't deserve that. He turned around and went quietly back to his bedroom. She didn't need to know he'd overheard her. But he hated seeing his sunny-natured friend upset.

Friend? Who was he trying to kid? It was *killing* him. For some reason she loved and believed in him and, like everything else in his life, he was incapable of reciprocating because he was an unemotional jerk.

Just like his dad . . . He sat on the bed and took a deep shuddering breath, his gaze straying to the darkness outside. There were no lights on the hillside in front of him. The silence was a living, breathing thing, quite unlike the city he'd reluctantly learned to call home. He'd never told his parents how hard it had been to get used to the noise and the constant flow of people. He'd never told them much at all. He'd been too worried his dad would demand he stop wasting his money and return home, or that his mom would be disappointed in him.

He'd kept everything inside and focused on being exceptional, so that no one would ever say he hadn't made the best of every opportunity he'd been offered. And what had it got him? Money, most of which he'd plowed straight back into his company, an enviable work ethic that was slowly eating away at his soul, and a team who loved and feared him in equal measures.

The door opened and Lucy came back in, her eyes suspiciously red.

"Sorry about that. I was just checking the weather reports. It looks like there's more snow on the way."

"I had a text from the Rosbergs." Caleb played his part because what else could he do? "Everything's fine at the B&B except Colin has basically moved into their house and is refusing to budge from in front of the fire."

She laughed, and something inside him solidified into a certainty, making everything else irrelevant.

"I told Dad I'd do the last check of the barn." Caleb rose to his feet. "It won't take long."

She hesitated. "I might take a bath and then go to bed, if that's okay?"

He kissed the top of her head. "Do whatever makes you happy."

"I've been doing that ever since you arrived, Caleb Erickson."

It was his turn to chuckle as he headed for the door. "Don't fall asleep too fast, okay?"

"I'll try not to."

He walked through the silent kitchen to the mudroom and put on his boots, fleece-lined jacket, and dented old Stetson. Five minutes after arriving at Stanford he'd ditched his hat and cowboy boots because he couldn't deal with the jokes. Everything still fit him fine. It was like returning to his old self—to the boy who'd changed into something else entirely and lost something indefinable along the way.

He let himself out and stood on the porch, staring up at

the ink-black night sky and the brightness of the stars. It was too cold to stand around for long. He walked down the well-salted path to the barn, flicked on the lights, and started checking in on the horses.

"Evening, son."

He almost had heart failure when his father appeared from the feed store.

"Did you think I'd forget to come out here?" Caleb asked.

"Nope, you've always been a man of his word." His dad paused. "I came out here to think."

"It's a good place to do that," Caleb agreed. "I've had a bit of thinking to do myself this year."

"About your work?"

"Yeah, about that and other things." Caleb glanced at his father, whose face remained in the shadows. "I've always loved it out here at night."

"You used to shimmy down that overflow pipe and scare your mother half to death, disappearing into the night," Isaiah said. "I told her you'd be fine, and I was always right."

"You knew about that?"

Isaiah snorted. "You were about as quiet as a baby elephant on that roof, son. Hard to miss."

"Why didn't you stop me?"

"Why would I? I knew you'd be safe on your own land, and that you were smart enough to make it back."

"So why didn't you assume the same thing when I went to Stanford?"

Isaiah was quiet for a long while. "I guess because I didn't understand why you wanted to leave."

"I didn't want to leave. You seemed to have the ranch running perfectly, and you weren't interested in me getting involved in that. I guess at eighteen I thought you didn't need me, and you didn't think I was good enough."

"I guess I screwed up, then."

Caleb blinked at his dad. "Say that again?"

Isaiah shrugged. "I didn't think you had anything to tell me when you were eighteen, and I let you know it." He hesitated. "I felt like I wasn't good enough for you anymore. I wasn't educated like your new friends, and I wasn't interested in changing that."

"You made me feel . . . unnecessary," Caleb said slowly. "That you didn't care whether I came back or not because the ranch was all yours and had nothing to do with me."

"And you did nothing to change my opinion of you, either."

Caleb considered that home truth. "I went out of my way to make sure you knew I didn't need you, *or* the ranch to be successful."

"Yeah."

"What a pair of stubborn fools. If Mom was here, she'd be calling us both out." Caleb took a deep breath and faced his father. I'm sorry, Dad."

Isaiah slowly nodded. "I'm sorry, too, son."

Caleb took an unsteady step forward and his dad held up his finger.

"Now, don't you start with all that emotional touchy-feely bullshit."

"Oh, shut up." Caleb wrapped his arms around his dad and gave him a bear hug and a noogie for good measure. "Take it like a man."

Lucy took a long bath, which gave her an excuse for the puffiness of her face, and put herself to bed. She loved the peacefulness of the ranch and the way she could almost taste the velvety darkness pressing in around her. Not that she felt very peaceful right now. Caleb was on target to bigger and better things than she'd ever accomplish, and he deserved every one of them. If anyone had told her a month previously that she'd get to spend the holidays with Caleb Erickson and make love with her dream crush, she wouldn't have believed them. She should be grateful for having her wish come true rather than complaining that it would have to end. The thing with most dreams was that they never lived up to reality, whereas Caleb had been even better in the flesh than she could ever have imagined. She should be satisfied.

But she wanted more. Lucy opened her eyes. Why *should* she have to settle for smiling and waving goodbye? One thing she'd learned after defying her parents and taking on the B&B despite their doubts was that she was stronger than she looked. Sometimes she fussed over things and apologized too much, but she'd survived the worst summer and winter on record for the B&B, and she was still standing. *And* she'd taken the opportunity to live her dream with Caleb.

The door creaked open, and she heard the rustle of Caleb removing his clothing.

"You still awake?" he whispered.

"Kind of." Lucy reminded herself that she was a strong, independent woman who took what she wanted.

He climbed into bed and took up almost all the room, his arm coming around her shoulders as naturally as if they slept together every night. She nestled close to his side, her cheek over his steadily beating heart.

"I talked to Dad."

"How did it go?"

"Well, I ended up giving him a hug. I don't think he'll ever forgive me for that, but the rest of it? I think we're coming to an understanding."

"That's wonderful." Lucy smiled against his skin. He smelled like a cowboy again, which she kind of loved. "Chip and I told him a few home truths after you left the table."

"Then I guess that's something else I have to thank you for."

He came up on one elbow and looked at her, his expression hard to read. "Can I kiss you?"

"In your father's house?" Lucy went for full horror and outrage. "What kind of a girl do you think I am?"

"My kind?" He kissed her very thoroughly until she had no choice but to reciprocate. "The most annoying best friend's little sister and hanger-on ever, kind?"

She nipped his lip and he growled as his hands roamed over her body. He swiftly removed her nightgown and settled himself between her thighs. She sighed as he kissed his way down her stomach, his bearded chin making her hum with pleasure as his tongue circled her most sensitive flesh. She raised her hips as he palmed her butt and pressed her closer to his talented mouth and plunging fingers. She came in a sudden rush, gripping his shoulder hard as she trembled and gasped his name.

"Nice," he murmured. "That's my girl." He took possession of her hand and guided it to his hard shaft. "Make me feel good, Lucy."

She was happy to oblige, her fingers sliding over his heated flesh as he rocked into the tightness of her grip.

"Where's . . . the condom?" Caleb groaned. "Don't tell me I left them in the bathroom."

"There's one in my bag, on the nightstand," Lucy said. "I can get it."

"Nope, I'm on it." Caleb was already on the move.

"It's in the zip-up pocket on the left-hand side," Lucy added as he started dumping her stuff out on the vanity.

"Got it." He climbed back into bed and remained crouching over her as he ripped open the packet, his expression intent.

Lucy sighed as he slowly eased inside her, his gaze never

leaving hers until he was fully seated. He framed her face with his hands and kissed her.

"Thank you for everything," he said softly. "I mean it."

She kissed him back with everything she couldn't say and threw herself into making love with him as if it was for the very last time—because it was—and she wasn't going to allow herself to regret a thing.

Caleb woke up early, kissed a sleeping Lucy, and snuck out of bed. He'd always loved mornings on the ranch, and he was determined to enjoy this one. He dressed in his warmest clothes and went through to the kitchen where the lingering scent of coffee meant his dad was already up and at it. He put on his boots and coat and went outside. The razor-sharp chill in the air made him catch his breath and stop to stare at the glistening white hills and ranks of hidden pine trees that climbed up the slopes.

He took out his cell and checked the time. It was probably too early to call, so he sent a text.

Hey, need to talk to you urgently about this investor thing.

Aware that he might be taking a small step toward a big crisis, he put his cell away, and walked over to the barn where his dad, Chip, and a guy he didn't know, called Angelo, were busy mucking out the stalls. He didn't bother to chat, picked up a shovel, and got stuck in.

Chip winked when their paths crossed, and his dad merely grunted like his presence was already accepted and not worth commenting on. It felt good to test his strength and stamina on real work rather than going to the gym. As Chip finished feeding the horses, Caleb let them out into the paddock behind the barn, where the snow had been cleared to allow them to roam more easily.

"Not sure they should be out in this," his dad commented as Caleb secured the gate. "Might get them back in if it starts to snow again."

"What you need is a heated field," Caleb said.

"Sounds expensive."

"It is, but it might be worth considering for the future."

"What future?" His dad wouldn't look at him. "If you don't take this place on, who am I going to leave it to?"

Before Caleb could answer him, Angelo came up to ask something, and his dad walked away. His cell buzzed. It took him a few minutes to dig it out of his pocket and look at the screen.

Call me at midday. Thanks.

Caleb checked the time. That meant he had six hours to talk to Lucy and maybe talk himself out of making a terrible mistake.

Chapter Six

"Morning, sleepyhead."

Lucy opened one eye to see Caleb with a mug of coffee at the door. "I hope that's for me?"

"Seeing as I've been up for two hours working in the barn, then yes." He placed it on the bedside table and sat beside her. It wasn't until he whistled that she remembered she was naked and grabbed a handful of the sheet to hold to her breasts.

"Don't hide on my account. It's not as if I haven't seen it all before."

And now she was blushing like a teenager. She took a sip of coffee and sighed with bliss.

"Thanks, I needed that. What's the weather doing?"

"So far, so good, today. But there's a storm due in late tonight. I called Denise and everything's okay at the B&B."

"Is the generator fixed?"

"The repair guy left a message saying the earliest he can get to you is December twenty-sixth."

"That's not good."

"You could stay at the ranch over Christmas," Caleb suggested. "I mean you're already here, and we're glad to have you."

"I'm not sure that would be a good idea." Lucy stared down at her mug.

"Why not?"

Darn it, she'd forgotten Caleb had no problem being all direct and confrontational. Didn't he understand that she was trying to walk away before she embarrassed them both and begged him to stay?

"I feel like I should be at the B&B," Lucy said carefully. "I mean, what if someone turns up unexpectedly and there's no one there?"

His brows drew together. "Denise will explain the generator's down and find them somewhere else to stay?"

"She wouldn't have that kind of information."

He studied her while she avoided his gaze and sipped her coffee.

"What's wrong?" he asked gently.

"Nothing!" She gulped too much coffee and it almost went up her nose. "You and your dad have a lot to talk about. You don't need me hanging around so you have to be polite and talk to me instead."

He stayed quiet for a while before finally speaking.

"Can I ask you something?"

"Sure, go ahead."

"Have you ever"—he hesitated—"thought about moving back to Seattle?"

She set the mug back on the bedside table so firmly coffee slopped over the side. "I told you how hard it was to get away from my parents and take on the B&B. Do you think I'd stroll back there, tell them I'd made a mistake, and ask them to let me come back?"

"I guess not."

She pushed the covers down and got out of bed. If he was

about to mention that *he* lived in Seattle, she was going to either scream or weep. "Excuse me, I need to shower."

"Does that guy you spoke to on the phone live around here?"

"What guy?"

"The one you told to clean up his act."

"Do you really think I'd sleep with you if I was involved with someone else?" Lucy was half ashamed at using Colin the cat as an excuse to get out of a difficult situation, and half relieved to have an excuse at all.

Caleb shoved a hand through his hair. "Jeez, maybe I should stop talking. Everything I say is making things worse."

"Yes, it is." She raised her chin. "Now, please excuse me."

He grimaced. "Okay. I told Dad I'd help with unloading the hay. I'll see you back here for lunch." He got out of her way, his expression thoughtful, which wasn't reassuring at all.

Lucy had a shower, got dressed and packed her bag. She went into the kitchen and found Chip with his hand in the tin of gingerbread she'd made the previous day.

"Caught me." He chuckled. "I just can't resist this stuff."

"I'll make you a batch of your very own if you'll drive me back to the B&B right now."

Chip frowned. "You and Caleb fighting or something?"

"Not at all. I just need to get back for the generator repair guy. I already told Caleb." Lucy slipped the lie into the middle of the sentence and hoped Chip wouldn't notice. "I'll call if I need to come back."

"Okay, then." Chip nodded. "I'll just get my keys."

Ten minutes later they were exiting the ranch at the county gate, and she was trying not to cry, which was stupid because she'd been given everything she'd ever dreamed about. Caleb was going back to Seattle with his relationship with his father on a way better footing, and his business was about to expand, and probably make him filthy rich. If anyone had asked her what she wanted for him for Christmas, then all the items on her list had been checked off.

"What time is the guy coming to do the repair?" Chip asked. "If it won't take long, I could hang around town and take you back out to the ranch."

"I have no idea," Lucy said quickly. This was why she tried not to lie. Everything got way too complicated. "That's very kind of you, but it could be hours."

"Okey dokey, then." He whistled a tune as they turned onto the county road, which was in a much better state than it had been the day before. Lucy kept up a bright stream of chatter as they made their way into town. Chip was easy company and he seemed to have accepted her choice to leave without too many questions.

He pulled up in the driveway of the B&B and smiled at Lucy. "Home sweet home!"

She looked out at the white painted Victorian with its wide porch and stained-glass panels in the front door and nodded, her throat tight. Even if times were hard, she'd keep going to save her grandmother's legacy and make new memories for herself.

"Thank you, Chip." She got out of the truck while he retrieved her bag from the back seat. "I'll get baking those cookies as soon as the generator is back on."

"No worries." Chip winked at her. "Now, hurry on back. Caleb will be missing you."

She managed to keep smiling as she disabled the alarm and let herself back into the house. To her relief, the secondary generator was doing its job as the freezers were still working, the kitchen light was on, and the woodstove was throwing out heat. Lucy set the kettle on the range and sat at the table as her thoughts went in circles. Had she made the correct decision to leave? If Caleb had come right out and asked her to move to Seattle with him, what would she have done? She loved him. She always had, and the thought of being with him was precious.

She hoped he wouldn't ask her to make that choice, and leaving before he did still made sense. They'd both gained something from their time together and she wished him nothing but the best. She plugged her phone into the charger and turned it off just in case he tried to call her. She had plenty of extra sweaters in her closet, so she wouldn't be cold. Right now, she just wanted to curl up, maybe cry a little, and then take a long nap. Everything would look better after that . . . it always did.

Caleb looked up as Chip's truck rolled to a stop in front of the barn and the man himself got out.

"Where've you been?"

Chip raised an eyebrow. "Just dropping Miss Lucy back at the B&B to wait for the repair guy."

"What?"

"She said she'd told you."

"That the guy had rescheduled?"

"Nope, that she was leaving." Chip scratched his head. "Oh, good lord. Don't tell me you didn't know."

"I—" Caleb got out his phone. There was nothing from Lucy to confirm what Chip had just said, which meant she'd left him. His heart sank to his boots. "Dammit!"

"Something wrong, young fella?"

"Yeah, but it's all my fault." Inwardly Caleb berated himself as he typed a message to Lucy. By raising the question of moving back to Seattle, he'd scared her enough to make her run. "Are you fighting with Miss Lucy?"

"Nope, I just put my big foot in my mouth as usual,"

Caleb said grimly. "She got the wrong idea about something I said."

"Wouldn't be the first time an Erickson's done that." Chip nodded. "I mean, look at your father."

"What have I done?" Isaiah came out of the barn and stared at them both. "Why are you standing around like you're at a church meeting in the snow when there's a perfectly good, warm house right there?"

Caleb went into the house. Something smelled good, but there was no sign of Lucy. There was a note addressed to Isaiah on the table. He picked it up and read it out loud.

"*Thanks so much for letting me stay until the generator at the B&B was fixed. I left you two batches of cookies in the pantry, and there are pork ribs slow roasting in the oven for dinner*."

He looked over at Caleb. "What happened?"

"I screwed up."

"I can see that. What are you going to do about it?"

Caleb held his dad's gaze. "I've got a call with my board at midday. Can I get back to you after that?"

"Sure," Isaiah said as he helped himself to a cookie and offered the tin to Chip. "But if you care about her, don't waste too much time letting her know."

Caleb went into his bedroom and closed the door. Without Lucy's presence the space felt cold and empty. She was the heart of him now and without her he was nothing. His cell buzzed and he accepted the call.

"Hey, it's Chase Morgan. What's going on?"

Caleb took a deep breath. "I want out."

"Of what, exactly?"

"Everything."

"Caleb . . . you're just panicking because you're in the position most startups dream about." Chase sounded soothing. "I've seen it a hundred times. The new VC wouldn't have decided to invest in you unless they thought you would succeed—just like me and the rest of the board did when we first met you all those years ago."

"I don't want any of it. I want to come home and work with my dad on the ranch."

There was a long silence. "You mean you want out of *everything*?"

"Yeah." Caleb's heart was beating hard enough to burst.

"Okay, Caleb, listen up. Promise me you won't do anything drastic until I've talked to the rest of the board," Chase said. "There's a lot to this decision, you know that. I want to make sure we explore every possibility before you walk away with nothing."

"I wouldn't have nothing. I'd still inherit an awesome ranch."

And maybe win the woman of his dreams, but Chase didn't need to know that.

"I understand." Chase paused. "But promise you'll wait until I get back to you. I think you owe me that."

Aware that if it hadn't been for Chase and his fellow VC angels, he wouldn't have gotten his start at all, Caleb agreed. He'd barely ended the call before his cell started ringing again, and he answered it.

"I'm not going to change my mind, Chase."

"I've no idea who the hell Chase is, Caleb, but my name's Dan, and I'm having some serious thoughts about what you've been up to since I left town."

Caleb sighed. "What do you want, Dan?"

"This is going to sound weird. Mom tried to call Lucy at the B&B, but she's not answering her phone, so she called Auntie Linda to check in on her, and Linda said Bernie said Lucy had gone to stay with you at the ranch because her power was out, or something."

"She was here last night."

"Great. You take good care of her, now," Dan said. "I'll tell Mom to stop fussing."

"Hold up, Lucy went home today."

"So, the power must be back on."

"Not that I've heard. She said she was waiting on the generator guy to come out, but I don't think that was true." Caleb paused. Seeing as he was pissing everyone off today, he might as well include his best friend. "She got mad at me for suggesting she should move to Seattle."

"Why would she do that?" Dan asked suspiciously.

"Because I'd like her to move in with me." Caleb braced himself as Dan went very quiet.

"You're . . . sleeping with my baby sister?"

"She's twenty-eight, Dan."

"But she's had the biggest crush on you forever!"

"So everyone keeps telling me."

"Then why the hell did you suggest she move to Seattle? Have you any idea how our parents would gloat if she came back with her tail between her legs? They'd be all nice and forgiving on the outside, but we'd all know how much they'd enjoy rubbing it in for the rest of her life."

"She told me that."

"Then why—"

Caleb interrupted him. "Because I'm an idiot, and I wanted to see if she liked me enough to want to be with me, and I asked the wrong question, *okay*?"

"There's no need to shout," Dan said. "I had to hold the phone away from my ear."

"I screwed up. She left, and now I'm trying to fix things."

"She's not going to move to Seattle, dude."

"I get it." Caleb took a deep breath. "Is there any way you can get here by Christmas Day?"

"If you pay for a private jet, helicopter, or limo, then sure. I'm at my parents' house right now."

"Then ask them to come with you."

"*Hell* no. You'll have to talk to Mom about that yourself."

"Then please get her on the phone," Caleb said.

He waited as Dan went in search of his mom, his thoughts all over the place.

"Caleb! How lovely to hear from you. Dan says you wanted to ask me something important?"

"It's a big ask." Caleb braced himself. "I'm hoping you'll all come and meet me at the B&B for Christmas. I think Lucy needs our support."

Lucy opened the front door to a man in green coveralls with the name badge, NICK, on his front right pocket. He was carrying a clipboard.

"Good afternoon. I've come to fix your generator."

"You have?" Lucy blinked at him. Maybe she was still asleep and dreaming and she'd somehow manifested the very person she'd assured Chip was coming to the B&B that very day. "You're not the usual guy."

"I have my official ID here." He handed it over. "If you want to call my company and confirm I'm a bona fide repairman, here's the number."

Lucy studied the card he'd given her. "You came all the way from Humboldt?"

He shrugged. "We definitely get around."

"Can I see the paperwork?"

"Sure."

He was looking at her funny now, but she had to make sure things were on the level.

"I didn't authorize this." Lucy looked up.

"You're not Ms. Erickson?"

"Only in my dreams."

Lucy realized Caleb must have waved his magic wand and made things happen while she was asleep. A deep sense of gratitude flowed over her. She stepped back and held the door open wide.

"Please come in. Would you like something to drink before you start?"

"No, I'll get on." He winked at her. "I'm on triple time right now."

"Oh! Then I'll show you where the generator is."

An hour later, the main generator was running again. After giving him some cookies and coffee to see him through the return journey, Lucy waved Nick off from the front porch. She'd asked for the bill, but he'd told her that was dealt with by the office, and that she'd probably get an invoice after Christmas. She suspected Caleb would be getting it sent to him. How she was going to persuade him to let her pay it was another matter entirely.

She slowly spun around in the well-lit hall, her gaze catching on the lighted Christmas trees, and the glittering tinsel, as she inhaled the scent of the pine candles above the fireplaces. A sense of her grandma's satisfaction swirled around her like a warm blanket, and she smiled like a fool. This was her home. If Caleb couldn't deal with that then he wasn't the man for her. She'd had her dream date with her longtime crush and maybe it was time to move on . . .

After she'd sent him a text thanking him for getting the generator repair done. That was only polite. She turned on her phone and then wished she hadn't. There were texts from both her parents, one from Dan, and one from Caleb.

Ignoring her family, she clicked on Caleb's, which he'd obviously sent just as Chip had arrived back at the ranch without her.

Where are you? Is everything okay?

What she loved about Caleb was that, even though she'd walked out on him, rather than continue to text, he'd done something practical to make sure she was safe and warm at the B&B. She began to type.

Thank you for organizing the generator repair guy.

She held her breath as she saw the three dancing bubbles in the corner of the screen indicating he was replying.

You're welcome.

She waited but that appeared to be it.

You remember when you thought I was on my phone talking to some guy who wasn't you?

Nothing.

I was talking to Colin about his lack of mouse hunting skills.

More nothing. Lucy was just about to put her phone down when he replied.

That's funny.

You're not mad?

As you said you wouldn't have slept with me if you'd been seeing another guy.

Lucy smiled foolishly at the screen. Caleb's no-drama approach to life was very refreshing.

I should have told you straight out.

Much more fun to keep me guessing, right? Gotta go. Stuff to do.

Lucy waited a minute, but he appeared to have followed through and had left the chat. She sighed, feeling vaguely hurt. She had no more reasons to contact him and maybe that was for the best. She'd enjoy her Christmas Day alone at the B&B while he got to share it with his dad, Chip, and the ranch hands.

Except, now who was being melodramatic? She didn't have to be alone. All she had to do was call her auntie Linda across the street and she'd be set. Spending the day with her cousins seemed a far better alternative to fake pining away like Miss Havisham from that Dickens book. She had family, she had friends, and a real community around her. If that didn't include Caleb Erickson, she'd survive, even if she missed him forever.

Chapter Seven

Lucy woke up to the sun streaming through her open drapes, and stayed where she was to appreciate it. She wasn't due at her aunt's for hours, but she had some baking to do that would use up her morning. She felt a small pang of regret that she wasn't waking up at the ranch in Caleb's arms and immediately tried to think of something else. She was lucky, she was blessed, and she wouldn't allow one man to spoil that for her.

But had she been too hasty? Was there room for compromise? He'd be coming back to see his father more often, and she would always be welcome to visit her parents in Seattle. Could they manage a long-distance relationship? After another night without him beside her she was beginning to wonder whether her future had to be completely Caleb-free.

She stretched out her legs and heard a disgruntled meow from Colin, who had reluctantly returned from next door and attached himself to her side. He wasn't happy with her, which meant he pretended to ignore her even while still hanging around, an attitude Lucy couldn't help but admire and wish she could emulate.

The water in the shower was hot, the heating was clanking away as usual, and when she went down to the kitchen all the electrical equipment was operating perfectly. She paused at the door and noticed there were fresh flowers on the table, which she hadn't put there herself. She approached them with the caution usually reserved for someone discovering an unexploded bomb.

There was no card attached to the festive red ribbon tied around the vase, but she had to wonder if they had something to do with Caleb. Although, he didn't have a key . . . She frowned. Had she left a door open last night? She went to check the alarm and found it was turned off. If she'd forgotten to set that, had she also neglected to check the doors? Usually if someone got into your house, they took things rather than leaving flowers.

She fed Colin and turned the oven on to make sure it was up to temperature when she started baking. Not having to rush around and deal with guests was always a pleasure, although she loved chatting to new people and had already turned some chance visitors into regulars. She gazed out of the window at the bright sunshine and hoped that by the New Year the roads through the forest would be open so that she could recoup some of her losses.

Her phone buzzed with a text from her parents wishing her happy holidays. She replied with a GIF of a tree and some additional kisses. Dan sent her a goofy text and she replied in kind, which made her smile and wish he was here. No one from her family had visited since her grandma had died, which meant she hadn't seen them for nine months. Her mom had tried to coax her back to Seattle with the promise of plane tickets, but Lucy had been working flat-out to keep the B&B running without the necessary staff. As she hadn't wanted her parents to know how difficult things really were, she'd just said she couldn't make it, causing hurt feelings and a silence that hadn't been comfortable at all.

She didn't think they wanted her to fail—in fact they

would be shocked and hurt at the very suggestion—but they did expect her to screw things up. They always had . . . She put on some coffee, made herself some festive oatmeal, and let her thoughts wander to what Caleb might be doing. He hadn't texted her again, but that wasn't surprising. He'd said he was busy, and he was a man of his word. If she did get a chance to see him before he left, maybe she'd float the idea of a long-distance relationship by him and see what he thought.

She might have gotten over her girlish crush on Caleb, but only because she'd fallen in love with the real man he'd become.

A knock on the back door made her jump.

"Hey! Open up!"

She opened the door and revealed her brother Dan grinning at her.

"Surprise!" He hauled her into his arms and hugged her tight. "Looking good, little sis!"

"Why didn't you tell me you were coming?" Lucy asked as she looked up into his beloved face. "And how did you even get here?"

Dan was already on the move, his gaze taking in the kitchen.

"Nothing much has changed in here. I keep expecting Gran to come around the corner in her apron to find me something to do rather than eat all her cookies."

"She wasn't a great believer in idle hands," Lucy agreed. "I haven't wanted or needed to change much in here. Everything works just fine."

Dan continued walking. "Okay if I take the small room at the back of the house?" He yawned. "I think I'll take a nap. Wake me up for dinner."

"You can have any room you like. I don't have guests right now."

A hint of sadness crossed her face. "I won't move back to Seattle full time, Caleb."

"I'm not asking you to."

She bit her lip. "Do you think we could make a go of a long-distance relationship?"

"We might have to for a while, but it won't be forever."

"Why's that?"

"Because I'm coming home for good."

She went still. "I don't understand. What about your business and your new investors?"

"I don't want them if I can't have you."

There was a long pause, and he held his breath.

"Are you *insane*?"

Caleb fought a smile at her horrified expression. "That wasn't quite the response I was hoping for, but what the hell." He tried to explain. "I think I've been verging on a burnout since Mom died. Coming back here, meeting you again, and finally talking things out with Dad made me see things differently. Money's great, but being with the people you love? That's the important part. I didn't realize how precious my time with Mom was until it was gone. I won't make the same mistake with you."

Lucy slowly shook her head and stared at him. "That's the most words I've ever heard you speak, Caleb Erickson, and you certainly saved the best till last." She reclaimed his hand. "I still think you're stark staring mad, but I'm going to set that aside while I enjoy the feeling of being loved that much."

"Sounds good to me." Caleb followed her into the house, where everyone tried to pretend that they hadn't been staring out of the window. "How's dinner doing, Dad?"

"All good." Isaiah was standing by the oven checking the ham. "About twenty minutes before I'll start to carve."

Dan whistled at Caleb. "Hey! Come and talk to me and leave my annoying little sister to get those dinner rolls on."

Caleb gave Lucy one last amused look before releasing her hand and walking over to where Dan sat with two beers waiting. Even as he talked to his old friend, he was aware of Lucy working alongside his dad and her mom in the kitchen. His relief in saying his piece to her was slightly offset by her lack of a definite response. Although she'd said she loved him, she hadn't said whether his decision to come home was okay with her or not.

She'd asked if he was insane. Something he'd been asking himself ever since his phone call with his primary VC Chase Morgan. He liked his cofounders and small team, and the thought of abandoning his company was hard. How was he going to tell them that he was leaving everything behind for love, especially when he'd only got to know her in a new light for a few days? Even as he considered how difficult that was going to be, he realized he wasn't going to change his mind. He wanted Lucy, he wanted to come home, and everything else would have to fall in behind that.

Caleb waited until everyone had eaten their fill before he stood up and cleared his throat.

"I've got some news."

"You're really a billionaire and you've bought the town and you're turning it into a parking lot?" Dan asked. "Because that would be *wicked*."

"I've decided to come home."

His dad looked up; his expression suddenly alert. "For good?"

"Yeah, to help you run this place—if you want me, that is."

Everyone turned to look at Isaiah, who nodded. "Fine by me." He picked up his mug and sipped his coffee as if Caleb hadn't just given him exactly what he'd always wanted.

"Good, then." Caleb looked at Lucy. "And Lucy and I are together now."

"Like we hadn't all got that when you forced us all to come up here," Dan said.

"Forced?" Lucy looked over at her brother. "I thought you'd agreed to come because you wanted to."

"Of course, we wanted to," Isla said quickly. "Dan's just trying to be funny and failing miserably."

"I mean it would've been nice if one of you had come to see me earlier in the year, but I wasn't exactly putting out the welcome mat." Lucy met her mother's gaze. "I couldn't afford any staff after fire season. I didn't want any of you to see that I was struggling."

"I guess it was easier for us to accept all the excuses on both sides than actually do anything about it." Isla sighed. "I think we all owe Caleb a big debt of thanks for getting us together again."

"Hear, hear." Chip held up his glass and gestured at the Erickson men. "And thanks to Miss Lucy for persuading these two knuckleheads to open up to each other as well."

Lucy burst out laughing. "I'm not sure which of them looks more revolted by that idea."

Caleb quickly rearranged his features into a positive smile. "It's all good."

"Says the grouch." Dan was as irrepressible as ever. He patted Lucy's hand. "And I was just joking. I'm really glad you and Caleb are getting it on."

"Eew." Lucy shuddered. "Stop that right now."

"I have to go back to Seattle to sort out some stuff, but I'm aiming to be back here in the New Year," Caleb said.

"Good. I won't need to hire an extra hand for spring calving," his dad said. "How about we put some more coffee on and open a few presents?"

As everyone started to move away from the table, Caleb's phone buzzed with a text from Chase.

Okay if I come and visit you tomorrow? I think this meeting needs to be face to face.

Caleb frowned as he typed his reply. I'm not in Seattle.

Neither am I. I'm home on the ranch just like you are. ☺ I'll come to you. I have the address. Expect me around ten.

Sure.

Caleb stared at the blinking cursor but there was nothing else to see. He had no idea what Chase was going to propose, but he owed him the courtesy of listening to him.

"Everything okay?" Lucy asked.

"I think so. Chase Morgan, who's on my board of directors, is coming to see me tomorrow."

"That doesn't sound great."

"He's a good guy. He just wants to make sure I know what I'm doing."

"He's not the only one." She put her hand on his arm. "I don't want to be responsible for you turning your back on something you love."

"You're not."

"I want you to be happy."

"I am."

She rolled her eyes. "I guess you used up your daily allocation of words earlier."

"I know what I want." He touched her cheek. "It's standing right here in front of me."

She held his gaze and lowered her voice. "Caleb, when you say things like that, all I can think about is stripping you naked, and getting you into my bed."

"Which is why I know you're the right woman for me because no one else would ever think that." He put his arm around her shoulders. "Let's go and do the presents. I can't wait to see what your auntie Linda has knitted for everybody."

"Me neither." She looked up, her blue eyes bright. "I do love you, Caleb."

"Good." He started walking as a deep sense of satisfaction welled within him. "I've always loved you," she said. "You know that!"

"Maybe I did." He smiled down at her. "But it's still nice to have my suspicions confirmed."

Chapter Eight

Lucy woke up the next morning wrapped in Caleb's arms at the ranch. Her parents and Dan had gone back the previous evening to take care of the B&B. Isla had reassured her that if anyone did turn up needing somewhere to stay then she knew how to handle it. Lucy had promised to return for lunch—something she was already looking forward to because for once in her life her parents were happy with her and mad at Dan.

She'd wanted to stay with Caleb to support him through his upcoming meeting with Chase Morgan, the VC who currently owned thirty percent of his company. She'd done a bit of surreptitious research while Caleb was out working in the barn and found nothing bad. Chase even commuted between his offices in Silicon Valley and his family ranch near Bridgeport. If anyone might understand where Caleb was coming from, it was Chase.

She whiled away the hours while Caleb and his dad were working by reorganizing the kitchen pantry and writing Isaiah a shopping list for the next time he went down to one of the bigger towns.

Caleb came in about fifteen minutes before Chase was expected, dropped a kiss on the top of her head, and headed for the shower.

"Won't be long. Dad's staying in the barn—keep Chase sweet if he turns up before I'm done."

"Will do." Lucy was good at being charming. She'd learned at her grandma's knee.

At 9:55 there was a tap on the side door. Lucy went to open it and revealed a relaxed-looking cowboy complete with Stetson, boots, and Wranglers. "Hi, I'm Chase Morgan. I think Caleb is expecting me."

"Oh." She looked him up and down. "I was expecting you to be wearing a suit."

He grinned at her. "Not when I'm on vacation."

"I'm Lucy Smith. Caleb's"—she paused to think of a suitable word—"significant other."

"You live here?"

"I live in town. I run the B&B."

"Nice." He wiped his feet on the mat, came in, and glanced approvingly around the kitchen. "Looks just like home—except with fewer kids running around."

"Caleb should be here any second. He was just taking a shower."

"Glad to hear it, if he's been out working."

Lucy couldn't help but like Chase Morgan. He was way less threatening than she'd imagined. Caleb came in and reached out his hand to Chase.

"Good to see you. Thanks for coming all this way."

"It felt like the right thing to do," Chase said.

"I'll bring you guys some coffee," Lucy offered. "You can take it through to the family room and talk."

"Thanks." Caleb nodded. "And bring three mugs. I want you to know what's going on, too, Lucy."

She was glad he'd included her. If he hadn't, she would've been loitering in the hallway unashamedly eavesdropping. She set the coffee mugs and a plate of cookies on a tray and took them through. Chase was sitting by the fire and Caleb was standing by the window looking tense. After putting the tray beside Chase, she went over to Caleb and squeezed his hand. "You've got this."

"I wish." He took a seat opposite Chase and Lucy sat beside him. "I haven't changed my mind. I don't want to live in Seattle. I want to be here with my family."

Chase looked at Lucy. "And now I understand why."

"I can't run my company from here because it's too hands-on, which means I have to get out."

"Got it." Chase took a sip of coffee. "Here's how I see your options. You shut everything down, fire your employees, and walk out with nothing, which after all your work seems way too harsh."

"Agreed."

"Or you sell your business to Melco, the company that's been dying to acquire you for years."

"I could do that, but my reasons for not doing so before still stand."

"Yeah, but this isn't just about you, Caleb. It's about your intellectual property, your patents, and finding a place where everyone you employ, including your cofounders, get to continue being paid for developing your ideas."

"But Melco wants me to stay on full-time for three years and split the payout accordingly."

Chase shrugged. "That's negotiable."

"Not to me." Caleb grimaced. "If that's the deal, I might as well take on the extra investment and go public myself in eighteen months. And I don't want to do *that* because I'm close to burnout."

"You'd get a shitload of money from them," Chase observed.

"But with massive strings attached."

"Okay." Chase took another longer slug of coffee. "How

about this scenario? We buy you out, put in a new CEO, and keep the company running."

Caleb sat up straight. "You, as in your VC fund?"

"Yeah, we already own thirty-one percent. We buy your fifty-one percent, making us the majority shareholders and pay you everything upfront. If anyone else wants to cash out, we'll work with them as well. Then we'll invest massively in the business and take it through to IPO."

"What's the catch?" Caleb asked.

"You'd have to agree to a six-month handover process and be involved in choosing your successor."

"And what else?"

"Nothing, if you don't want to be involved, but you might find you want to keep at least a finger in the pie."

"That's not possible from here."

"Caleb . . . I commute between Morgan Valley and Silicon Valley all the time," Chase said. "I co-own my family ranch and manage to run my business. If that's something you want, it certainly is doable."

Lucy glanced at Caleb and crossed her fingers. She'd had a whole lot of wishes granted this Christmas, but she was hoping for another one.

"You trust me not to mess this up, don't you?" Chase asked.

"Yeah." Caleb frowned. "Absolutely."

"If you want to leave free and clear, we can do that. If you want to retain stock and some say in the business even if you're no longer the CEO, we can do that, too." Chase rose to his feet. "Take your time. Think things through, talk to Lucy and your family, and get back to me with any questions you have, okay?"

He smiled at Lucy. "You make great coffee."

"You should taste my cookies before you go. I made

Christmas snickerdoodles this morning." She pointed at the plate.

"Yeah? My kids would love those."

"I'll get you a to-go bag." Lucy went ahead of him into the kitchen and hurriedly wrapped some up while Chase finished up with Caleb. "Here you are." She presented him with the bag. "And here's one for the road."

"Thanks." Chase took a bite. "That's so good I doubt these little beauties will make it back to the ranch."

He winked at Caleb, who was still looking stunned, tipped his Stetson to Lucy, and went down the porch steps to his rental car. With one last wave, he departed, leaving Caleb and Lucy staring after him.

"Are you okay?" Lucy asked.

"Yeah."

"It's a lot." Lucy went back in and closed the door behind Caleb. "Do you want to talk about it?"

He rubbed his hand over the back of his neck. "I wasn't expecting Chase to make that offer."

"He obviously thinks very highly of you and your company."

"He always has." Caleb went to sit on the couch. "I'd absolutely trust him to do the right thing by me and everyone on my team. The question is, do I want to be involved on the sidelines after being in charge for over ten years?"

Lucy came to sit beside him. "I suppose that depends on whether you feel they still need you."

"They *think* they need me because I've always been that kind of boss." He sighed. "That wasn't healthy for me or for them. Sometimes I wish I'd stayed a tech nerd and let someone else become the CEO. It's a lot of pressure."

"Maybe you could strike a deal that gave you the option to be involved in the development side only?" Lucy suggested.